INVISIBLE CITY

INVISIBLE CITY

Julia Dahl

Minotaur Books
New York

INVISIBLE CITY. Copyright © 2014 by Julia Dahl. All rights reserved. Printed in the United States of America. For information, address St. Martin's Press, 175 Fifth Avenue, New York, N.Y. 10010.

www.minotaurbooks.com

Designed by Omar Chapa

The Library of Congress Cataloging-in-Publication Data is available upon request.

ISBN 978-1-250-04339-9 (hardcover)
ISBN 978-1-4668-4191-8 (e-book)

Minotaur books may be purchased for educational, business, or promotional use. For information on bulk purchases, please contact Macmillan Corporate and Premium Sales Department at 1-800-221-7945, extension 5442, or write specialmarkets @macmillan.com.

First Edition: May 2014

10 9 8 7 6 5 4 3 2 1

For my grandparents

FRIDAY

CHAPTER ONE

I was in Chinatown when they called me about the body in Brooklyn.

"They just pulled a woman out of a scrap pile in Gowanus," says Mike, my editor.

"Lovely," I say. "So I'm off the school?" I've spent the past two days pacing in front of a middle school, trying to get publishable quotes from preteens or their parents about the brothel the cops busted in the back of an Internet café around the corner.

"You're off," says Mike.

The rest of the press is on the scene when I arrive at the gas station across from the scrap yard. Pete Calloway from the *Ledger* is baring his crooked teeth at the NYPD's Deputy Commissioner of Public Information, or as reporters call him, DCPI. DCPI is six inches taller and seventy pounds heavier than Pete. It's barely twenty degrees out and Pete's got his hoodie up, his shoulders hunched against the cold, but DCPI is hatless, scarfless, gloveless, coatless.

His uniform jacket collar is pulled up, two inches of starched wool-blend against the icy wind.

"We're hearing she was found without clothes," says Pete. "Can you confirm that?"

DCPI looks over Pete's head and rubs his hands together. Behind him, in the scrap yard along the canal, two excavators stand frozen against the sky; the grapples attached to their long arms sway slowly, thin scraps of metal hanging from their teeth.

Pete stares up at the cop, who is ignoring him. Both of them are ignoring me. I've seen Pete at multiple crime scenes, but we've never introduced ourselves. Mike and the rest of the editors think Calloway is some kind of crime-reporting savant. But it seems to me, after just a few months at scenes with him, that all he is is single, dogged, and nosy. I catch his eye and smile a smile I mean to indicate camaraderie, but he doesn't respond. Drew Meyers from Channel 2 slides up, cashmere coat to his shins, leather gloves, wine-colored scarf. DCPI loves him.

"Drew," he says, grasping his hand like an old friend.

"Cold enough for you?" says Drew. DCPI's ears are absurdly red. His nose and cheeks and neck glow pink. "So what's going on?"

DCPI lowers his voice. "Female."

"Is she still in there?" asks Drew. Pete and I step in to listen.

"Don't have that," says DCPI.

"The M.E. van hasn't been here," says Pete.

Drew looks at DCPI, who confirms Pete's statement with silence.

"Was there a 911 call?" asks Pete.

"Yes," says DCPI.

"What time?" I ask.

DCPI looks down at me. "Can you let me finish, please?"

I nod.

"A call came in to emergency services this morning, reporting that workers loading a barge on the canal had found what they thought was a female body. We are in the process of determining identity."

"It's definitely female?" asks Pete.

DCPI nods.

Drew furrows his brow, doing a good impression of someone empathizing. He folds his notebook shut, though he didn't write down a word of what DCPI said, shakes the cop's hand, then turns and walks to the Channel 2 van, his coattails flapping behind him.

DCPI stays put, and so do I. There are several DCPI cops that work crime scenes. I know two or three by sight, and have one's name, but I've never seen this man before. "Can I get your name?" I ask.

He looks down at me. "Can I see your press card?"

I dig my stiff fingers—exposed by the fingerless gloves that note-taking necessitates—into my coat and manipulate the laminated *New York Tribune* badge from beneath several layers of clothing. My skin scrapes against the metal zipper as I pull it out and present it.

"You don't have a press card."

He's talking about the official credentials that the NYPD gives to reporters. If you want the press card, you have to submit six articles with your byline on them that prove you cover "spot news" in the city and routinely need to get past police lines. The card doesn't actually get you past police lines, but it gives you a small measure of legitimacy in the eyes of whichever DCPI you're dealing with. I applied for the card right before Thanksgiving, but I haven't heard anything. I called after the New Year and the officer who answered the phone at the public information office told me to wait.

"I applied in November," I tell DCPI. "I'm still waiting to hear."

He nods.

"Is she still . . . in there?" I ask.

"You'll get information when I get information," he says, sounding bored.

I turn away. Police tape stretches across the wide gravel entrance to the scrap yard, fastened to a tall iron fence on one end and the bow of a long canal boat on the other. There is a trailer that seems to serve as the site's office. Officers stand at ease, protecting the perimeter. Men in hard hats, whom I take to be employees of the yard, stand pointing for men in suits, whom I take to be detectives. The workers seem to be motioning between the grapple cage above their heads and the mountain of scrap rising fifty feet beside them. I follow to where their fingers are pointing, and see a leg.

I call in to the city desk and ask for Mike. I give him the information DCPI gave me.

"She's still up there," I tell him. "You can see her leg."

"Her leg?" I can hear him typing. "What else? Hold on . . . Bruce!" He's shouting to the photo editor. "Bruce, who's out there for you? Rebekah . . . who's there for photo?"

"I haven't seen anybody."

"Hold on." He clicks off. I try to communicate with Mike in these conversations. Every shift it's the same: he tells me where to go and why; I tell him what I find. I've seen him in person twice in six months. He's fifty pounds overweight, like most of the men in the newsroom, but unlike most of them he is polite and soft-spoken. When I walked into the office after three weeks of speaking several times a day, he said hello and avoided eye contact, then turned back to his computer.

I rock back and forth in my boots. I'm standing in the sun, and I've got fleece inserts over socks over tights, but I still can't feel my toes. Mike comes back on the phone.

"Johnny's coming."

"Johnny from Staten Island?"

"Yeah. Larry is working sources at 1PP." Larry Dunn is the *Trib*'s longtime police bureau chief. "Talk to somebody from the scrap yard. We're hearing a worker called it in. Is Calloway there?"

"Yeah."

"Don't lose sight of him."

"Got it."

"I'm going to the meeting with a woman in a scrap heap. We need an ID."

"I'm on it," I say.

The rest of the TV newspeople start rolling up in their vans. The on-air reporters always ride shotgun, camera techs squat with the equipment in the back. Gretchen Fiorello from the local Fox station steps out carrying her battery-powered microphone. She's in full makeup, eyes lined and shadowed, lipstick just applied, and her strawberry blond hair is coiffed so that it lifts as one entity against the wind. She's wearing panty hose and slip-on heels and a matching scarf and mittens set.

DCPI has nothing new, and the men at the scrap heap are still staring up at the steel fist with the body in it, so I push into the gas station convenience store to warm up. Working stakeouts or active scenes in the cold requires a tedious amount of energy. Hot coffee or tea warms you best from the inside out, but if you've got your hands wrapped around a cup, you can't take notes. Plus, the more you drink, the more likely it is you have to find a bathroom—which usually isn't easy. I shake powdered creamer into a white cardboard cup and pour myself some coffee from a mostly empty pot sitting on a warmer. I pay, then stand beside the front window and sip. From where I'm standing I can see most of the scrap yard.

My phone rings. It's my roommate, Iris.

"Where are you?" she asks. Iris and I both majored in journalism at the University of Central Florida, but she works in a cubicle on Fifty-seventh Street and I'm never in the same place for more than a couple hours.

"Right by home," I say. We share an apartment just a few blocks away. This is the first time I've ever been on a story in Gowanus. "The canal."

"Jesus," says Iris. "Hypothermic yet?"

"Nearly."

"Can you still come?" We have plans for drinks with an amorphous group of alums from Florida tonight.

"I think so." My shift is over around five.

"Will Tony be there?"

Tony is a guy I've been hooking up with. He's very much not Iris's type, but I like him. Iris likes metrosexuals. The guy she's sort of seeing now has highlights and the jawline of a Roman statue. Tony is very not metrosexual. He just turned thirty and he's balding, but he shaves his head. I wouldn't call him fat, but he's definitely a big guy. We met on New Year's Eve at the bar he manages, which also happens to be the bar where UCF alums meet for drinks and where Iris and I ended up after a weird party at someone's loft in Chelsea. He kissed me across the bar when the clock struck midnight and then we spent the next two hours kissing. He's an amazing kisser. And despite his decidedly less than polished appearance, Iris seems to like him. Iris is the beauty assistant at a women's magazine. We haven't had to purchase shampoo, nail polish, lipstick, soap, or any other grooming toiletry since she started last summer.

"I think so," I say.

"You don't know?"

I don't want to get into it, but I didn't return his last text—and Tony isn't the kind of guy who's gonna blow up a girl's phone.

"I'll be there by six," Iris says.

"Me, too," I say.

I tuck my phone back into my coat pocket and put my face to the steam rising from my coffee. Bodega coffee almost always smells better than it tastes.

The glass door rings open and two Jewish men walk inside, carrying the cold on their coats. I know they're Jewish because they're wearing the outfit: big black hat, long black coat, beard, side-curls. It's not subtle.

The men walk to the back corner of the convenience store, and the tall one whispers fiercely at the other, who looks at the floor in a kind of long nod. Behind them by a few steps is a boy, a four-foot clone of the men, in a straight black wool coat, sidecurls, a wide-brimmed hat. His nose and the tips of his fingers shine like raw meat. He is shivering. The two men ignore him, and he seems to know not to get too close to their conversation. He stamps his feet, laced tight in neat black leather oxfords, and shoves his little hands into his pockets.

I scoot back to my perch between the coffeepot and the chip rack, where I can see the press vans in the parking lot of the gas station and the cop cars clustered at the scrap yard's entrance across Smith Street. I'm monitoring motion. As long as the players—the rest of the reporters and photogs, the cops in uniform, the cops in suits—are just standing around, I can assume I'm not missing anything. If any group begins to move, I have to, too. If I had to choose, I'd rather be on a story like this than the one I just got off in Chinatown. In Chinatown, a reporter—especially a white reporter—is in hostile territory. Certain kinds of people love to talk to reporters—I can get an old Italian man in Bay Ridge or a young black mother in Flushing to gab and speculate about their neighbors, the mayor, their taxes, just about anything I come up with as long as I'm writing down what they say. *This gonna be in the paper?* they ask me. Immigrants are tougher. The *Trib* doesn't have a reporter who speaks Chinese, and when you're asking people already predisposed not to trust you if they know about the Internet café across the street selling ten-dollar blow jobs to middle school boys, without any of their language, you give them nothing but reasons not to say a word.

Active crime scenes are different. At an active crime scene, I have a role. I'm not staff at the *Trib*—I'm a stringer. I work a shift every day but have no job security or benefits. Every morning I call in, get an assignment, and run. I work alone, unless a photographer is assigned to the same story, and answer to a rotating assortment of editors and rewrite people whom I've usually never met. I have a laminated *Tribune* badge that identifies me as a player on the stage.

I get shit about the *Trib* from cops sometimes—they complain about how we played some story, or the editorial page bias—and I can't always get the same access as reporters with the official press card. But I'm in a much better position at a crime scene or official event than someone from one of the news Web sites that most of the cops have never heard of, or even worse the bloggers—who get nothing but shit.

At a crime scene, the cops secure the area. The reporters arrive. The cops inspect the body and the scene, then occasionally relay some of what they've found to another cop, the spokesman cop: DCPI. DCPI, when he feels like it, saunters across the street to the reporters busying themselves getting neighbor quotes ("I never *heard* them fighting" or "This building is usually so safe") and checking their e-mail on their phones. Crime scenes are a relief for a new reporter. You just follow the herd.

The Indian-looking man at the counter leans on his forearms, watching the scene outside the windows. I approach him.

"Do you know what's going on?" I ask.

He doesn't answer, but I think he understands what I've said.

"I'm from the *Tribune*," I say. "They found a body in the scrap yard."

He nods.

"A woman they say."

This is a surprise. "A woman? No."

I nod.

"Terrible," he says. He is probably in his thirties, but the ashy brown skin beneath his eyes could belong to a man twice his age. He hasn't shaved in a few days.

The men in the back of the store stop whispering and march toward the boy in the black coat. The tall one says something and they rush out, leaving the boy behind. They walk swiftly toward the scrap yard. I assume they won't talk to me, so I don't bother trying to ask a question. I should follow, but I just can't brave that wind again quite yet. If it were warm, I'd tag along a little behind, nose toward the scrap yard, try to get some detail to give the desk. Before I got anywhere near anything good, of course, I'd be told to get back. Get back with press, they'd say. I guess I'm a better reporter in the summertime. It was never once this cold in Florida, and even under all these layers I feel painfully exposed by the temperature. My bones feel like brittle aluminum rods, barely holding me up, scraping together, sucking up the cold and keeping it. One poke and I'll crumble to the ground.

The boy takes his hands out of his pockets and carefully places them around the glass of the decaf pot. After a moment he brings his hands to his face, cupping his cheeks with his hot little palms.

"That's smart," I say.

He looks up at me, surprised.

"I use my cup," I say, and lift my coffee. "And it keeps me warm on the inside."

He nods.

"You work for the newspaper?" he asks.

I look at the man behind the counter. Kids hear everything.

"I do," I say. I point to the wire newspaper basket by the door. "The *Trib*."

"My mommy reads the newspaper."

"Oh?" I say. "Do you?"

The boy shakes his head. His mouth is a thin line. I don't think

I've ever seen so serious a child. But, of course, I've never seen a Hasid—man, woman, or child—*not* look serious. My mother was Hasidic. She fell in love with my dad—a goy—during a period of teenage rebellion. They had me, named me after my mom's dead sister, and then she split—back to the black-coated cult in Brooklyn. There aren't really any ultra-Orthodox Jews where I grew up in Florida, but now that I've moved to New York, I see them every day. They live and work and shop and commute inside the biggest melting pot in the world, but they don't seem to interact with it at all. But for the costume they wear, they might as well be invisible. The men look hostile, wrapped like undertakers in their hats and coats all year long, their untended beards and dandruff-dusted shoulders like a middle finger to anyone forced against them on the subway at rush hour. The women look simultaneously sexless and fecund in aggressively flat shoes, thick flesh-colored stockings, and shapeless clothing, but always surrounded by children. I picture their homes dark and stale, with thick carpet and yellowing linoleum and low foam ceilings and thin towels. Are the little boys allowed action figures and race cars? Does somebody make a knockoff Hasidic Barbie for little girls? Barbie pushing a baby carriage and walking behind Ken. Barbie who leaves her kid.

"What's your name?" I ask.

The boy hesitates. He lifts his face toward mine and our eyes meet for the first time.

"Yakov," he says. "Yakov Mendelssohn."

My phone rings. It's an "unknown" number, which means it's probably the city desk. I smile at the boy, then turn and walk toward the beer cooler to take the call.

"It's Rebekah," I say.

"Hold for Mike," says the receptionist.

I hold.

"Hey," says Mike. "Is photo there yet?"

"Nobody's called me."

"Fuck. Is the M.E. there?"

"No," I say.

"Any ID?"

"Not yet."

"Is anybody at the scrap yard talking? Any workers?"

I haven't asked. But I can't say that. "I haven't found anybody so far. They've got it mostly taped off."

"Well, keep trying. See if you can talk to whoever found the body."

"Okay," I say. I know—and Mike knows—that whoever found the body has likely been whisked off to the neighborhood precinct for questioning. But editors in the office often suggest you do things that are essentially impossible on the off chance you get something usable. Once, after the FBI had raided a pharmacy that was selling illegal steroids to cops, I spent an entire day in Bay Ridge looking for people who would admit they'd bought steroids there.

"Look for beefy guys," advised Mike. "Maybe hang out outside the gym."

I took the assignment seriously for about two hours. I actually approached several men—one in a tank top with shaved calves, one exiting a tanning salon, one carrying a gym bag—and asked if they'd heard about the raid and if they knew anybody who uses steroids. Not surprisingly, no one did. I finally gave up and just started walking the streets. I struck up a conversation with some men

smoking cigarettes outside a bar and told them about my assignment. They laughed and said good luck.

When I called in to report that I'd found nothing, Mike was
gone and Lars, a younger editor, laughed when I told him what I'd
been asked to do. "Don't you love assignments like that?" he asked.

I tell Mike I'll do my best and hang up. When I turn back
from the cooler I see that Yakov is gone.

I approach the man behind the counter again. "Cute kid," I say.

"He is son of owner," says the man.

"Of the gas station?"

"No," says the man. "The scrap yard. I watch him grow up, but
he never speak to me. None of them do."

"Them?"

"The Jews," he says. "You must be special."

I shrug.

"You say there is . . . a woman?" He points his chin toward the
yard across the street.

"Someone found her this morning. I can't believe they haven't
gotten her inside yet. Have the police been in?"

"Here? Yes."

"Did they say anything? Did they ask you anything?"

The man shakes his head.

I drop my coffee in the trash can by the door and step outside.
The cold air stings my face. I look down and aim the top of my head
into the wind.

There are half a dozen police cars at the entrance to the scrap
yard. I linger a few moments at the corner of the administrative
trailer, watching as small groups of men—they are all men—rock on
their heels, rubbing their hands together and gazing up at the long

arm of the steel excavator, still motionless, with torn metal and a frozen limb hanging from its clenched fist. From this close, I can tell the victim is white. Good, I think. That's one piece of info to give the desk. The *Trib* loves dead white women.

I wait beside the door to the office trailer, studying the men's interactions to whittle down the number of people I'll have to approach to get the information I need. A man in a hooded sweatshirt and work boots comes around the corner and I stop him.

"Excuse me," I say, flashing a smile for a moment, then cringing as the cold sinks into my teeth as if I'd just bitten down on a Popsicle. "Sorry to bug you, but do you work here?"

The man doesn't look me in the eye, but says, "Uh-huh."

"Were you here when they found the body?"

"I was in the cab."

"The cab," I say, pulling my notebook and pen from my coat pocket. "What happened?"

The man shrugs and looks over my head. "I was just pulling up loads. That barge was supposed to be out hours ago." He lifts his chin in the direction of the flat boat sitting on the canal, a pile of scrap in a low mound on its belly. "I was just pulling, and Markie started screaming over the radio. Shouting. I looked out the window and saw a couple guys running."

I'm scribbling as fast as I can, trying to maintain eye contact with the man and write something legible enough to dictate back to the desk. In my notebook, his quote becomes: *pull loads, mark scream radio, look wind saw guys run.* I nod, inviting him to tell me more. "Could you see her from the cab?"

"I thought it was a guy, because of the hair."

"The hair?"

"Well, not the hair. There's no hair. She's bald."

I stop writing. "Bald?"

The man nods and lifts his eyes to the crane. "Her head was . . . I could see it."

"What could you see, exactly?"

"I saw her foot first, then, well, once I saw the foot and I knew, I could tell. Her color, she didn't match the scrap."

"What were you thinking?"

"I fucking picked this lady up. I didn't fucking see her in the pile and I closed her in the hook and . . . I was thinking, I don't know. I was thinking how cold she was." He shivers and wipes his hand across his face.

I need more. I need him to say something like, "I couldn't believe it—I've never seen anything like that before."

"Wow," I say. "I mean, could you even believe it?"

He shrugs and shakes his head. That'll do.

"How long have you worked here?" I ask.

"Almost a year."

"Have you ever seen anything like this before?"

"A dead body in the pile? No."

"Can I ask your name?"

He hesitates. "Nah, I think . . . I think that's enough."

"Are you sure?" The desk frowns on anonymous quotes. "Even just a first name?"

He shakes his head. Last ditch, I smile and lean in a little. "Are you *sure*? It would really help me out."

"I think I probably helped you out already."

"What about . . . Markie?" I say. "Do you think he might talk to me?"

"Maybe."

"Could you maybe point him out for me?" I'm smiling again, cocking my head, trying to make my eyelids flutter.

He looks around, his hands deep in his pockets. He nods his head toward a group of Hasidic men and workers huddled at the wheels of the excavator.

"Don't tell him I gave you his name."

"How can I tell him?" I ask, trying one last time. "I don't even know your name."

He nods. No smile of recognition. Just a nod. I wait another moment, then say thank you and turn toward the crowd at the base of the scrap pile, which is more like a mountain range than a mountain. It spans hundreds of feet along the canal, rising and falling in peaks and valleys of broken steel. The scale of the piles is dizzying. Mack trucks parked at the base look like plastic Tonkas in their shadow. The grapple is shaped like that claw you manipulate to grab a stuffed animal in those impossible games in the lobby of Denny's. I stuff my notebook in my coat pocket and my phone rings. It's a 718 number.

"It's Rebekah," I say.

"Becky, it's Johnny!" Johnny, the photographer from Staten Island, is the only person in the entire world who has ever referred to me as Becky more than once. "Where are you?"

"I'm at the scrap yard."

"Where? I'm here. I'm in the Camaro." Johnny and I have worked a couple stories together. I turn around and see his silver Camaro parked across the street, near the air pump at the gas station. Johnny once told me that he "owns" Staten Island. On one of my first stories, he told me to follow him in my car to a subject's house; then he slid through the end of a yellow light on Victory Boulevard. I gunned through the red, annoyed. Later, in the parking lot where we were scoping for a recently released sex offender, he leaned against my car and said I should be more careful going through reds. They got cameras, he said. Did you see a flashing light? I said maybe and he said he'd take care of it. Write down ya' plate number for me. I'll ask a buddy. I wrote down my number and gave it to him; he wrote "Rebecca" beside the numbers. I didn't correct his spelling. I never got a ticket, though I doubt that had anything to do with him.

I catch his eye across the street and walk over to his car. My former car, a 1992 Honda Accord, died when winter came. It had never seen snow. I sold it to someone for two hundred dollars. On my first day working after it was towed away, I had to tell the desk when I called in before my shift that I couldn't drive. I worried I might be out of a job. At my interview, Mike specifically asked if I had a car. A good stringer is an asset—we run around the five boroughs to crime scenes and press events, knocking on doors, bothering neighbors; we can get the information or the quote or the photo that sells the story—but a stringer with a car is considered an even bigger asset. Stringers with cars can get to Westchester to sit on big houses owned by sloppy, greedy politicians or doctors or professional athletes. Stringers with cars can knock on doors in Long Island for four hours and get back in time to get a quote from someone in Queens before the first edition deadline. But when I stopped having a car, nobody seemed to care. My guess is that Mike simply forgot I'd ever told him I had one.

"Becky! Get in."

I go around the Camaro and sink into the passenger seat. The car smells like home. There is a coconut-scented palm tree hanging from the rearview mirror. Johnny's got the heat blowing high, and I put my hands up close to the vents in the dashboard.

"Warm up, girl," says Johnny. Johnny is a flirt, and though he's always overfamiliar, I never feel like he's actually leering at me. I don't think I'm his type. Johnny likes big hair and tight sweaters and big blue moons of eye shadow. In Staten Island, he does well. Or so he says.

"Have you talked to the desk?" I ask.

"Dead lady in the pile," he says.

I lean toward the windshield and point. "Look, you can see her. Right there. In the crane."

Johnny looks and points. "There? That . . ." He's stuck for what to call what he sees, which is a leg. "Jesus!" He twists around and grabs his camera from the backseat. "Watch the car. I'll be back." He throws open the long door and slams it shut behind him. As he trots across the street in his cropped red leather jacket, Johnny is adjusting his lens, snapping a photo, and then checking the image in his viewfinder. He gets to the edge of the yellow police tape and snaps away. Click click twist twist look. Click twist look. After a couple minutes, I can see the cold start to slow him. He stomps his feet and rubs his hands together. More clicking. He kneels down, maybe getting the tape in the shot, and jogs toward the trailer where the worker I spoke to is standing, smoking, staring at the crane.

I can't imagine why they haven't brought the poor woman down yet, though I'm sure Johnny is thrilled he got here in time to get his shot. In the time I've been working for the *Tribune*, I don't think they've ever actually published a photograph of a dead body. I worked a scene out in Queens in September where a kid had tried to ride his bike *Back to the Future*–style behind a delivery truck and ended up with his head spread open on the pavement. The photographer took dozens of shots of the lump beneath the white sheet in the middle of the road, and the blood-dark pavement around it, but we published a picture of the truck, and the driver sitting on the sidewalk with his head in his hands. They also didn't use the quote I got from a witness who described the sound the boy's head made when it hit the blacktop. But photographers, like reporters, know they have to get every angle, every detail—just in case. In case their editor is in a particularly perverse mood; in case the *Ledger* has the image or the detail and we need to match it.

Johnny seems to be trying to talk to my worker and his friend, but neither's lips are moving much in response to his questions. My guy points to where he pointed me, to the group of men beneath the crane: workers, Hasids, police. Johnny jogs over, staying just on this side of the yellow tape. An officer in his star-brimmed hat stands guard, and I watch Johnny show his badge and try to sweet-talk him into letting him get closer for a shot. The officer listens without engaging. His eyes dart around him. Johnny is persistent. He's pointing and gesticulating as if this stranger was an old friend to whom he was recounting some wild encounter.

My phone rings. It's the desk.

"I need whatever you've got for first edition," says Mike. I read him the quotes from my construction worker. "Still no ID?"

"No," I say, about to explain that the poor woman is still dangling forty feet above the canal, when suddenly everyone begins running: the crane is moving.

"I gotta go," I say, opening the car door. "They're bringing her down."

Outside, Johnny is frantically changing his lens. "This shot is gonna be shit. Shit!"

I leave him be and get as close as I can to the excavator, pressing against the police tape. The cage is swaying, and as the long yellow arm guides it slowly toward the ground it makes a low, rattling moan. The workers and police step back, forming a circle around the base of the cage. The two Hasidic men from the bodega, now joined by several other men dressed just like them, stand to the side. Everyone is watching the leg. The thigh, the knee, the bare foot. And as it gets closer to the ground there is more. Her skin has color, bluish white, like skim milk. When the cage gets within a couple feet of the ground, it stops abruptly. A policeman shouts something I can't understand to the crane operator, and the operator shouts something back. The metal arm shudders, pulling the cage up. More shouting. Now the officers all have their hands up, they're shuffling back and forth, looking like circus clowns scrambling to catch a trapeze artist. Finally, the bottom tip of the cage touches the frozen ground. The new slack shifts its contents, pressing down on the body. There is more shouting, and the officers move in, touching the cage, touching the metal scraps, not touching the woman. It's hard to imagine how they're going to get her body out without crushing her.

Within moments of each other, two vans pull up. One has blue and gold Hebrew lettering on the side. The other says KINGS COUNTY MEDICAL EXAMINER. A uniformed officer lifts up the yellow tape and lets both vans enter the yard. Out of one jump Orthodox men in broad-brimmed black hats, with neon green vests over their coats and white strings hanging from their hips. Out of the other jump men in blue jumpsuits. They all run toward the body.

With the crowd beside her swelled, my stomach begins to hurt. Why can't they get her *out* of there? My intestines get all fucked up when I get upset. I learned from a therapist many years ago that it's called anxiety. I'm always afraid of stuff. Weird stuff, though. Not monsters or murderers or even airplanes. It's more ephemeral than that. I feel fear when I feel insecure. When I feel alone or rejected. And when I feel powerless—like I do looking at this poor woman's skin, torn by metal, bare beneath the sun on the coldest day of the year. Get her out, I think. Get her warm.

Johnny appears next to me.

"This is seriously fucked up," he says, winded, excited.

"Who the fuck *are* all these people?" I say. "Get her inside and sort it out there."

Johnny chuckles. "If only it were so easy, Beck."

"What?" I say.

"The Jews are here," he says, as if that explains something.

"And?"

"And, the Jews take their own bodies."

I do not understand.

"You've never seen them before? They were at that murder-suicide around Thanksgiving on the Upper East Side. Remember? Woman who owned the apartment is having dinner with a guy, her ex barges in and kills everybody. She was Jewish, so they came to collect the body. They cut up the rug, too. Took the sofa cushions."

"They did not."

"They did. Almost came to blows with a couple cops, too.

Turf shit. In the Jewish religion, they're supposed to bury you with everything, every drop of blood and hair and stuff."

"They let them do that? Just take the body? Just take evidence?"

"In this case, they knew who did it," says Johnny. "But, yeah. I think so."

This seems very implausible to me. I doubt the NYPD just lets people run off with their crime scene evidence. But it's not really worth the conversation with Johnny. He calls black people "niggers."

Finally, some decision is made. The Jews run back to their van and emerge with a stretcher, which they unfold, wheeled legs dropping to the ground. A black bag—a body bag—lies thin atop it. They push the stretcher to the cage and consult with the officers. Everyone stands still for several more minutes, holding themselves against the cold, peering at the leg. Johnny is snapping away, ducking beneath the yellow tape and being yelled at to "get back." Calloway and Gretchen and Drew come running.

I'm trying to make eye contact with one of the Hasidic men from the gas station. The taller man is stony faced, but the shorter one is clearly distraught, and very often distraught people talk. He looks my way and I raise my eyebrow and open my mouth expectantly. I put up a gloved hand and wave. He sees me—and then he looks away.

The metal arm groans again and lifts up a few feet. Two policemen spread a tarp beneath the cage, and then the tip creeps open, dropping scrap and, finally, the woman. She falls like the rest of the material, turgid and graceless. But as soon as she's down, the operator swings the cage back, keeping the rest of the scrap from crushing her. A couple pieces come loose, though, and the police scramble to protect her. Johnny is snapping and I'm just staring. I can see her belly and her breasts and a mound of black pubic hair. I shiver again. It's so fucking cold. Cover her, I think.

"Look," says Johnny, showing me his viewfinder, pressing buttons to zoom in on her face. Her lips are blue and she has a completely shaved head.

"See," he says. "She's a Jew." I look at him and he looks toward the Hasids. "They make their women shave their heads."

"No, they don't," I say, but I don't actually know whether he's wrong.

"Yeah, they do," he insists. "Haven't you ever noticed all those women wear wigs?"

I stare at the woman's image in the camera. Her mouth is open slightly and the corners of her mouth seem to be pulled back in what I can't help but picture as a scream. White, bloodless cracks run down her lips. One of her front teeth is chipped, and her left eye is swollen shut. It looks like a giant pink and purple gumball.

"Fucking dead Hasid," says Johnny. "You better try to talk to those dudes now. They're gonna close up tight as a pussy soon as this gets out."

He's probably right, but I stay put. I'm straining to get one last glance at the woman as the men lift her up and set her into the black bag. One long zip and she's gone.

CHAPTER TWO

Iris is smoking a cigarette outside the bar when I get there.

"Rebekah!" She's begun drinking already.

"You got off early," I say. It's barely five. DCPI said definitively they weren't going to have an ID for hours, so Mike said I could take off.

"I snuck out," she says. Brice, the highlighted honey, is beside her, and just like DCPI, he's in a wool coat and no hat, gloves, or scarf. He smiles, displaying teeth so straight and white and square, I would have said they were dentures on anyone over fifty. Iris drops her cigarette to the sidewalk and smears it with the round toe of her knee-high boot. "Let's go back in."

I follow the two of them inside, through the seasonal plastic and canvas vestibule and past the velvet curtain that keeps the cold out. Frau Flannery's is packed. There's a mountain of coats in one corner and, because there is about a sixty-degree difference between the air outside and inside the bar, the big front window is steamed up like a Caddy at a drive-in.

Tony is behind the bar, interacting with the cash register. Iris drags Brice to the bar, where two girls from our class are sitting. Hannah is a legal secretary; Jenny fact-checks at one of the food magazines.

"Hi, ladies," I say, scooting up into the bar stool.

"Hey," says Hannah, putting one arm around me in a half hug. "Did you just get here?" I nod.

Jenny raises her pint glass. "I've been here since three."

"Jenny got laid off."

"Fuck," I say.

Jenny raises her eyebrows and gulps from her beer. "No work tomorrow."

"What happened?"

Jenny is still drinking, so Hannah answers. "The magazine is folding."

"Folding?"

Jenny finishes her beer and sets it down on the bar a little harder than she probably meant to. "Yup. The EIC called us into her office right after lunch. She was *crying*. She was like, I never thought I'd see the day."

"Was circ down that much?"

Jenny shrugs. "Probably. I mean, it's totally their fault. Instead of making the magazine *better*, they fucking spend zillions on this fucking consulting firm from Wall Street—because they so have their shit together—to tell them where to trim the fat. Apparently, we're fat."

"The whole magazine?"

"Fat."

I shake my head and Iris and I exchange a look. None of this is surprising in the least. We all know what's happening to the fancy New York City publishing world we dreamed of in college.

"And, of course, I get nothing. No severance, no two weeks paid. Fucking nothing."

"You're still freelance?" She gives me a look, like, duh. We're all freelance. My insecure job at the *Trib* is probably more secure than any of the jobs my friends have. Magazines die, but tabloids always need people willing to run around the city picking up quotes. I could probably keep this gig until I'm forty. And anyway, insecurity is something I'm used to. My dad was always there, and his wife, Maria, has been my stepmom since I was five, but you don't grow up knowing your very existence sent your mother packing without developing a sense that the bottom can always drop out and you should probably be prepared.

The hole my mother left in me never healed. It's like the space my wisdom teeth left in the days after I had them pulled: a raw gap, tender and prone to infection. The woman in the metal cage— her open mouth and exposed breasts and bare head, her stark, cruel anonymity—poked at it. I've had countless fantasies about my mom's life the last twenty years: I've imagined her married, beaten by her husband, dying in childbirth, turning mute with the shame of abandoning me, committing suicide and leaving a note addressed to me; in my mind she's come to Orlando and watched my school play from the back row, then ducked out when the curtain fell; she's fled again, and is trying to contact Oprah to reunite us. She could be doing anything right now. She could have been in that cage.

Hannah and Jenny go to the bathroom. Tony is no longer behind the bar, so Iris and I order beers from a woman with frizzy hair and blue eyeliner. She takes our order and fills it without ever really looking at us. I assume Tony knows I'm coming here tonight—Friday night is UCF night—but I've given him the brush-off since our last date. I've been processing a conversation we had over dinner at a brick-oven pizza place on Flatbush a little over a week ago, and I'm still not sure how I feel. We'd just ordered wine and were talking about our days. I told him about being sent to cover a fire in a housing project in the Bronx the day before.

"Did they send you because they know you've written about that before?" he asked.

"What?" I said. I'd written a series in college about fire hazards in Section 8 housing, but I was pretty sure I hadn't told him about that.

"The fires in those apartments. From last year. You won a prize, right?"

"You read that?"

"I Googled you. It was really . . . sad. I couldn't believe the things that one guy said to you. 'You get what you pay for.' Unbelievable."

I should have been flattered. Even Iris was impressed when I told her about it afterward. She said it meant he was genuinely interested in me, and that he didn't feel threatened by my success. But I felt violated. Like he'd poked into my world when I hadn't invited him. Like he should have asked permission. I stiffened up immediately. When the pizza came—a scrumptious-looking white pie with artichoke hearts and spinach—I had no appetite. My stomach was buzzing with anxiety and we didn't stay for dessert. Mercifully, Tony read me, and just gave me a quick hug when we parted at the steps of the subway.

"Where's Tony?" asks Iris.

"He was here a minute ago," I say. Brice is standing behind her, gazing around the bar, tipping a bottle of Bud Light to his lips every minute or so. He's like her page.

"Are you still pissed he Googled you?"

I shrug and drink my beer.

She puts her hand on my leg and leans toward me, tilting her head. Iris's mother died during our freshman year. She'd been fighting breast cancer since Iris was thirteen, but the cancer won. I saw pictures of the two of them before prom and at Iris's high school graduation. Her mom didn't look good. Her skin was gray and her eyes hollow. After she died, Iris used to cry about all the ugly things she thought about her mom. She said she used to beg her to wear a pretty scarf or a hat to cover up her bald head. She tried to drag her for manicures and to department stores for clothes. But her mother didn't care, or didn't have the energy, or both. Iris said she felt like her mom had died years before the cancer killed her. She gave up on herself, Iris said. She didn't think it was worth it to pretend she was still pretty. Her mom couldn't have known how much her daughter needed her to pretend. Both motherless at nineteen, we got high one night and pretended we were each other's mothers. Tell Mom what's wrong, we said, and we took turns putting our hands on each other's knees, leaning in and nodding sympathetically, listening, pledging love "no matter what." As Mom, it turned out, we both gave pretty good advice. Who knows who I was modeling: some mash-up of Mrs. Garrett from *The Facts of Life* and the silent, smiling women who bake cookies for groups of children in Nestlé commercials? Maria left advice-imparting to my dad. I think she was uncomfortable playing mom to the little girl who never knew hers.

"I thought you really liked him," Iris says.

"I did," I say. "I do." I look up at Brice, a little uncomfortable talking about anything in front of him, but he's got his eyes on the TV above the bar. Good boy.

"So give him a chance," says Iris. "When was the last time you actually liked a guy?"

It's been a while. "I know," I say. We both drink from our beers, and then Iris changes the subject.

"How was your day?" she asks. When we created the Mom game, "how was your day" was very important. Mothers always ask about your day. Apparently.

"I was on a body. A woman. She was naked."

"You saw her?"

I nod. "She was just lying there, in this crane. In the cold. And there were all these men around. Oh, and there were Jews."

"Jews?"

"Like, my mom's Jews. With the . . ." I make a spiral motion with my finger indicating sidecurls.

"Really? Did you talk to them?"

"I talked to a little boy, actually. Just for a minute."

Hannah comes back and takes her seat. Iris straightens from her Mom posture; our game wasn't a secret the year after her mom died, but four years later, I think we might both be a little sheepish about how much we still rely on it.

Right behind Hannah comes a group of men. They squeeze in next to Brice, one snagging Jenny's stool.

"Excuse me," says Hannah. "This seat is taken."

"I know," says the new occupant, a big guy with a goatee. "By me."

"Uh, I don't think so," she says, snapping instantly into bitch mode. Hannah raises the left corner of her upper lip and reaches her arm across the bar, in some attempt to keep him from ordering. "My friend is in the bathroom and this is *her* seat."

"Look," says the man, turning toward her in his enormous puffy coat. His eyes are bloodshot and he smells like dust. "I'm fucking beat and your friend didn't leave no handbag. . . ."

"She didn't *need* to leave a handbag," says Hannah. "*I said I'd* watch her seat."

Now the man's friends are watching. I'm trying to figure out how to avoid becoming involved. Brice steps back, probably thinking the same thing. Iris and I angle away, sipping our beers and watching.

The man sighs. He looks exhausted. "Well, you did a shitbag job, lady."

Hannah puffs out her chest. "Lady! Don't you fucking . . ."

"Look, hon, all you had to do was ask me to move. I'm not a pig. But I don't take orders from no bitch. Not today."

Hannah's mouth hangs open and for a moment, she's speechless. And then Jenny comes back from the bathroom.

"Uh, hello!" shouts Jenny, taking long, uneasy strides toward the bar. She's moving so fast, she stumbles and plows right into the man in her seat, spilling a pint glass of beer she must've swiped from some pushover Florida boy all over him. The man jumps up, and as he tries to wipe the liquid off his lap, shoves Jenny, who falls dramatically to the floor.

"Oh my God!" she screams.

"Did you *see* that?" shouts Hannah.

Jesus. I hop off my bar stool and kneel down beside Jenny. "Come on," I say. "You're fine. It's okay."

"He fucking *hit* her!" shouts Hannah.

"He didn't *hit* her," says Iris, but not loud enough that Hannah pays her any attention.

The man is wiping beer off his jacket, unzipping the front and shaking out the cuffs. His friends have backed away. Tony appears and offers Jenny his hand to get up.

"Everything okay?" he asks.

"I'm sorry," I say quietly. "She's fine."

But Hannah's not done. "Excuse me! Excuse me!" she calls to the bartender. "Did you see what just happened here? I was saving my friend a seat and he took it and then . . . now . . . he just *pushed* her!"

The bartender stares at Hannah. She rubs her forehead with nicotine yellow fingers and looks to Tony.

"Can I get a towel, Maureen?" says Tony. Maureen tosses him a towel.

"Here you go, man," he says. "This round's on me."

The wet patron nods and wipes off his coat.

"I'm sorry," I say again, putting my hand on his back. Tony smiles at me and winks.

"Why are *you* saying *sorry*?" says Hannah.

"Can I get you ladies another couple drinks?" asks Tony. It shouldn't surprise me that he's good at managing drunk people, but the ease with which he's taken control of the situation, careful not to imply fault or favor, is suddenly incredibly attractive. We fucked on our first real date, and it was pretty awesome. He made me come with his hand and afterward, when I turned my head to see his face, he had this enormous smile spread across it, like he'd just won the lottery. Then he slid inside me and made me come again. Could

I just drag him into the bathroom right now and spread my legs and get fucked against the tiny sink? I slide my hand down his back and touch his ass through his jeans. He looks down at me, surprised, and pleased. Standing beside him now, the fact that I'd been irritated by his interest in me seems very silly. I hope he forgives me.

"Another round would be great," I say, leaning in like he's mine.

But Hannah is over Frau Flannery's.

"This place sucks," says Hannah, taking her purse from the hook beneath the bar. "Come on, Jenny."

Jenny looks at me and Iris. Her eyes are glassy and unfocused. I hug her close and then. Hannah whisks her away. Iris winks and turns toward Brice, leaving me and Tony alone in the crowd.

"That was exciting," says Tony.

I slide my hand around to his back again and he pulls me to him. I look up—he's a head taller than me—and to my great pleasure, he kisses me. Right there in front of everybody. I can't see Iris, but I bet she's smiling.

"I'm sorry I've been an asshole," I say, loving the way his soft chest feels against mine. He is about to say something when my phone rings. It's the desk.

"I'll be back," I say.

"Promise?"

"Promise."

I angle through the crowd to a space by the door and answer.

"Hold for Cathy," says the receptionist. I hold.

"Rebekah, you were on the Gowanus body, right?"

"Right."

"Who was out there? What was the scene like?"

"Um, how so?"

"They might need a couple extra inches for the second edition. Vic Hubbert told me to check it out."

Cathy Richards is on the Sunday desk, but she sometimes picks up overnight shifts. Vic Hubbert runs the night shift and compiles the police blotter. He is way past retirement age.

"The workers seemed shook up. The owners were a little weird, but they're always kinda weird."

"The owners? What do you mean weird?"

"Sorry. I mean . . . They were Hasidic."

"Hasidic?"

"The Jews, in black hats . . ."

"I know what Hasidic means."

I hear typing.

"What was the name of the yard?" she asks.

"Um, I forget. Hold on." Shit. I should know this. I pull out my notebook and flip the pages. "Smith. Like the street."

"You think it's owned by Hasidics?"

"I don't know for sure. I talked to a kid at the gas station across the street and the guy at the counter said the boy's dad owned the yard."

"Get his name?"

"The kid? Yakov."

"Last name?"

"Last name . . . he said it, I think."

"Where did you talk to him? Wait, how old?"

"I don't know, like eight or nine maybe?"

"We can't quote him. Did he say anything interesting?"

"Not really. He came in with his dad and another man but they left him there."

"They left him?"

"He seemed comfortable. I mean, if it's the family yard, I figured he'd been there before."

"Okay. But you didn't get a last name."

"I did. . . . Um, fuck."

"Find it. I'll call you back."

I flip through my notes three times, but the last name isn't in there. I pull out a pen and circle some possible quotes. The cashier's reaction: "I can't believe it." And the Jewish van. I look up and catch Tony's eye. He's back behind the bar. I mouth "work" and roll my eyes. He winks.

Cathy calls back.

"Library is working on an address for the owner. What time did you start?"

"Nine."

"Vic wants to door-knock." She is typing. "Let me see who's on the schedule tonight. . . ."

"I'll go," I say. I've never volunteered for a double shift before. But I've also never been on a story that in any way involved the Hasids. In fact, I don't think I've ever even read a story about them, not in the *Trib*, anyway. It's a funny secret, I think, that I'm one of them and they don't know it. Or maybe I'm not. Can you be Hasidic without all the dress-up and the rules? Is it in my blood?

"Yeah? Okay, hold on, I'm gonna get Vic on speaker."

I hold.

"Hello?" Vic's voice is a croak. It's more than just smoking. He sounds like someone's scraped his throat out with a fork.

"Hi," I say.

"You talked to the owner?" asks Vic.

"I talked to a little boy. The bodega worker said his dad owned the yard."

"They were Hasidic?"

"Yeah."

"What else?"

"Um . . . they took her body away in a van. But it wasn't the police van. It had, like, Hebrew on the side."

"Really?" says Cathy.

"Did you see Johnny's film?"

"Johnny?"

"The photographer. He got some shots when they took her down. She was bald. And naked."

"Bald?" says Vic. "Cathy, call Larry. Ask him if 1PP will confirm the victim was bald."

"Johnny assumed she was Jewish because she had a shaved head. He said the Hasids make their women shave their heads. But that's not true, I don't think."

"They wear wigs," says Cathy. "Who knows what the fuck they've got underneath. But if a special van came to pick up her body, she's probably Hasidic."

"Do they have their own coroner or something?"

"I don't know," says Cathy.

"This is all stuff we should find out," says Vic.

"Exactly," says Cathy. "Which is why I'm interested in who owns that yard. Rebekah, we'll call you back when we get an address."

She hangs up. I stand staring at my phone. I've just given away my night. I angle back to the bar, and Tony, who presents me with a fresh, frothy pint.

"Guess what?" I say, taking a sip.

"What?"

"I'm back on the clock."

"Back to work?"

I nod, and then my phone rings. I set down my pint.

"I'll be right back," I say. I push through people to the door and answer.

"Hold for Cathy."

I hold.

"Smith Street Scrap Yard is owned by an LLC registered at 5510 New Utrecht Avenue. That's Borough Park. The library has a number, but I called and it's just a generic machine message. I'm thinking maybe you go down there. Door-knock at 5510 and see if you can talk to somebody. Ask if they own the yard and if they have any info. See if you can get a name."

"Okay."

"You're Jewish, right?"

I hate answering this question. In junior high I changed the spelling of my name to Rebecca because I thought it looked less Jewish. I decided that the way it was spelled "marked" me as Jewish, which I hated because the only Jewish part of me was long gone. My dad wasn't supportive of my choice, but didn't put up much of a fight. It was a tough time for us. My questions about my mother had become more insistent and angry by the time I turned twelve, and I think my father was exhausted from the constant struggle to balance respect for the woman who had borne his child and trying to be understanding about the identity crisis of a preteen girl. A few years later, when it was time to start applying to college, I switched it back to Rebekah. Every time I wrote it the new way it felt like a lie, and I decided it was time to learn to live with who I really was.

"Um . . . my mom was," I say.

"Okay, well, that means you're Jewish. As you know. Good. They can usually tell."

She hangs up. They can tell?

I find Iris and tell her I'm taking another shift.

"On a Friday?"

"I'm going to Borough Park."

"Really?" Iris knows that my mom grew up in Borough Park. She's offered to go there with me and walk around, just to see. But that always felt too much like a search. I am not searching for my mother. Not actively, anyway.

"You want company?" she asks.

"I'm good," I say.

Iris, who is loose and Friday-drunk, laughs. "I love you, Rebekah Roberts." She turns to Brice, who is standing at attention behind her stool. "Rebekah Roberts is my fucking hero." She hugs me.

"I'll text you," I say.

"Be safe," she says. "And don't forget poor Tony."

Tony is at the other end of the bar, kneeling with a clipboard in front of a mini fridge. I wave and he smiles. He finishes whatever he's doing, then comes over.

"Scoop's got a scoop?" he says.

The night we met I told him I worked for the *Trib* and he teased me, named me Scoop. I rolled my eyes, enjoying the attention, but cringing at the truth: I've never gotten a scoop. Not at the *Trib*, at least. There are reasons for this. Scoops, for the most part, come from sources, and sources come from being in the same place for more than a couple hours. As a stringer, my job is to go where I'm told, get some information, repeat. I'm in a different borough every day—one day a murder on Staten Island, one day a press conference in Midtown, one day an old woman dead in a broken elevator in Brownsville—and nobody knows my name or face until I show up. Every day I have to ingratiate myself to a whole new group of people. Different ages, different languages, different values and occupations and prejudices and levels of intoxication or hostility or shame.

"I'm going to Borough Park," I say.

"Yeah? What's the scoop?"

"Dead lady in a crane." I feel strong when I shock people—ooh, look how *hard* she is—but Tony's face tells me what I already know, which is that my characterization was crass. "Sorry," I say. "I was at this scene today. They found a woman, a naked woman, in a scrap pile. They had to lift her out with a crane."

"And you watched that?"

I nod. "She looked cold."

Tony shakes his head. I take a gulp from the pint, thinking, I could use a little buzz as I head into the neighborhood where my mother was born. The neighborhood that has haunted my imagination for my entire life.

"They don't know who she is yet," I say. "Well, we don't, the paper. But there's an address for the company that owns the yard. I'm going there, to see if they have any information."

"By yourself?"

I nod and finish the beer. Tony seems about to say something, but stops himself. I appreciate his concern almost as much as his self-control. I don't want to stiffen up with him again, but I can't seem to help it—sometimes it just takes one wrong word.

"They'll probably send a photographer," I say. "Plus, Borough

Park is really safe. Come on, how much Jewish street crime do you read about?"

"Just because you don't read about it doesn't mean it doesn't happen."

I smile. "True."

He seems pleased to have bested me, but not too pleased. He's very hard not to like.

"I'm sorry I have to bail," I say.

"Me, too," he says.

"What are you doing tomorrow night? Do you have to work?"

"I don't."

"Wanna have drinks near me?" I ask, bracing myself, just in case he says no. I can stand angry brothers and haughty teenagers telling me to fuck off when I try to interview them for a story, but in my personal life I do not take rejection well. Another thing I learned in therapy was that each rejection "brings up" *the* rejection, and all of a sudden I'm just an orphan. But I try not to think about it that way.

"I could be into that," he says.

"I'll call you," I say. I step up on the footrail along the bottom of the bar and lean in. "I'm sorry I was shitty," I say again.

Tony smiles. He has really long, almost feminine eyelashes and cloudy-day blue eyes.

"Stand me up and I'll go Brooklyn on your ass," he says.

I lean in closer and kiss him, feeling wet and a little drunk.

"Maybe you'll go Brooklyn on me anyway," I say.

Oh Rebekah, she's so hard.

CHAPTER THREE

I got my job at the *Trib* five weeks after I moved to New York City. My dad gave me three thousand dollars for graduation. Enough to put down my half of our first month's rent and security deposit, buy a monthly MetroCard, and float me for a little less than a month. I wanted to do daily newspaper work. I'd listened to my professors and read various memoirs of successful journalists and they all espoused the virtues of the daily grind. They also recommended staying away from major markets, like New York City, where competition is fierce—for jobs and for stories. But New York City was nonnegotiable. New York City was the goal. I decided I could temp if I didn't get a job right away. Plus, Iris was going. And yes, partly, it was about my mom. Being close feels like forward movement.

I'm not actively trying to find her; I've gone over the ways that would turn out in my head many times and each time the conclusion, even if I find her, is sadness. She and my dad never got married, and if she was smart, which my dad says she was, she probably never told anyone she'd had a child in that lost year when she ran off with a Methodist from Orlando. I used to feel nothing but hurt and hate for her. I hated that what she'd done was even possible. Then I got pregnant my freshman year at college and I experienced what it felt like to know that I just couldn't take care of a child. I wasn't in love—or rather, I was in love, but he wasn't—and while I imagine that my mom's trepidation probably began as soon as she found out she was pregnant, having my father there with her, ecstatic, proposing marriage, ready to be a family, postponed the realization that she couldn't—or wouldn't—shed everything she'd been bred to believe her life was about. I had an abortion at ten weeks. I think it was the right thing to do.

So New York City it was. On my fourth day in town, I interviewed for, and got, a position at *The New York Star*. Official title: Reporter. It was magical. Iris and I invited everyone we could think of to our apartment to celebrate. We drank and smoked weed and then pranced through the streets like we owned them. Which we kind of did. I fell completely in love with New York that night. Who was I? Some motherless white chick from Florida, and yet every sidewalk and storefront and street corner and subway car was *mine*.

Then the *Star* folded. Apparently, New York City can sustain five major daily publications, but not six. The next week I interviewed at the *Staten Island Advance* and *The Jersey Journal*, but they were just "informational interviews," as there were no actual openings. I found a weekly paper in Brooklyn that needed writers, but their "freelancer guidelines" were seven single-spaced pages long, and they only paid twenty-five dollars per article. Iris had started buying my food when I got an e-mail from a reporter at the *Queens Chronicle,* where I'd sent my résumé. The reporter said that they weren't hiring, but that I might contact his buddy Mike Rothchild at the *New York Tribune.* "They're always looking for stringers," he said in the e-mail. "Feel free to use my name." I did, and two days later I was walking into one of those black glass Midtown high-rises with half a dozen revolving doors to the lobby. The reception desk called up for Mike, and I waited until someone came to fetch me and take me upstairs.

My first impression of the newsroom was that the ceilings were low. The entire floor was open, a maze of cubicles and outdated desktop computers. Windows all around but nothing beyond the next glass building to see. My escort tapped Mike on the shoulder, motioned to me, and then walked away. Mike took me into an office that did not belong to him, looked at my résumé, and asked two questions: when can you start and do you have a car? Now, and yes, I said. He nodded and explained my role. We'll try you out three days a week, he said. Call in at nine for a ten-to-six shift. He gave me the phone number of the city desk, where I was to report, and told me to go to the fifteenth floor to get an ID made. And just like that, I became a New York City tabloid reporter. I get $150 a day.

I get off the D train at Fifty-fifth Street and New Utrecht Avenue just after seven. Every sign is in Hebrew and there isn't a soul on the street. Streetlights glow weak orange over the stores. It doesn't exactly make sense, but I kind of feel like I've been transported to a 1930s Polish village. There is a milliner, a kosher meat market, a bakery, a florist, a tailor, a cobbler. There is a store for purchasing gravestones. There is a women's clothing store with the windows iced over as if it were a porn shop. Fifty-five ten is a brick building with three floors. The ground floor appears to be a commercial space of some kind, with racks of clothing and shelves of products inside. A small, hand-lettered sign leaning against the inside of the window says *Boro Park Mommies*. I try the front door, but it is locked. The buzzer panel has three buttons, all unmarked. I step back and make sure I'm in the right place. Fifty-five ten New Utrecht Avenue. I call Cathy.

"I'm here," I say. "It looks like it's some kind of shop. Is there an apartment number or something?"

"Nope, just 5510 New Utrecht Avenue, LLC."

"Okay," I say. "There's *nobody* on the streets."

"Shit," says Cathy. "I can't believe I didn't think of that. It's fucking Sabbath."

"Oh, right," I say.

"I thought you were Jewish?"

"I am," I say. I don't tell her that I've never once observed the Sabbath.

"I'm sorry," she says. "I should have remembered that. You're gonna have a hard time getting anybody."

"Well," I say, "I'll buzz."

"Great." She hangs up.

I buzz the top buzzer. Nothing. Again. Then the other two. Nothing. I buzz again. I wait. I buzz again. I buzz for five minutes. If there's anybody up there, they are either incredibly stoic, or deaf.

I call Cathy and tell her no one is answering. She says to hang around and see if anybody goes in or out. I walk up the block and across the street, then take shelter in the heated vestibule of a Citibank. While I wait, I pull out my phone and Google "Smith Street Scrap Yard and Boro Park Mommies." The fifth link is to an article from 2011 on a Web site called YiddishReader.com: "Mendelssohns donate space, funds to new mothers." That's it. Mendelssohn. The boy said his name was Yakov Mendelssohn. According to the article, the family founded an organization that provides assistance to new mothers, and clothing and supplies for families in need. Aron Mendelssohn is quoted as saying, "My wife, Rivka, and I visited a similar organization in Jerusalem and we strongly believe in the importance of nurturing Jewish children through assisting their mothers."

Rivka. Rivka is the Hebrew version of Rebekah. I am named for my mother's sister Rivka. According to my father, my mother had—has (I vacillate between referring to her in the past and present tense)—four sisters and three brothers. Rivka, the second oldest, died of an allergic attack when she was eleven. The girls were upstate, at a camp where Jewish families from Brooklyn sent their children. Rivka and my mother, who was nine, were walking back from a pond where they'd gone to try fishing. They were swinging their homemade poles and Rivka managed to smack open some kind of hive. My mother was a few steps ahead and escaped the worst, but the bees or wasps or whatever they were attacked Rivka. And she was allergic. She fell there, as little Aviva ran for help. When my mother came back, Rivka's eyes were swollen shut and she was gasping for breath. She died at the hospital.

I scroll through the search results for something else on the family, but don't find anything. I look up and see a man walk quickly to the door of 5510, open it, and slip inside. Fuck. I call Cathy to tell her the boy's last name was Mendelssohn.

"Great," says Cathy. "The library got a hit on the LLC that owns the building. Aron Mendelssohn?"

"That could be the father," I say. "I found an article about him and his wife creating a charity that seems like it's based here. And I remembered that the little boy said his name was Yakov Mendelssohn."

"Okay. Let me see if the library can confirm that Aron Mendelssohn actually owns the yard. In the meantime, let's get to his house. It's not far from where you are. If he *does* own the yard, he'll know what's going on with the dead body on the property. He might be our best chance of ID'ing the victim, because the cops aren't giving anything out."

"Right. Somebody went in the office. I'll wait and see if he comes out."

She gives me the Mendelssohn home address and I walk across the street to 5510. I'm not there two minutes when the man appears. He's rushing, and lets the door slam behind him.

"Sir," I say, skipping to catch him. "Excuse me, sir?"

He keeps walking a moment, then turns toward me. We make eye contact briefly. It's the tall man from the gas station.

"I'm sorry to bother you," I say quickly. "I'm a reporter from the *Tribune*. I was at the scrap yard earlier today and I just wanted to ask you a couple quick questions. Your family owns the yard, right?"

The man says nothing.

"Sir?"

He shakes his head and begins walking away.

"Mr. Mendelssohn, wait. . . ."

That gets his attention. He stops and turns again.

"You *don't* own the yard? I'm just trying to . . ."

"I have no information."

"Um, can I just confirm . . . Is your name Aron Mendelssohn?"

"I'm sorry," he says, turning, "I must get home."

"Sir," I call, but he's walking away. I go out on a limb. "Mr. Mendelssohn, I spoke with your son. . . ."

Dead stop. He turns back, his face changed. "You spoke with Yakov?"

Oops. "Uh . . ."

"You spoke with Yakov!" He steps toward me and I flinch, afraid for a moment he's going to hit me.

"I'm sorry, sir."

"What is your name?" he demands, towering over me. Spitting.

I have fucked this up. "Like I said, I'm from the *Tribune*. We're trying to get an ID on the woman who was found in your yard. I thought maybe you'd spoken to the police."

Mr. Mendelssohn's eyes are animated, but the rest of his face is slack. The difference is unnerving. "If you come near any of my children again, I will have you arrested."

He turns and walks away, heels clicking with angry deliberation against the sidewalk. I am no longer cold. Sweat pops from my pores and my heart is pounding huge inside my coat. I'd always imagined my grandfather as a kind of monster. I spent years searching for ways to pity my mother, to excuse her abandonment, and the excuse was always her father: Avram Kagan. My father had never met him, but he knew my mother feared and revered him. Here is what I know about my mother, Aviva: I know that my dad met her at the Strand Book Store in Manhattan in June 1988. My mom was dabbling in mainstream culture, peeling off her long black skirts and long-sleeved shirts and panty hose in McDonald's bathrooms and pulling on jeans and sandals and tank tops in an attempt to create, as my dad put it, a "non-Orthodox" identity. They met in the modern religion section. My dad was looking for a copy of *The Screwtape Letters*. He told her he was studying religion, and she lied at first and said she was, too. She'd been reading a lot about Judaism, trying to figure out if all the rules and limits she'd been taught were really the only way to worship God, so religious philosophy was easy for her to talk about. By the time she admitted she was a Hasid who'd never left New York, it was too late, my father was in love. They met secretly. Girls in her culture, my dad said, live at home until they are married, which is usually right after high school. They aren't encouraged to do much besides get ready to be a wife and mother, so while she was waiting around, my mother started reading. And the reading gave her ideas. So she read more. Her father didn't really pay attention—nobody did. As long as she watched after her little brothers and stayed out of the way, she could do what she wanted. And in early September, she ran away to Florida with my dad.

She was pregnant with me almost immediately. Dad proposed, she accepted, I was born, she bailed. Dad went to look for her once, but he didn't go to the family home. He told me he was concerned that confronting her father would drive my mother further away; that if she had been punished upon her return, the punishment would be redoubled when her goy baby-daddy showed up and gave face to the shame she'd caused. Maybe though, my father wasn't quite so valiant. Maybe he'd come to Borough Park and seen a man like Aron Mendelssohn. Maybe he'd been afraid. What utterly different lives we've had, my mother and I. Me, coaxed and encouraged into adulthood by my dopey, dependable, loving-kindness father. Aviva, ignored and intimidated by a man always cloaked in black.

I call Cathy and tell her what happened.

"Can you call DCPI and float a name?" I ask.

"Sure," says Cathy.

"Ask if the dead woman is named Rivka Mendelssohn."

"That's the kid's mom?"

"I think so. I'm pretty sure I just met her husband."

"I'll call you back. Head to the house."

I start walking. I don't get hunches a lot. I'm not often in a position where I know enough about a subject I'm reporting on to make any kind of guess about anything other than whom to call next and whether or not people are telling me the truth. I can't always see a lie, but sometimes it's easy. Sometimes people lie about really weird things, like, no, my son's not here, when I can see him peeking out from behind the blinds. I've had people tell me they witnessed crimes and accidents they didn't; I've nodded and taken notes while they say, oh yeah, I heard like fifteen gunshots around 10 P.M., when police have already told me there were only two shell casings and that the victim was shot after midnight. Usually they're harmless; they just want to feel important, maybe get their name in the paper. I shouldn't have let it slip to Mr. Mendelssohn that I spoke with his son; any father would be upset by that. But when he turned around to look at me after I'd said that, his face wasn't just angry; it was afraid.

I get to the Mendelssohn address in about ten minutes. The yard must be doing great business because the house is enormous. It's a corner lot, and the structure takes up almost every inch of the property, with just a small strip of grass separating the sidewalk from the outside walls. The front porch has pillars, like a Southern mansion, but the house itself is a peach-tinted stucco, with elaborate dormers and window dressings on all three floors.

I walk up the grand front steps and knock. Nothing. I knock again. Nothing. I go back to the sidewalk and look up. There do not seem to be any lights on, but on the top floor I see a face peek between the curtains. I wave, and the face disappears. I go back to the front door and knock. After a few seconds, I hear footsteps.

"What do you want?" asks a voice, muted behind the heavy wooden door.

"I'm sorry to bother you," I say, "I'm looking for Rivka Mendelssohn."

Another pause, and then someone turns the bolt and cracks open the door.

"Hi," I say, thinking, friendly, friendly, nonthreatening. "Is this the Mendelssohns?"

"You know Rivka?" I can barely see the woman's face. She's wearing a brimless velour hat pulled down over her eyebrows.

"I'm a reporter, for the *Tribune*. I actually talked to her husband, I think, just a few minutes ago. . . ."

"You spoke with Aron?" She opens the door a little wider at this. Her face is wide and unattractive: eyes too close together, nose too long, a sloping, shallow chin. She looks about thirty, give or take five years.

"I think so. He owns a scrap yard? In Gowanus?"

The woman does not confirm or deny. She looks past me, squinting into the street, looking for someone looking at her.

"Do you live here?" I ask.

She nods almost imperceptibly.

"May I ask your name?"

"My name is Miriam," she whispers, looking up at me briefly.

"I'm sorry to bother you, Miriam. I'm not sure if you've heard, but there was a woman's body discovered at the Smith Street Scrap Yard this morning, and we're trying to get some information about who she was, but the police haven't released her name yet. I was hoping Mr. Mendelssohn might be able to help."

"Did he?"

"Not really. He seemed . . . busy. Are you related to the Mendelssohns?" No response. "What about his wife, Rivka. Is she home?"

Miriam shakes her head and begins to close the door.

"Wait," I say, but I'm not sure what to say to stop her. "Um, will you be home tomorrow? I'd love to . . ."

"I'm sorry," she says. Click, bolt, and she is gone.

I wait a moment and lean in. I think she's still there; I don't hear any footsteps. I knock quietly. "Miriam?" Nothing.

My phone rings. It's Cathy.

"Where are you?" she asks.

"I'm at the Mendelssohns."

"Get out of there."

"Why?"

"Because you were right," she says. "The dead lady is Rivka Mendelssohn."

CHAPTER FOUR

When Cathy says get out of there, she doesn't mean I should flee the scene. What she means is that I should hang back. The *Trib* doesn't have much in the way of a code of conduct, but one thing we are very definitely not supposed to do is inform family members of a death. That's the police's job. Our job is to swoop in immediately post-inform and gather as much detail as the shocked family will give. It's an ugly job. I've asked mothers about their dead daughters and husbands about their dead wives, but I've never done it less than a few hours after they actually learned of the death. Of course, Aron Mendelssohn was at the yard earlier, so he is probably aware that it was his wife's body in the scrap pile—but Miriam, and anyone else at home, may not know yet.

"Stick around the block," says Cathy. "The police should be there soon. We're past deadline, but get everything. We'll go with the name and any information you can get. Find out if she's actually married to the yard's owner, how old she is, if she has kids, whatever you can. A quote would be great."

I'm standing across the street when I see three Jewish men in black hats and vests similar to those worn by the men who took Rivka's body away come up the block toward the house. They stand together at the street corner, waiting. I decide to approach.

"Hi," I say. "My name is Rebekah, I'm with the *Tribune*." The men barely look at me. "Are you here because of the woman in the scrap yard? I was out there earlier and I saw some . . ." Jews? No, can't say that. "I saw that the body was taken away by . . ." You guys? Can't say that either. I stop talking, hoping one of them will help me out. No such luck. They all look elsewhere—the sky, the ground, each other, their hands. For several seconds, I stand there like an idiot, trying to catch someone's eye. All three men are bearded and wear long tightly coiled sidecurls, which remind me of Shirley Temple ringlets. One is a redhead, like me. The other two have dark hair.

"We have no information," says the man with the red beard. They are all wearing long coats, but not gloves or scarves. Instead of boots, they all wear black shoes that are like a cross between sneakers and wingtips. And like DCPI, they display no signs of being affected at all by the icy weather.

"Is this where Rivka Mendelssohn lives?" I ask.

The redhead shakes his head. I don't think he's saying no, just that he's not going to tell me anything. I step away, feeling like an asshole, and a moment later, an NYPD squad car pulls up. The officers stay inside. The wind is picking up and I look around for a doorway or vestibule to hide in, but the streets are hopelessly residential. The cops look warm in their car. I wonder if, in the spirit of camaraderie, they'd let me sit in the back, but I'd probably have better luck asking Miriam to let me in and pour me a beer. I start pacing, halfway down the block and back again. The Mendelssohn home is the largest in sight, but many others are impressive. There are two-car garages and brass driveway gates and wrought-iron fences and glassed-in porches and patios. No children throw snowballs in the street; no cars blast music. It is just past dinnertime, but the streetlamps are the only lights on the block. Everyone is inside, living in the dark.

I swing my arms and jog in place. My scarf is wrapped around my mouth and nose, turning damp as I breathe. I wonder if Aviva grew up on this block. Did they live in a house or an apartment? Which synagogue did they pray at? If I had asked Miriam, *Do you know Aviva Kagan?* would she have said yes? I wish I could talk to someone about all this. Iris is likely to spend the night with Brice. I pull out my phone and text Tony.

how late do u work?

Tony texts back: *off at 10*

wanna grab a drink?

sure – bell house?

The Bell House is a bar three blocks from my apartment.

great. i'll text you when I get off – 11ish?

cool

The cops are still in their cars. I call Cathy.

"How long do you think I should stay?" I ask.

"If the cops haven't given us more info by ten, they won't until morning. Hang on till then. Photo's on the way. Is any other press there?"

I look around to be sure. "No," I say. "I haven't seen anybody."

"Good," says Cathy.

As soon as I hang up, another set of cops arrive. This time, it's plainclothes detectives in a black Lincoln Town Car. Just like DCPI and the Jewish cops, they are dressed for October, not deep January. As soon as they get out, so do the uniformed officers. All three groups congregate on the sidewalk for about thirty seconds, and then the cops get back in their cars, tailpipes pumping exhaust into the cold. I decide to make contact with the plainclothes officers. I cross the street and knock on the passenger-side front window. The man inside looks at me and raises his eyebrows without rolling down the window. I wait, then speak through the glass.

"Hi. I'm from the *Trib*."

He squints like he can't hear.

"Is this Rivka Mendelssohn's house? Her family owns the scrap yard, right?"

Finally, he rolls down the window about four inches.

"I don't have anything for you," he says, looking in the sideview mirror. He's probably fortyish, overweight like just about every cop out of uniform I've ever met, with a severe gray buzz cut. His partner doesn't even turn to look at me. He just stares down at his BlackBerry, rolling the cursor ball. "Call DCPI."

I cross the street and watch. After about ten minutes, the plainclothes cops get out of their car, which triggers the uniforms to do the same. The Jewish men join them, and the whole group climbs the front stairs. A moment later, they disappear inside.

After a few minutes, another Jewish man appears, this time on a bicycle. This man is clean-shaven but wearing a black hat like the others. Around his waist is a belt with a badge and a cell phone clipped to it. Huh, I think, an Orthodox member of the NYPD?

The man leans his bicycle against the back fence of the Mendelssohn house, and waits.

Five minutes later, my phone rings. It's George, the photog. He's on his way. I'm surprised Pete Calloway hasn't gotten here yet. Ten more minutes and two more cars pull up. One is George; one is Fred Moskowitz, editor, publisher, reporter, and ad sales rep for *The Brooklyn Beacon*, a tiny free weekly. I practically run to George's Volvo and jump in.

"Cold?" he asks.

I put my hands up to the heating vents and grunt a noise somewhere between *brrrr* and *yeah*.

"They want a photo," says George. "But these are Hasids, right? We're not gonna get anything." George is probably in his fifties. He wears a bomber jacket with Army patches on the chest and back. We sit together, listening to 1010 WINS, the local news station, which gives us hockey scores and traffic and weather between loud ads for skin doctors and car buy-back programs. Forecast: cold. Windy and cold. It's going to be fifteen overnight.

After about twenty minutes, the detectives come outside. George reaches into the backseat for his camera. "I'll follow your lead," he says.

We hurry over, with Fred trailing us. I call out a question: "Can we get an age, Detectives?"

The men keep walking.

Fred asks, "Is this about the woman in the scrap pile?"

"You have to get that from DCPI," says the one I'd talked to before, barely breaking stride. "We have no information for you."

"Assholes," says Fred, after they've gotten into their car.

"The uniforms are still in there," I say. "And the Jewish cops."

"They're called *Shomrim*," says Fred, loving my ignorance. "They're a neighborhood watch. And we won't get anything from them. I'm gonna get some coffee and come back later." He crosses the street to his Ford Taurus in a huff.

"What's the plan?" asks George, once we're back in his car.

"I'm not sure," I say. George has been on the job probably fifteen years, but it's usually up to the reporter to make decisions about who goes where on a stakeout. Even when the reporter is just twenty-two years old. "I should probably call in."

Just then the front door opens and the uniformed officers and the Jewish watchmen exit the house. The Jews walk together down the street and out of view. The officers linger on the sidewalk. One lights a cigarette. In the side-view mirror I see the man on the bicycle walk toward the officers. The officers nod in acknowledgment and they begin to discuss something. One gestures toward the house. Bicycle jots whatever information they're giving him down on a notepad. When the smoking cop finishes his cigarette, the two uniformed officers nod good-bye, get in their cruiser, and drive away.

Bicycle watches after them, then closes his notepad and starts walking around toward the back of the house.

"I'm gonna see if this one will talk to me," I say to George, who obligingly reaches back for his camera.

"Let's do it," he says.

We get out of the car and I walk quickly toward the man in the black hat.

"Excuse me," I say. "Sir?"

He turns around.

"Hi," I say, "I'm from the *Trib;* I'm wondering if you can give us any information about Rivka Mendelssohn. Even just an age? Was she married? Did she have children?"

I speak quickly, including multiple questions because I assume, based on the behavior of the rest of the cops, that he'll barely stop walking. I am wrong. This cop stops.

I extend my hand. "My name is Rebekah. I was at the scrap yard earlier today. This is George. I wonder if you could give us any information about the victim." The cop doesn't answer. He looks flustered, like I've caught him picking his nose or something. I continue. "We know her name is Rivka Mendelssohn, but we're hoping to get a little more information for the story. This is where she lived, right?"

As I am talking, his face changes. He begins to smile.

"Rebekah?" he says.

"Yes." My hand is still extended, but he hasn't taken it. He is just staring at me. I look at George, who raises his eyebrows.

"Sir?" he says, but the man doesn't seem to hear.

"Are you working on this case?" I ask, letting my hand fall, embarrassed. "We're just wondering if we can get a little information about Mrs. Mendelssohn. Is it correct that she was married to the Smith Street Scrap Yard's owner, Aron Mendelssohn?"

"I am Saul," he says. "Saul Katz."

"Okay," I say, writing down his name.

"I knew your mother."

I look up from my notebook. "Excuse me?"

He steps forward, reaching out to touch my arm. I flinch. Who is this man?

"You look just like her."

I drop my pen but can't bend over to pick it up. I feel like I've been turned to stone. I know I look like my mother. I've seen pictures. We have the same wavy copper hair, the same heart-shaped face, the same long nose, the same hazel eyes. There is also, I've come to realize, a sexiness about us both that, at least as adolescents, made us seem older than we were. Part of it is easy to point at: we're both stacked. I wore a C-cup before I got to high school. I'll never forget the way the junior high boys gawked and stumbled when I came to the end-of-eighth-grade party in a bikini. I'd had to buy the two-piece because my top and bottom were totally different sizes. When he is reminiscing, my father refers to my mother, on that first day in the Strand, as a "bombshell."

Saul steps back. "I'm sorry," he says, but he's still staring.

"Could you just tell us . . ." I'm too flustered to form a clear question and my stomach feels like it's on fire. Is my mother about to jump out of the bushes? Have I become a participant in some kind of reality TV show? Is this like, *Intervention* for abandoned children?

I look at George, who, mercifully, takes over.

"We've been told the woman who lives here was found dead this morning. We're looking for some information about her—age, marital status, that sort of thing."

Saul slowly pulls his eyes off me and addresses George.

"She was married," says Saul. "I'm not sure of her exact age."

"Do you know the family?" I manage to ask. My voice is tight, like something has its hands around my throat.

"I do," says Saul. "Though not well." He is older than my dad, maybe fifty-five. He is not wearing a wedding ring.

I can't think of the next question.

"Are you enjoying New York?" Saul asks.

I nod. I can't bring myself to look at him.

"Your father said you were a reporter."

"My father? You talked to my father?"

"We've kept in touch a little. He sent me an e-mail when you moved here." He's still staring at me, and his face has this almost-laughing look. The beer in my stomach is threatening to shoot up my esophagus. I am not prepared in the slightest for this situation. I wonder what George thinks. The last thing I need is him reporting my meltdown to the desk. I raise my eyes and stare Saul down.

"Is there anything you can tell me about Rivka Mendelssohn?" If he's going to make me feel like a frightened child, I am going to pump him for every ounce of information I can. Fuck you. I am not my mother.

"I'm sorry," he says, wiping a hand across his face. "It's just . . . I'm sorry."

"Age? Kids? I spoke with Aron Mendelssohn. Were they married?" Each word is difficult to say, but I am not going to let this man—or my mother—turn me into a mute idiot who can't do her job.

"Yes," says Saul. "Rivka Mendelssohn was Aron Mendelssohn's wife. He owns the scrap yard. This is their home. I don't know her exact age."

"I knocked on the door and met a woman," I say. "Miriam?"

"You spoke with Miriam?" Saul seems surprised, which pleases me. See? I'm not just an orphan girl. I'm a big-city reporter, bitch.

"Just for a minute, but that was before we were sure the dead woman was Rivka Mendelssohn. I'd like to see if I can get a quote from her now."

Saul is silent.

"Are you working on this case?" I ask.

"I work in property crime, not homicide. I was called in to assist with translation. Most Hasidim speak Yiddish at home. I help the department liaise with the community, when needed." He pauses. "Would you like to speak with Miriam again?"

No cop has ever offered to facilitate an interview for me. Usually, they either scoff, like the detectives in the car outside, or shame me, shaking their head that I would have the gall to prey on these devastated people at this delicate time. Perhaps, I think, I have stumbled upon a source. Courtesy of my deadbeat mother.

"Yes," I say.

"I will take you around the back."

"Can George come, too?"

"No."

I look at George. He doesn't seem bothered. Saul walks toward the back gate and George bends down to pick up my pen.

"I'll be right here," he says. "Holler if you need anything."

Saul lifts the latch on the gate and holds it open for me. The backyard is a narrow strip of snow-covered grass. A rusty metal swing set stands crooked in one corner; a row of garbage cans are lined up along a two-car garage. All the window shades are drawn. Saul knocks softly at the back door, which looks a lot like the front door; it has its own doorbell and small portico. Miriam appears at the door and Saul motions for me to go inside.

The three of us stand together in a small entryway. Miriam

looks very nervous. She says something to Saul in Yiddish and he says something back; then he turns to me.

"It is *Shabbos,* she is worried what the neighbors will say about all the activity. I've told her you are Jewish. She says she can answer a few questions if it helps."

I look at Miriam and try to catch her eye, but she keeps her head down.

"Thank you for taking the time," I say. "I can't imagine how hard this is. I just want to get a little information so that we can . . ." I want to say "humanize," but somehow it seems inappropriate. "So we can just let our readers know a little about her life." I pause for a cue to continue. Nothing. I continue. "Rivka lived here?"

Miriam nods.

"And, may I ask, how you are related?"

"Rivka is my brother's wife. We are like sisters."

I scribble *sister-in-law* in my notebook.

"How old was she?"

"Thirty."

"Did she have children?"

Miriam nods.

"Sorry, can I ask how many?"

"Three girls and one boy."

"Great . . . ," I say, scribbling. "And her husband, your brother, is Aron Mendelssohn? He owns the Smith Street Scrap Yard?"

Miriam nods again.

"When was the last time you saw her?"

Miriam looks at me for the first time during the interview. Her features seem even more pinched than they did an hour ago. I catch a faint whiff of cigarette smoke on her breath. "Tuesday."

"Tuesday?" That's odd, I think. It's Friday now. "Had she gone somewhere?"

Miriam looks at Saul, as if for help. Saul doesn't say a word. I'm surprised he's let me go on so long.

"Were you concerned? Had anyone in the family heard from her?"

Miriam shakes her head.

"So you hadn't heard from her? What did you think happened? Had she ever been gone like that before?" I have a bad habit of throwing all my questions out at once when I'm nervous.

Miriam bites down. I see her jaw flex. "She was a good mother."

I write that down. "I'm sure," I say, nodding. "Did you report her missing?"

Miriam does not respond, so I keep talking.

"How did she seem when you saw her last? Can you think of any reason this might have happened?"

Again, nothing from Miriam. I wonder if maybe her English is poor and I'm speaking too quickly. I try another subject.

"How are the children?"

"The children are fine."

"Fine?"

Miriam nods. "They are very sad."

I look at Miriam. She's looking at my notebook. I write down *kids v sad*. "Can you tell me a little about Rivka? Was she born here? What did she like to do?"

"We were both born in Borough Park."

"And you both live here, together?"

"My husband and I live on the third floor. It is a separate apartment."

A door slams. We all turn and see that Aron Mendelssohn has come in through the front. As soon as he sees me, he stops. He looks truly shocked that I'm there, as if I'm some sort of winged beast that just dropped through the ceiling. Like, how the fuck did this creature get in my hallway and how can I kill it before it kills me?

"Miriam!" he roars. Miriam jumps toward me. She actually grabs my arm, as if I might protect her.

Saul moves quickly past us, and the two men begin shouting in Yiddish.

"Go!" hisses Miriam, pushing me toward the door. "Write something nice. She was beautiful. Say she was beautiful."

I run out the back door, turning once to make sure Aron Mendelssohn hasn't followed me outside. I can hear him yelling. I lift the latch on the back gate and jog past George to his car. I have no idea if Saul is behind me. Fred Moskowitz has returned from his coffee run and sees me coming out.

"We're not getting a photo," I say when George gets inside.

"Oh yeah?" says George. "Figures."

"I'm gonna call in what I've got." I pull out my notebook and my hands are shaking. I can barely read my writing, but I remember exactly what Miriam said. I call Cathy's number directly. She picks up on the first ring. I tell her I talked to the sister-in-law.

"Perfect. Give me what you got."

"Her name is Rivka. She's thirty, married, has four children. Lives in a big house in Borough Park. Her husband is scary."

"Her husband is scary? Is that a quote?"

"No. Sorry. That's me. The rest is from the sister-in-law. I got in the house after the cops and talked to her, but when the husband came home he started screaming and I left."

"What's the sister-in-law's name?"

"Miriam."

"Last name?"

"Fuck." I forgot to ask. "I forgot to ask. It's probably not Mendelssohn. That would be her maiden name and she said she was married."

"And she lives there?"

"Yes. There are two entrances. It's a really big house. It's split into two residences."

"Okay, we can just say the sister-in-law. Anything else?"

"The last time she saw her was Tuesday."

"Tuesday?"

"Yeah."

Moskowitz is coming toward me and George. His coat is buttoned improperly, so the collar pokes up at his chin on one side. I can't talk to him while I'm talking to my editor. I point to the phone and make a sign to wait. He nods. I think Moskowitz might have worked for the *Trib* before striking out on his own. Or maybe it was the *Ledger*.

"That's three days before she was found."

"Right."

"But they didn't report her missing?"

"She didn't say."

"Okay. Any quotes?"

"Not much. She said, 'She was a good mother.' And, 'She was beautiful.'"

"Really?"

"Really." When she said it, it seemed somehow adequate as a

description. Not so much now. "She was pretty shook up. She said the kids were very sad."

"That's a quote? The kids are sad."

"The children. She said the children are very sad."

"Is photo there?"

"Yeah, but I got chased out before I could even ask for a photo. And I don't recommend anybody going back there. At least not tonight."

"Is anyone else there?" She means other press.

"Just *The Brooklyn Beacon*."

"Not the *Ledger*?"

"Nope."

"Okay. Go home. Great work. Don't forget to put in for overtime."

"Does Larry at the Shack have anything? A cause of death?" The Shack is how newspaper people refer to the tiny office reporters have at police headquarters.

"Not yet. But it's definitely a homicide."

"Duh."

Cathy laughs. "Great job, Rebekah."

I hang up and roll the window down to talk to Frank.

"You got in," he says.

"I didn't get much. Just her age—she's thirty." The offer of information surprises Frank. "Thirty, married, four kids. Born in Borough Park. That's it." I can give him information because nobody reads his paper.

Frank repeats the information and I nod, indicating he's remembered it correctly.

"Who's this from?" he asks.

"The sister-in-law. Miriam."

"Last name?"

"I forgot to ask."

Frank snickers. Forgetting to ask for the last name is a first-week mistake.

"That's all," I say.

"Okay. Thanks."

I roll up the window. George calls in and is told to go to a location in Queens. A city councilman's wife was picked up for DUI. They want a shot of the car. I'm about to call myself a livery cab to go home when I see Saul coming out the back gate. He looks around, then waves at me. I get out of the car.

"Here is my phone number," says Saul, handing me a business card that identifies him as a detective in the NYPD. "Please call me if you have any questions. For your story. Or . . . anything you need."

He's not staring at me with the same intensity now, which is nice. I write my phone number on a piece of notebook paper, tear it off, and give it to him.

"Thanks," I say. "If you hear anything about the investigation, give me a call. I don't even think they have a cause of death yet. I guess they're waiting on the autopsy."

Saul nods, but says nothing.

"Okay," I say. "Bye."

"Good-bye, Rebekah," he says. He's staring again. I turn and get back in George's car to call for a livery cab.

"Everything okay with that guy?" asks George.

"Yeah," I say. "He knew my parents."

George nods. Unlike Johnny, George doesn't need to fill a shift with talking. I appreciate that.

On the way home to Gowanus, sunk in the worn leather back-seat of a beat-up Town Car, I check my phone and see that I have a text from Tony.

still on for 11?

It's almost ten now. I even have time to shower.

see u there . . . hope you're ready for a saga

As we merge onto the Prospect Expressway, I close my eyes and see Aron Mendelssohn. What if he killed his wife and now he's mad enough to kill his sister for talking to me? I don't remember ever reading about a murder in the ultra-Orthodox community, but I haven't been in New York that long. I wonder if Saul knows more than he told me.

Saul.

I pull out my phone and dial my dad.

"Hi, hon!" he says.

"Hi, Dad."

"How's life in the big city?"

"Cold."

"It's a little chilly here, too. Maria brought in a bunch of grape-fruit from the tree this morning and a couple had gone bad from frost overnight." Maria is originally from Guatemala, but she's been in the U.S. since she was a teenager. She and my dad met at a conference of religious academics in Denver when I was about three. Maria was working as an assistant to one of the conference coordinators. They got married when I was five and had my brother, Deacon, a year later. "How's work?"

"Guess who I met today?"

"Who?"

"Saul Katz."

"Oh!" He sounds happy, which I suppose I should have expected. I've never understood my father's relationship to my mother and her memory. He doesn't talk about her much, but when the subject comes up, he speaks with tenderness and sympathy, like she died of cancer instead of abandoned him with a six-month-old doppelgänger. I challenged him for years, screaming and crying that she was a horrible bitch, a selfish, weak, heartless little girl who ruined both our lives. He listened, and he stroked my hair and held me when I'd worn myself out. But he never said anything more combative than, she shouldn't have left.

"Did you know he was a cop?"

"I did. He kept in touch over the years."

"That's what he said."

"You sound upset."

I sigh heavily. My dad is king of the understatement.

"He kind of ambushed me. Why didn't you tell me you had, like, told someone who knew Mom that I was moving to New York?"

"I'm sorry," he says. "He e-mailed me a few months ago. I think he saw your byline in the newspaper. Wanted to know if it was the same person."

"Great, so he's stalking me."

"I doubt that," says my dad. "He's a very nice man. How did you say you met him?"

"He showed up at a crime scene."

"A crime scene?"

"Well, actually, at a victim's house. They found a dead woman in a scrap pile this morning, and it turns out she's Hasidic. I went to her house to get a quote from the family and Saul was there."

"How awful. Are you okay?" My dad is very concerned about my work for the *Trib*. He doesn't approve of tabloid journalism. I wouldn't say I "approve" either, exactly, but, as I've explained to him, *The New York Times* wasn't hiring and I wanted to learn how to be a reporter.

"I'm fine."

"I don't know how you can do that kind of work. It must be so hard."

"What kind of work, Dad?"

"Not the *Trib*—I just mean, a body in a, what did you say? A scrap pile? Lord." My dad says "Lord" a lot. "The family must be devastated."

I decide not to get into the reactions of the family members I've met so far.

"So, how did Saul know Mom, exactly? He's older than you guys."

"Saul was part of a group of ultra-Orthodox who were questioning the rigid lifestyle. They used to meet in a house out near Coney Island to talk freely and read newspapers and watch movies— things they couldn't do at home."

"They couldn't read *newspapers*?"

"No. Most Orthodox try very hard to keep themselves from interacting, even passively, with the rest of the world."

"Right, because we're so evil."

"Depends on your perspective." I roll my eyes. My dad is the ultimate religious apologist.

"Okay, anyway . . ."

"They were all experimenting with new ways of living. From what I remember, Saul had married, at about nineteen, a woman he did not love. His family was not wealthy, and the matchmaker didn't consider him a good match, so he ended up engaged to a troubled young woman from a slightly wealthier family."

"Troubled?"

"Depressed? I'm not sure. What I know is that the marriage was a disaster. They were married more than ten years and had only one child, which was considered shameful. When he filed for divorce, she moved back in with her parents. Her father went to court and told a judge that Saul should be barred from seeing his son because he had become less religious and the child would be confused."

"And the judge agreed?"

"Apparently."

Everything I learn about Hasidic life is So. Fucking. Sad. But this is what she left me for. My stomach sizzles. I shift in my seat; I'm going to need a bathroom soon.

"Divorce was rare in the community, and he'd brought shame on his family and hers."

"Where does Mom come in?"

"Saul had worked at his father-in-law's clothing store. Of course, he was fired as soon as he filed for divorce. He had nowhere to go, and I think he actually slept outside or in the subway for a while until another man, I forget his name, invited him to help him fix up the run-down Coney Island house he'd been living in in exchange for a place to stay. Saul and the man—maybe his name was Menachem?—turned the place into a refuge for questioning Orthodox. That's where he met your mother."

"Mom stayed there?"

"She did. At first, she just went when she could sneak away from home, while her brothers were at yeshiva. But once we met, yes, she stayed there some nights. Until she came to Florida."

"And now he's a cop."

"Yes. He enrolled in the academy, if I remember correctly, the summer your mother and I met. He was older than most recruits, but physically fit and didn't have a criminal record. And back then, I don't think you needed any college to get hired."

"He didn't go to college?"

"Most ultra-Orthodox don't."

"Well, he's a detective now."

"Good for him."

"I think he was pretty surprised to see me." The burning in my stomach is getting worse. I cross my legs.

"I'm sure. You look just like your mother."

Sigh.

"Tell him I said hello, will you?"

"If I see him again." It's an obnoxious thing to say. I'd *like* to see him again. My dad would like me to see him again. Saul would probably like to see me again. I'm not sure why I antagonize my dad sometimes. I think I just hate the way he forgives her.

"How's Iris?" asks Dad.

"She's good. A lot of people are getting laid off in magazines but she seems to think she's safe."

"A lot of people are getting laid off everywhere. Did I tell you your brother lost his job at Taco Bell?"

"He *lost* a job at Taco Bell?" My brother is a sophomore in high school. He is very good-looking, very smart, and very lazy.

"If you can believe it, they actually closed the location."

The driver pulls up to my block under the F train.

"Tell him to get into newspapers. It's a thriving business."

"Ha."

"I'm home now, Dad. So I better go."

"Okay. Thanks for calling. I love you, sweetie."

"I love you, too."

I take the stairs two at a time to get to the toilet. Fortunately, I haven't eaten much, so the acidic shit that comes out is minimal. I have pills I'm supposed to take when the anxiety flares up, but they don't mix well with alcohol, so I dig around for the little bit of weed left in Iris's jewelry box. I pack our glass pipe and take a pull. Pot does pretty much nothing to help my symptoms, but it alters my thinking a little so I can sometimes pry my focus away from whatever it's stuck on. I stand beneath the hot water in the shower for what seems a very long time and concentrate on breathing. My stomach is aflutter and my throat is tight. My heart is beating hard and fast in my chest, quickened by the pot and the image of Rivka Mendelssohn's blue-skinned body and Aron Mendelssohn's roar, mixed with the pleasant buzz that comes from the knowledge that I'm about to see Tony. I inhale the steam and the lavender scent of Iris's fancy foaming body wash. The calm promised on the bottle is something I long for, something I can't ever seem to catch.

Tony is at the bar before me, drinking a beer and chatting with the bartender.

"Hey," I say, tapping him on the shoulder.

He gets up and hugs me. I rest my head on his chest for a moment, close my eyes. "What are you drinking?" he asks.

"Beer," I say, turning to the bartender. "Something local. No IPA."

"You heard the lady, Rico." Rico, sporting a newsboy cap and a long, stringy ponytail, obliges. The beers come and we drink. Tony seems to know someone at every bar or restaurant in the city.

"I met the dead lady's family," I say.

"Tell me."

I tell him. I tell him about Rivka's blue skin, about the little boy at the gas station, about the big house, about Miriam, Aron, and Saul. I tell him that I forgot to ask Miriam's last name, and that I was worried about her after Aron chased me out.

"So, Saul knew your dad? But you're from Florida, right?"

"He knew my mom, actually. She was from Brooklyn. She and my dad met here while my dad was doing an internship."

"And now they live in Florida."

I don't tell everybody I meet about my mom—it's a sad tale, and the awkward pity is unpleasant—but it's kind of front and center right now. And I feel safe.

"My dad does. My mom's . . . gone. She left right after I was born."

"Really?" He looks genuinely surprised, and then sad, like he just heard really bad news. Almost like he feels for me. "Fuck. I'm sorry. I didn't mean to . . . fuck."

"It's okay," I say. "I've had a lot of time to get used to it."

"Do you talk to her?"

I shake my head. "She could be dead or alive. I have no idea."

"And this guy, Saul, he knows her?"

"Knew her." But he could know her, I think. He could know

where she is right now. My heartbeat speeds up and I breathe in sharply.

"You okay?" asks Tony, putting his hand on my knee. "Wanna change the subject?"

Wouldn't it be nice, I think, if it were that easy? Change the subject, change the way I feel. Change my life. I nod, but I can't pull the pinched grimace off my face. I look away and drink. One-two-three big swallows of beer. Swallow the tightness. Liquefy it.

"Sorry," I say. "It's been a long day."

Tony motions for another round.

"Tell me if you wanna bail," he says. "I know it's late."

"No," I say. I let this feeling of fear slow me down for years. I let it keep me inside. No more, not here. Not in New York City.

"Wanna come over?" I ask Tony.

"I do," he says slowly. "You sure, though? We don't have to . . ."

"I'm sure," I say, sliding off the bar stool. I can't imagine sleeping alone tonight.

SATURDAY

CHAPTER FIVE

Tony and I get about five minutes into watching season five of *The Wire* in my bedroom when we start kissing, which turns quickly to me pulling off my shirt, him unhooking my bra, and his very thick dick inside me. I sigh and lean back when it goes in. It feels like a relief. He's got his arms tight around me and he comes with a loud cough.

"Sorry," he says, red-faced and out of breath. "That was quick. Did you . . . Do you want . . . ?"

I kiss his lips and hold his face in my hands. There are few moments in life where I feel more powerful than when I've just made a man come. I don't orgasm easily—maybe it's the pills, or maybe just my general anxiety about letting my guard down in front of people—but tonight I don't care. What feels good in this moment is being in control.

We fall asleep and wake up around ten the next morning. He goes up the block for coffee and returns with a copy of the *Trib*.

The front-page photo is of "Porn Dad." "Porn Dad" is how the newspaper refers to a man named Frank White who was arrested on Thursday for selling pornographic pictures of his girlfriend's son and daughter to his friends and several continents of other online perverts. The story got even bigger yesterday when somebody realized that "Porn Mom," whose name is Melissa Dryden, is actually Missy Sanders, former "hot daughter" on an ABC sitcom that ran between 1984 and 1986. She did a guest spot on *Melrose Place* in the early 1990s, then made some soft porn before disappearing. Pages three and four are the spread, which includes one sidebar of screen shots from poor porn mom's Cinemax days, with plot summaries of films including *Ecstasy Island 2: Pleasures in Paradise* and *Snow Bunny: Wet in Winter*, and another with a couple shots from her teen sitcom days.

Rivka Mendelssohn gets four inches on page seven:

WOMAN'S BODY FOUND IN
BROOKLYN SCRAP YARD
By Rebekah Roberts

The body of a Brooklyn woman was found in a Gowanus scrap yard on Friday. Rivka Mendelssohn, 30, of Borough Park was discovered by workers at Smith Street Scrap around 9 A.M.

"I saw her foot first," said an operator who declined to

give his name. "Everybody starting pointing and yelling and running toward the pile."

Mendelssohn dangled nearly 50 feet above the ground for several hours before employees and emergency service workers retrieved her body.

"I couldn't believe it," said another worker on the scene. "I've never seen anything like that before. I just kept thinking how cold she must be."

According to family members, Mendelssohn had been missing since Tuesday.

"She was a good mother," said Mendelssohn's sister-in-law. "The children are very sad."

Close. Someone embellished the quote from the operator and made it seem as though we had quotes from two workers, instead of two quotes from one. My name is on the piece, but I didn't actually write a single word. It took me by surprise when I first started at the *Trib* and learned that being a reporter meant that you go get the story, or part of the story, and then call in what you've learned. Someone else writes the story and either shares the byline with the reporter or, as in this case, just gives it away.

Tony and I turn on the television and settle into watching Goldie Hawn and Kurt Russell in *Overboard*, which is playing on TBS. The radiator hisses and heats the room. I slept badly, and yesterday feels like a dream. The edges run together. The body and the black hats, Miriam, the little boy. Did he know that his mother was the one hanging there? Did he know as he stood by the coffeepot that she was gone?

At noon Iris appears, and just as she's walking in, my phone rings. I get up from the futon and see that it's a New York number I don't recognize. Maybe it's Saul, I think. Maybe he's got my Aviva Kagan with him. Maybe they're right outside.

"Rebekah, it's Saul Katz."

I go to the window in my bedroom and wrap my arm around my chest, pressing in on my manic heart.

"Is everything okay?"

"I have something I'd like to show you. I know it's the weekend, but you may be able to use it for an article."

"Okay . . . ," I say. He is not with Aviva. But he could be; he will be. Maybe. If I am patient.

"Would you like me to pick you up?" he asks.

I give him my address and he says he will be there in thirty minutes.

"If you have one, wear a long skirt," he says. "It will help to fit in."

After I hang up, I go into the bathroom and lean over the toilet. Something wants to come up, but it isn't food. I gag, tears forming in my eyes. I flush, and fling cold water on my face.

"Was that work?" asks Tony when I come back out.

"That was Saul."

"Does he have a scoop?"

Iris is dumping her purse and her coat on the table. "Who's Saul?"

"Saul is a cop," I say. "He helped me out on the stakeout last night. He knew my mom."

"Really." Iris looks sideways at Tony.

"I told him."

"Oh good," says Iris, coming to sit on the opposite side of the futon from Tony. I am still standing.

"Saul is a detective and he's Orthodox and he was called to help the police translate when they notified the family of the scrap yard woman that she was dead," says Tony.

Iris looks at me. "And you just . . . ran into him?"

"He recognized me. He said I looked just like her."

"Jesus," says Iris.

"I know."

"This is strange, right?" Iris asks. "Or am I just negative because I'm hungover?"

"Borough Park is like a small town," says Tony. "There are thousands of Jews, but there are far fewer families. He could have known her."

"Oh, he knew her," I say, thinking about the way he was staring at me. "Anyway, apparently he's got some information for me. On the story."

I dress and tell Iris not to worry. Tony walks me downstairs. Saul's Chevy Malibu is idling outside the door. Tony gives me a hug and says he'll call me later. I open the car door and slide into the seat beside Saul.

"Thank you for coming," says Saul. He's wearing the same thing he was last night, a cheap white button-down shirt, and a coat and pants that are both black but not quite the same hue. He looks like he hasn't slept, though I probably do, too.

"How are you?" I ask.

"I read your story."

I want to say it's not really my story, that I didn't write it. But before I do, it occurs to me that whether or not I actually put the words together, my name is on it—and thus I am responsible for it. Or I should have been. "It was short."

"Will you write another article?"

"I don't know," I say. "I don't usually get to make that decision."

We drive in silence for a few minutes. Just as I am about to ask where we're going, Saul speaks.

"My supervisors do not know I've contacted you," he says. "I have some information you can use to write a story—maybe many stories—about Rivka Mendelssohn. But you cannot use my name in print. I am a police official with knowledge of the investigation."

This is not what I expected him to say. But I suppose it makes sense that we establish the rules of our interaction early. Yes, he is the man who provided the first morsel of actual information about my mother I'd been given in, oh, twenty years, but he is also a cop and I am a reporter.

I've used anonymous sources before. In my Section 8 fire series, I kept the secretary at the landlord's office completely out of the story, even though she was the one who confirmed to me that she had seen him give his teenage nephews seventy-five dollars each to install the smoke detectors and failed to check their work. In school my professors warned against allowing people to go off the record or remain anonymous. Once someone is off the record, it's hard to get them to go back on, they said. And anonymity undermines trust between the reader and the newspaper. Reporters don't take a formal oath to do no harm or follow a set of ethical guidelines while performing our job—actually we don't take any kind of oath, or test, at all. I had a professor who thought journalists should have to be licensed, like lawyers and accountants. Then, he said, we'd get more respect. I'm actually not against the idea at all, but it doesn't matter, because it's not going to happen. And who would we be swearing to do no harm to? Our source? Our reader? Our editor? Ourselves?

"That works," I say.

"It is very important that we find who killed Rivka Mendelssohn. If the newspaper keeps writing about her, it might help."

"Really?" Usually cops say the opposite. "What makes you think that?"

"Well, to begin with, Aron Mendelssohn has not been questioned. You always bring the husband in. Always. And he hasn't been in. Which could mean a couple things, but what I think it means is that he has exerted pressure."

"Pressure?"

"The precinct has to deal with this community delicately."

"Why?"

"They give money, for one thing. And they vote in blocks. There is an informal agreement that the ultra-Orthodox are mostly law-abiding and can police themselves. . . ."

I interrupt him. "Until somebody dies."

"You'd think so."

We ride in silence a few moments more.

"Do you think he did it?"

"Aron Mendelssohn?" Saul considers this. "I don't know. Aron Mendelssohn is a wealthy man. His father donated most of the money to build the yeshiva on Ocean Parkway. He is a business owner, of course. The fact that his wife was found dead at his business is suspicious, but doesn't necessarily point to him as the killer. He's never been in trouble with the law, but most Hasidim haven't.

He needs to be questioned. And not bringing him in tells me the investigators are thinking about things other than the most efficient, effective ways to solve the case. It also tells the community that they can stay behind closed doors and pretend it didn't happen."

"Is that what they'll do?"

"It's what they do when it comes to domestic violence and mental illness and sexual abuse. All of which occurs in the community, just like in any other community. But here the shame of coming forward is compounded. Generally, Jews in this community believe that speaking to the authorities about another Jew is a sin against the community. It's *mesirah*, they say."

"Mesirah?"

"Mesirah. It's Yiddish. It means reporting on your fellow Jew. In the past, in Europe, if a Jew was arrested and sent to prison, he would be killed there. So it was every Jew's duty to keep other Jews out of prison, which means not talking to the police."

"Even now?"

"Even now."

"But, this is a murder. You can't just not talk."

"You can if the police don't ask you to."

"But, won't someone *want* to talk? Like Miriam? Her sister-in-law was found in a dump."

"You saw what happened when Aron saw Miriam talking to you," says Saul. "I'm surprised she risked it."

It's a strange thing to say, given that he's the one who took me to speak to her. He was pushing things even then. Did he know she would talk to me?

"Yeah, but I'm a reporter. I don't have any actual power. The police have power. They can make you talk."

"Maybe. Actual power depends on perception of power, to some extent. Many people would say that with access to the minds of a million readers, you had more power than I did there. But really, in that situation, neither of us had actual power. Aron Mendelssohn had actual power."

"Yeah, but . . . what about the law? Couldn't a judge compel people to talk? Contempt of court or something? Interfering with an investigation?"

"Yes, that could happen. But the fact that the investigators haven't brought the husband in yet is a sign that they are not going hard at this. So is the fact that they didn't take any evidence with them when they were in the house last night."

"You're not an investigator?"

Saul shakes his head. "Not on this case. Not officially. Like I said, I was called in to assist last night."

"Do you get called in a lot?"

"Every month or two. Usually as a translator."

"They really can't speak English?"

"Most can, but many—the elderly and children, for example— have trouble. For boys, their general education ends at eleven or twelve. Then they begin Torah instruction, which is conducted in Yiddish."

"And the city is okay with that?"

"The city tends to stay out of religious education."

"And then what?"

"And then they marry. They find a job, usually within the community. As a teacher, or a clerk. Many Hasidim own property, so real estate management."

"What about the girls?"

"It is different for the girls."

"Obviously."

Saul looks at me. I'm not used to being around people who are so serious. I think I've hurt his feelings.

"Sorry, it just seems a little weird."

"No, no," he says, again. Then he pauses and smiles. "You look like your mother but . . ."

"But what?"

"You are very different."

"How?" He's set my stomach off. I squirm in my seat.

"She was not, not so . . . I think you are smarter than she is."

It's not what I expected him to say. I look at him, but he keeps his gaze forward. We've left Gowanus and are headed south toward Borough Park. I've never thought about how I stacked up to my mom intellectually. I feel more proud than offended, which is what I'm sure Saul meant for me to feel, but I'm frustrated by my complete inability to add anything to a discussion I would love to have. Was my mother smart? I have no idea.

"You said 'is.' Is she alive?"

"Your mother?" Saul sounds surprised. "You don't . . . ? I'm sorry." He feels bad, I realize immediately. Like it took him until this moment to realize that she really did disappear from our lives twenty-two years ago. "Her family moved upstate near Kiryas Joel many years ago."

Kiryas Joel is the name of the town in the Catskills where a sect of super-Orthodox Hasids live. I've read about it. The articles said it was pretty bad: Rabbis having to see women's "clean" panties to certify they were off their periods and thus safe to re-welcome into society. Average family size triple, quadruple the rest of us. Most people on food stamps. One article said it was the poorest town in America.

"Do you still see her?"

"No," he says. He's not exactly wistful, but almost. "The last time I saw your mother was more than twenty years ago, just before she moved to Israel."

"She was in Israel?" Now that's news.

Saul nods. "The Kagans have family there. Two great-uncles chose Jerusalem over Brooklyn after the war. I got the sense that it was to be a fresh start for her."

"Another fresh start," I say. "I think me and my dad were supposed to be a fresh start, for a while."

"Do you keep in touch with your mother?"

His question surprises me, and then pisses me off.

"You're kidding, right? For all I know, she got hit by a bus ten minutes after leaving us. I actually had myself convinced she was dead for like, a good few years. It was almost comforting. Until I realized that if she was really dead, I'd probably have heard about it. Then for a while I thought she was alive because, somehow, I'd just *know* if she was dead. Then, I started thinking she could be, like, dead in a ditch somewhere, and I'd never know. I totally imagined her trying to get back to me, and being murdered. But that was bullshit."

"You are very angry with your mother."

"I think I have a right to be."

"Your mother—"

"Hold on," I say. "If you're about to tell me how fucking great

Aviva Kagan was, and how she was just *so* tortured by her family and their ridiculous idea of God that she had to *abandon her child—* you can save it." The last few words are a croak. I take a deep breath. I've been in therapy on and off for years and if there's one thing I've learned, it's to take a deep breath. As many as possible. "You just don't leave your child. Unless you're cruel. And maybe she was cruel." I'm shaking now. My chest feels on the verge of emitting a laugh, a sob, and my breakfast all at the same time. Deep breath.

Saul signals and pulls the car over after the next light. We're in front of a fire hydrant on a residential street. Traffic is light.

"Rebekah," says Saul slowly. "Your mother was a weak woman. She was vibrant and creative and beautiful and willing to take risks. She changed a room when she walked in it. But she could not tolerate pain. Her spirit broke easily, and often catastrophically. The gossip was drugs, but I have no proof of that. I believe your mother was sick. A mental illness, perhaps. She just couldn't make it work for herself. And of course no one wanted to marry her after she came back. I think that was what Israel was supposed to be. Find a groom far enough away he won't mind a little . . ."

"Backstory."

"Exactly."

"But she came back?"

"Yes."

"And disappeared again, right?"

Saul nods.

I puff an exasperated exhale.

"It must be have been very difficult," says Saul.

"It was, Saul," I say, feeling like I know him all of a sudden. I look at him and he is looking at me. He's almost smiling, and suddenly

I realize how grateful I am to be looking at someone who knew her. Someone other than my father for whom the woman who is my mother is a real person. "It was very difficult. It was always there."

Saul nods. "I know many young women like her—and men, too. It is not always a natural fit, this life, and there are harsh consequences for failing to conform. Your mother didn't fit. And she hated herself—and the world—for it."

I don't know what to say. I suppose that makes sense. I wonder if Rivka Mendelssohn fit? I close my eyes a moment, then open them.

"We can go now," I say. "I'm fine."

Saul checks his mirrors and pulls out into the street.

"I didn't know Orthodox Jews could be cops," I say after a few blocks. "I mean, you can't go by all the rules, right?"

"My religious life doesn't affect my work as much as you might think," he says. "But I do not live the strict lives many others in the community live."

"You rebelled."

Saul looks cross. "I hate that word. It sounds so adolescent. I endured a marriage that was very unhappy and which brought pain to myself and many others. Including my son. Because of all this, I was moved to alter my way of life, but not to turn my back on my heritage or my God. It was a very long process. And I know you meant nothing by it, but the word upsets me."

"Perfectly understandable," I say, trying to apologize without actually apologizing.

"What were we talking about?"

I laugh. "Before your outburst or mine?"

Saul chuckles, too. Neither of us can remember. We ride in

silence again for a while. Finally, Saul pulls over alongside a small park.

He turns off the engine and looks at me.

"There will be a funeral for Rivka Mendelssohn later today. But before she is buried, I'd like you to see her body."

We walk in silence for several blocks, past quiet brick homes and small apartment buildings. "I know it's cold," says Saul, finally. "I'm sorry. It is Shabbos. I can't be seen driving."

"You can't be seen? By who?"

"By anyone," he says. "By the community."

"So you, like, *pretend* to be observant?"

"It is important that I have the trust of the people in the community," he says. "I am observant. But not so much as some."

I wait for him to explain further, but he does not.

After about ten minutes, we reach the funeral home, a large low building with a parking lot surrounded by a chain-link fence. There is one entrance marked for men. Another for women. We enter through the women's door and stand in a kind of vestibule. Saul speaks in a hushed voice.

"When a Jew dies, the family receives the body almost immediately. Tradition forbids embalming or extracting part of the body, which is what the medical examiner would do. And the deceased is to be buried as soon as possible, usually within twenty-four hours. If today was not Shabbos, she would have been buried this morning. Instead, the service will be after sundown."

"But it's a homicide."

"Yes," says Saul. "But again, there is pressure from the family and the community to have the body buried."

"Are you telling me that Rivka Mendelssohn is going to be buried without an autopsy?"

"Yes."

"Is that even legal?" I ask, dumbfounded. How could the police even begin trying to figure out who murdered her if they don't examine her body?

"There is no law that says there must be an autopsy done on a body. That is entirely up to police discretion. And in a case like this, when a member of the ultra-Orthodox community is dead, the police have been known to defer to the wishes of the family, or whoever is representing them. The Hasidim vote, and most vote for who their rebbe tells them to vote for. In Brooklyn, the ultra-Orthodox vote can mean the difference between being the current or former district attorney, or city councilman. And if a powerful man like Aron Mendelssohn calls the rebbe and the rebbe calls someone in the DA's office and asks him to tell the precinct commander to let Chesed Shel Emes take a body, the precinct commander may let that body go."

"Who?"

"Chesed Shel Emes. They are a privately funded group—some with schooling in mortuary science. Jewish law says that every drop of blood and strand of hair of the deceased should be buried with him. Officially, they prepare the dead for burial. They come to crime scenes and clean up, and then cleanse the body to make it pure."

"They destroy evidence."

"That is one way to look at it."

"I saw them take her away, from the yard. The M.E. and this other van, with Hebrew letters drove up at the same time. The . . . Chesed . . . they ended up taking her."

"Yes. And they brought her here."

I am about to say that this arrangement seems utterly fucked, and ask Saul how many other special interest groups get to keep bodies from the authorities after violent crimes, when a woman walks in. She is probably in her late thirties, and she's wearing a white coat. She is petite, small-boned, and, I realize, wearing a wig. I don't think I would have noticed that it was a wig yesterday, the deep brown hair looks very natural, cut in a bob and parted on one side with bangs that sweep across her forehead. But now that I have the idea in my head that ultra-Orthodox women wear wigs, it's easy to see that it's not really her hair. It's a little too shiny, and the place where the part meets the bangs seems too perfectly perpendicular. She says something in Yiddish to Saul, and Saul responds back in English.

"This is my cousin's daughter," he says, gesturing toward me. "She is considering police work. Rivka, this is Malka Grossman."

"Hello," I say. Why is Saul lying?

Malka nods. "If you want to view her, we should hurry," she says to Saul. "Her family will be here by four o'clock." I glance at my watch. It is two thirty.

"Please," says Saul.

We follow Malka through a door, down a hallway, and into a small room, where she directs us to don paper hats and paper booties. While Malka is out of earshot, I ask Saul why he referred to me as Rivka.

"Rivka is Hebrew for Rebekah," he says.

"I know that," I say.

"Malka won't feel comfortable speaking to you unless she thinks you grew up in the community." I decide not to argue and we descend a narrow set of stairs into the basement, where a body, covered with a white cloth, lies on a table. A young woman is sitting on a chair beside the body. She is praying. Malka says something to the woman in Yiddish and she leaves without acknowledging us. Saul and I keep our coats on.

"I never allow a man to view a woman's body. But your cousin is a friend to our family. And I hope he can help the police find who did this. Rivka Mendelssohn was a good woman."

Malka pulls down the shroud over Rivka's body, and the first thing I think is that she looks dry. At crime scenes, there are fluids. Bodies leak when damaged. But here in the basement of the funeral home a day after being found, Rivka Mendelssohn's shredded skin looks like someone has painted a coat of polyurethane on it. The gashes torn into her legs, her arms, her belly, her neck have been cleaned out. The flesh bunches against the deepest wounds, creating wrinkles. The smaller ones, the scratches, are red, but bloodless. Where there are no open wounds, her pale skin is covered in bruises; clouds of purple and blue and red and yellow. If Malka told me she had been attacked by wolves, I would have believed her.

Saul begins to speak. "This looks like blunt force trauma, here and here." He points to Rivka's head. You can see the skull wounds clearly because she has no hair. Someone has, mercifully, closed her mouth.

Malka is silent and Saul continues. "It looks like she was hit multiple times, very hard, on the back of the head." Malka, as if on cue, lifts Rivka's head slightly and turns it, pointing to one particularly devastating wound just above her left ear. "See the blows to the neck? Here and here. They seem to be both pre- and postmortem."

"She did not die easily," says Malka.

I can't speak. What is happening inside my chest is not anxiety. It is the low rumble of a feeling I thought I might have outrun: sadness. Heavy, weeping sadness pulling at the corners of my mouth, tightening around my throat. Rivka Mendelssohn was about my height and weight, but lying on the table she seems tiny. Like a child. She has an old scar, maybe from a cesarean birth (or two), just below her belly button. I remember reading *Catch-22* in high school and getting to the end where Snowden, the airman who gets shot, "spills his secret," and his secret is literally his guts. Man is matter. Drop him out a window and he will fall. Set fire to him and he will burn. Something like that. I always remembered those lines. To me it felt like a carpe diem thing. Like, you've got this body, this life, and it's all you've got. But looking at Rivka Mendelssohn I think maybe he meant it more literally. Rivka Mendelssohn was a woman, and then, suddenly, she was a pile of meat and bones. And it didn't take a war to do it. If I had a bat, I could have done it myself.

"I've seen bodies in worse condition," says Malka. "But usually in deaths involving motor vehicle accidents. See these?" She points to marks on her wrists. "I'm not certain, but she may have been restrained."

My phone rings. I dig into my pocket to silence it, but my hands feel light, and as I pull it out I drop it onto the concrete floor. It bounces twice and lands beneath Rivka. I drop to my knees to retrieve it. UNKNOWN—it's probably the desk, though I don't know why they're calling me. I flip the switch to silent and put the phone back in my pocket. Malka looks uncomfortable; she glares at my phone. If I were really named Rivka, I think my phone would be off for the Sabbath.

"Sorry," I say.

"I know this would just be an opinion," says Saul, "but might you be willing to entertain a scenario?"

Malka nods.

"Rivka, perhaps you should write this down," says Saul. I nod and dig into my bag for my notebook. My hands are trembling. "Based on what I see, my opinion is that Rivka Mendelssohn was struck from behind and knocked down. See her hands, and knees." He points to Malka, who obliges, gently lifting Rivka's left hand. She turns it over to reveal broken fingernails and scratching. She sets it back down and lifts the other. The knees, I can see, are scratched and bruised, though so is the rest of her.

"The wounds to the head and neck look pre-mortem. If I had to guess at a cause of death, I would probably say cerebral hemorrhage due to repeated head trauma. But obviously I can't be sure. Much of the rest—especially the bruising and ripping in the skin—seems to be postmortem. It is possible that much of this came from the . . . material in which she was found."

He means the mountains of steel.

"What are these?" I ask, pointing to deep skids on Rivka's bald head.

"It appears as if her hair was freshly shorn," says Malka.

Saul nods. "I'd say those are from a straight razor or a knife with a very sharp blade."

I start to conjure pictures of what happened to Rivka Mendelssohn in my mind. Someone ties her up. Then shaves her head. Then kills her. Then takes off her clothes and drives her to the scrap metal yard and throws her in. That is some sick shit.

We all stand silently for a few moments. If I focus on the

injuries—the torn flesh, the bruised skull—I can trick myself into thinking that the body lying before me is some kind of science project: just a cadaver ready to be cut open and explored by medical students or researchers. But when I look at her feet, the second toe longer than the first and the remnants of polish on her toenails, her breasts fallen flat and crooked against her chest, I see a mother who bore four children and breast-fed them. I see a woman bent over in a bathroom, painting her toenails. Did she have to keep that secret? Are ultra-Orthodox women allowed such adornments? I have the urge to touch her, just to make sure this is all real. Three hours ago I was eating a breakfast sandwich and watching Goldie Hawn yell at Kurt Russell.

Finally, Malka speaks.

"And she was pregnant. I'd say about twelve weeks."

"Fuck," I say.

Saul and Malka both look at me.

"Sorry," I say. "I just . . . so the police really aren't going to see her?"

Neither Saul nor Malka answers my question.

"If that's all . . . ," says Malka, "The service is at six."

"Thank you, Malka," says Saul. "You'll keep this visit between us?"

Malka nods.

"Thank you," I say.

Saul and I strip off our hats and booties in silence. In the entryway, I check my phone and see two more missed calls from the desk.

"Do you need to return that call?" he asks.

I nod. "It's work."

"Better take it outside."

The steel sky has turned into a low fog, and my anxiety is so high, I feel like I might float away. Inside my chest my heart is bloated. It is clattering like thunder and I realize I'm sweating and shivering. I look around for a bench or a rock or something to sit on. My stomach is making noises, and of course I've left my pills at home.

I dial the *Trib*.

"City desk."

"It's Rebekah," I say.

"Rebekah," says the receptionist. "Lars has been looking for you. Hold on."

Lars has Mike's job on Saturdays.

"Rebekah—you were on the scrap yard body, right?"

"Yeah."

"Do you have a car?"

"No."

"Shit."

"Lars," I say, "you know I'm not on today, right?"

"I thought you had a car. The list says you have a car."

"I did. . . ."

"Can you work today? We're short and I need somebody to go to Sunset Park. Police are questioning the gardener in the crane lady murder. When he gets home, we want to talk to him."

"The gardener?"

"Apparently he's illegal. If you've already worked your thirty-eight, you can put in for time-and-a-half."

"Okay . . ."

Lars gives me the address. "Miguel Arambula. Do you speak Spanish?"

"No."

"Shit. Hold on." Pause. "I'll call you back."

He hangs up and I wait. That would have to be one seriously fucked-up gardener to do all that to a client. Maybe she was horrible to him. I haven't thought much about who Rivka Mendelssohn actually was. Maybe she was a rich bitch. Maybe he kidnapped her and tortured her and tried to extort money from her family because he got tired of being called a wetback.

My phone rings.

"It's Rebekah."

"Hold for Lars."

I hold.

"Rebekah. Can you go to Borough Park instead? They're having crane lady's funeral."

"Okay," I say.

"Get the scene. Find out whatever you can about her."

"So is the gardener a suspect?"

"Don't know. Her body is at the Adonai Funeral Home, so that's where they'll gather." He gives me the address—but I'm already there.

Saul comes out of the funeral home.

"I'm supposed to cover the funeral," I say, still holding the phone up to my ear. I feel like I can't bring my arm down. "I guess they're still interested in the story."

"Good," says Saul.

"Why did you bring me here?" I whisper. I can't get ahold of what's happening in my body. I feel like I'm going to explode into flames and melt into the cement at the same time.

"I brought you here because, in three hours, Rivka Mendelssohn will be in the ground and the only people who will have seen what happened to her body will be Malka and myself. And who-ever did this. And now, a member of the press."

My mind feels like it belongs to someone else. How did I get here? Who the fuck am I to be entrusted with this? Fucking *mur-der*. And we're the only ones who've seen what he did to her.

My stomach heaves and I cover my mouth, but it's useless. I lean over and vomit up coffee and egg and bile onto the pavement of the funeral home parking lot. The yellow liquid splatters on my shoes. Saul jumps back. I kneel down and gag again, but nothing comes out. My face is wet and hard with tears and snot and I can feel the bits of whatever came out on my lips.

Saul puts his hand on my shoulder. "It's okay," he says. "Come, let's get in my car."

We walk in silence and I let him open the passenger door for me. He comes around and digs through his center console for Kleenex, which he hands to me. I wipe my face and blow my nose. My mouth tastes like acid. I roll down the window to get some air.

"Did you hear about the gardener?" I say, finally.

"The gardener?"

"Apparently you guys have the Mendelssohns' gardener in for questioning. He's illegal."

Saul is silent.

"Did you know about that?"

"I did not," he says. "But it is not surprising."

"Aron Mendelssohn probably gave them his name."

Saul almost smiles.

"So . . . what can I use of that? What we just saw?"

"What do you mean?"

"I mean, the fact that she was pregnant is a big deal. My editor might care about that. And maybe that she was hit on the head. And that her head was shaved recently. And that she was tied up." It is, I realize as I speak, a great story. A scoop.

"Use it all," says Saul.

"But . . . can I use your name? And Malka's?" Malka, who, I realize, doesn't even know I'm a reporter.

"You can't use my name," says Saul. "Definitely not. But your paper allows anonymous sources. Call me an official in the police department with knowledge of the investigation. Don't mention Malka. Just say everything came from me."

CHAPTER SIX

Saul leaves me at a deli a few blocks from the funeral home. I order a green tea and sit by the window. The streets are dark. My hands have stopped shaking, but my insides are on a low vibrate. My leg is bouncing beneath the wobbly wood table. I don't have my pills with me, and I try to focus my mind forward, to problem-solve. But it's a problem so much bigger than any other I've ever tried solving that I can't even imagine where to begin. It makes no sense to me that the police would give a body away at the crime scene, then allow it to be buried without so much as a toxicology report. What if she was poisoned? What if the killer's blood or hair is still on her? Or in her? Malka didn't mention rape, but maybe she'd had sex before she died. Wouldn't that be a lead? For the first time since I got this job, I know things no one else knows. But I have no idea what to do with what I know. Can I just write what I saw?

Will it even make a difference? She'll be in the ground by midnight.

I decide to call Cathy. I dial her extension and get voice mail.

"Cathy, it's Rebekah Roberts. I don't know if you're still on crane lady, but I, um, got some information and I wanted to see what you thought. I'm covering the funeral, so I'll have my phone on me. Just give me a call when you can." I hang up and immediately feel like an ass for referring to Rivka Mendelssohn as "crane lady." Like porn dad, and the hot dog hooker (who sold blow jobs and wieners from a cart on Long Island), and tan mom (who got arrested for supposedly allowing her toddler to use a tanning bed), tabloids, and to some extent cable news, often create crude monikers for the people unlucky enough to catch our attention. It's a shorthand, obviously, since we deal with so many names every day. I've never thought of it as anything beyond mildly amusing, but saying those words now ignites a little army of pins and needles in my stomach. I've seen this poor woman's naked, brutalized body. She is a woman with stories I will never know. Crane lady doesn't have children, or ideas; she doesn't love or weep or fight back. Crane lady is a cartoon; Rivka Mendelssohn is woman, like me. Like Iris. Like Aviva.

I sip my tea and wait. After about a half an hour, the streets start getting crowded. Hasidic men and women and children move as one from side streets onto the main road, where the funeral home is located. I toss the rest of my tea and head outside.

Everyone is dressed in black. There must be hundreds—maybe thousands—of people, but the street is almost silent. Even the children are quiet. I stand for a few moments in the doorway of a small apartment building, looking for a sympathetic face to stop. I covered the funeral of a construction worker once. He'd been atop a beam that wasn't properly secured and fallen to his death. He was buried on Staten Island on a beautiful fall day. I spoke with a woman whose husband had been on the job with the man and she gave me a good quote about how frightening it was to know that the safety inspections hadn't turned up any problems. Another woman, a cousin of the deceased man's wife, said his family was still in shock. That they'd just put a down payment on a house. After the graveside service, someone laid his hard hat, like a bouquet, atop the coffin. As everyone walked back to their cars, I watched the cemetery workers, who'd been standing off to the side smoking cigarettes during the ceremony, cover him in dirt.

I see a young woman, maybe my age, pushing a stroller, and I slide next to her, trying to keep apace.

"Excuse me," I say. "I'm sorry to bother you, but I'm from the newspaper. Did you know Rivka Mendelssohn well?"

The woman does not break stride, and I can tell by the sharp shake of her head that she is not going to talk to me.

I step into the doorway and wait. Excuse me, I say, over and over to the people walking by. But no one stops. I decide to merge in and just follow the herd. I step in next to an elderly lady struggling with a heavy canvas shopping bag. Perfect, I think. The Good Samaritan gets the quote.

"Can I help you with that?" I ask.

The woman looks up at me. She squints, then smiles. The bag is heavy and her back is bent. She nods yes, and hands it to me. "Thank you," she says.

"Did you know Mrs. Mendelssohn?" I ask.

"Of course," she says. "My daughter went to *bais yaakov* with her."

I have no idea what that means.

"It's so sad," I say.

"Terrible," she says. "She was very young."

"What was she like?" I ask.

"Like?" The old lady looks at me.

"I'm . . . I'm from the newspaper," I say quietly so no one else around us can hear and tear her away. "We'd like to write a story about her . . . sort of . . . humanize her for our readers. I spoke with her sister-in-law Miriam yesterday. . . ." Saying you spoke with a family member or someone else in the inner circle of the person you're trying to get information on makes it more likely others will talk. If the family is okay with me, I must be okay.

"You spoke with Miriam?"

"Yes," I say. "She was very upset."

The woman grabs my arm suddenly, her face now animated with unhappiness.

"It is so horrible!" she whispers, shaking her face at the sky. "I cannot understand it. So horrible. And you're from the newspaper. They think, yes, that it was her *gardener*?"

Word travels fast around here.

"Oh, I don't know," I say. "I think the police are questioning lots of people. . . ."

She shakes her head fiercely. "Imagine. She trusted him, from outside the community. . . . Oh, her poor *children*. That poor family. As if they haven't been through enough."

"I know," I say, though I don't know anything.

"And you spoke with Miriam?"

"Yes. Will she be here?"

The woman raises her eyebrows. "I suppose so. If you spoke with her."

"Have there been other . . . tragedies? For the family."

"Nothing like *this*," she says. "But like all families, they have illness. There are disappointments." Illness and disappointments. Not too specific. Then she lowers her voice. "She lost a child last year. A baby."

"That's terrible," I say, trying not to look too excited.

"It really was. But *Rivka*! She was a good woman."

"When was the last time you saw her?"

"Oh, not for several months. She had her family. But my youngest daughter, Chaya, Rivka has been a real friend to her. Such a blessing."

I've managed to back us into the vestibule of an apartment building.

"Is your daughter here?"

"Chaya? No, no this is much too much for her. She is at home. I will go to the Mendelssohn home later today, to take this." She points at the bag I'm carrying. "You are Jewish," she says, certain the answer is yes. I nod. "Then you know." But again, I don't know.

"I would love to speak with your daughter, maybe have her share some memories of Rivka. . . ." It's a long shot, but why not? I'm not doing anything illegal. Just gathering information. And then it occurs to me that I don't have my notebook out. Shit.

"Oh, that would be nice. . . . ," she says. "Did you know her well? What is your name, dear?"

"Rivka," I say. It just slips out. "My name is Rivka. From the newspaper."

"Rivka! Yes, yes, you said, from the newspaper. Well, if it's all right with the family, I suppose it's all right with me. You said you spoke with Miriam?"

I nod.

"Chaya lives just around the corner there," she says, twisting back and pointing at a series of row houses. I really need an address, but inserting numbers into the conversation, making it a more concrete thing—like, ring buzzer B at 560 Fifty-sixth—might freak this lady out. I know I'd be freaked out. Can I have your address so I can talk to your child about her dead friend? "I should be going," she says.

"Thank you," I say. I help her put her bag back over her bent shoulder. "And you never told me your name."

"Mrs. Shoenstein," she says.

And she's off, slowing the ladies in her wake.

I wait a few moments and then step into the stream. As we approach the funeral home, the crowd gets thicker, and separates into males and females. I hear a male voice over a loudspeaker, broadcasting his prayers—I assume they are prayers—onto the street. I stand on my toes and all I see is black hats for what seems like blocks. It's like a parade, but instead of cheering, people are weeping. Did all these people know Rivka? Do none of them want to know how she died? A year or two ago I read a novel that took place in an alternate universe where instead of going to Israel after the Holocaust, European Jews established a country in Alaska. In the novel, the author referred to the Jews as "black hats." I liked the description, but when I told my dad, he said he thought that was a slur, and that my affinity for it evinced my adolescent anger at my mother—which I should have by now outgrown. But standing here among about a thousand black hats, it seems apt. Solemn and formal. A pretty good description of these people, or those I've met so far.

It's been half my life since I attended a Jewish event. I had a friend in junior high school named Anya who was Jewish. We met in the "gifted" social studies class. There are several thousand Jews in Orlando, but since my father worked for the church, all his friends were Christian. He often said he lamented the lack of Jews in our life and wanted me to learn more about "that side" of my family. He bought me *The Diary of a Young Girl*, by Anne Frank, when I was eight or nine years old, and for years afterward I devoured a series of young adult novels about the Holocaust. I was, as most people are when they learn about the Holocaust, appalled. I remember I had a vague idea that I might find clues about my mother in the books. Maybe the horror of what the Jews had endured—the betrayal and savagery—was such a burden, culturally, psychologically, that it drove even those fifty years away from it to sacrifice everything in . . . deference? Remembrance? Honor? When Anya and I met, she had been preparing for her bat mitzvah for more than a year. She kept her "Torah portion" in a binder with her school papers. It was phonetic, so I could read it, too, sort of. She was always practicing, so when we would eat lunch together, or occasionally visit each others' houses, I would test her. Once, I slept over on a Saturday night, and the next morning she took me with her to Hebrew School, which was much like Sunday School at my dad's church, but more focused on preparing the student for either a bar or bat mitzvah or a confirmation, which was different, but I wasn't sure how.

"This is my friend Rebekah," she told the class when the teacher asked her to introduce her guest. "She's Jewish, but she doesn't belong to temple."

I knew a couple of the kids by sight from school. One was a shitty kid named Gabe. He wasn't terribly bright and his parents spoiled him, a lethal combination in his case.

"She's not Jewish!" he said, his face a smear of scorn.

Gabe and I, it turned out, had already had it out over my Judaism, or lack thereof. Early in the school year, the teacher had given him some tests to pass back, and when he saw how I spelled my name, he grilled me.

"Why do you spell your name like that?" he demanded, standing over me, waving a paper in my face.

"None of your business," I told him. My rebuff only enraged him further, and he began telling everyone that I was trying to make myself look Jewish by spelling my name "the Jewish way." And *clearly* I wasn't Jewish, because have you *ever* seen a Jewish redhead? And besides, her dad works at a *church*. The gossip was much more interesting to Gabe than most everyone else, since most everyone else didn't really give a shit about Jews one way or the other. He stuck to it, though. He made a real effort to get people to rally against me. Anya, whom I had told about my mom, told me I should stand up to him and say that I was Jewish because my mom was Jewish. But I didn't want to open that can of worms with him. So when he protested my Jewishness in Hebrew School, I was surprised at how it suddenly affected me.

"My mom was more Jewish than you'll ever be," I said, leaning toward him. "My mom was so Jewish, she gave everything up for Judaism. She gave *me* up. Would your parents give *you* up for Judaism? *Fuck you.*"

If I hadn't said "fuck," they probably wouldn't have escorted me out. But I did, and they did. When I saw them all again, at Anya's bat mitzvah, they kept away. Even Gabe. After that, it was me who kept away.

I am pressed toward the funeral home by the crowd, barely having to move my feet. The moaning seems to be coming from every direction. Is Aron Mendelssohn here? Is Miriam? From where I'm standing, everyone looks the same. I am able to get to the sidewalk and just past the gate into the parking lot when the voice on the loudspeaker falls silent. All I can hear is weeping. I rise onto my toes again and see a light-colored wood box moving slowly on the outstretched hands of the women outside. The box that holds Rivka Mendelssohn. The women around me lift their arms. I do the same, my fingers moving in anticipation. As the box moves back, the women turn to watch it, until suddenly, she is in my hands, and everyone seems to be looking at me. My fingertips feel the scratch of the wood, but the box itself seems weightless. Around me, the women turn as one, passing her back toward the street. I watch as she floats away, carried on the outstretched hands of the women of her community, until finally she reaches a waiting black car and is slid into the back. Someone shuts the door and she is gone. The women nearest the car slap their hands on its tinted windows, their rising wails a final good-bye.

Men and women jog after the car, and the crowd thins. I stand and look around for friendly faces to interview. Everyone seems to be looking down. There is a lot of hugging. I spot a woman across the street who is wearing pants and smoking a cigarette. I cross at the light and approach her.

"Excuse me," I say. "Do you have a minute?"

The woman looks at me. I continue.

"I'm a reporter for the *Trib*," I say. "We're doing a story about Mrs. Mendelssohn."

"Oh?" She looks mildly surprised.

"Yes, I'm just looking for a little information about her. What she was like, how she'll be missed. That sort of thing. I've spoken a little to her family. . . ."

"Really?" Now she's even more surprised. "What did they have to say?"

"Well, they were very distraught, obviously. . . ."

"Did they tell you she was planning a divorce?"

"No," I say. That's news. "Was she?"

"She was. Very definitely. She told me she had seen the rebbe, though I don't know what other action she had taken."

"That's, um, rare, in this community, right?"

"Not as rare as you might think. But yes, it's unusual."

"My name is Rebekah," I say, extending my hand to shake.

"I'm Sara Wyman."

I jot that down.

"And how did you know Rivka?" I ask.

"That's a long story," she says. "And my ride is waiting." She reaches into her enormous purse and pulls out an overstuffed wallet. "Here," she says, handing me a business card. "Give me a call."

The card says, SARA WYMAN, LICENSED CLINICAL SOCIAL WORKER.

"Would you mind telling me something quick about her? Something to characterize her for the article? I'd really appreciate it."

"You can say that she was a passionate, intelligent woman who cared deeply for her children and her friends."

I can already hear my editor say, boring.

"Anything else? Was she involved in any . . . activities?"

"She ran a group for new mothers."

"Boro Park Mommies?"

Sara nods. She seems to be considering telling me something else, but instead she just says, "Call me. We can talk in depth. But not now."

With the crowd dispersing, I decide to go find Mrs. Shoenstein's daughter, Chaya. The corner she pointed to has three row houses on it. I climb the short staircase to the first one, which has two buzzers, but neither are marked with names. I hear something above me and I look up. There is a woman in the second-floor window. She slides the glass up a few inches.

"Hello," I say, trying not to shout.

"What is it?" She's young. A teenager, maybe. And her voice is soft.

"I'm sorry to bother you," I say, speaking toward the second floor. This is an awkward conversation to have at a distance. "I'm from . . ." I pause a moment and consider: which do I say first, that it's about Rivka Mendelssohn, or that I'm from the newspaper? For lots of people, saying you're from the *Trib* works—they love the idea of being in the paper. But that is clearly not the case in this community. I decide to lead with her mom.

"I'm looking for Chaya," I say, hopeful.

"I am Chaya," she says.

"Hi," I say, probably too cheery. "I just, I just spoke with your mother. . . ." I point toward the funeral home. "I wonder if I could come up."

"My mother?"

"She said you were . . . a friend of Rivka Mendelssohn?"

"My husband is away," she says.

"Right . . . I was hoping we might talk? My name is Rivka. I'm from the newspaper. . . ."

The window opens wider and the girl comes closer to the sill. "Your name is Rivka?"

"Yes," I say, the lie feeling less uncomfortable than it probably should. "I work for the newspaper. We're writing an article about Mrs. Mendelssohn."

Chaya closes the window and disappears. A moment later, she's at the front door. She is very tiny and very pregnant, wearing a long black skirt and enormous sweater. Her head is wrapped in a cloth hat a little like Miriam's. She looks at me, looks both ways up and down the street, and then gestures sharply for me to step inside.

I follow her up a steep set of carpeted steps and into a kitchen with appliances that look older than either of us. There is a faint smell of meat and mildew. Garbage is piled in the corner. Poor Chaya is not much of a housekeeper.

"My husband will be home soon," she says.

"I won't take up too much time," I say. "I just, um . . . were you close with Rivka?"

The girl begins to sob. It's a guttural, inelegant noise, not the quiet weeping of the women at the funeral. She's so tiny and front-heavy, I worry she might fall over. I look around for a chair.

"Here," I say, gesturing toward the kitchen card table and folding chairs. "Sit. Please. Can I get you anything?" The girl shakes her head and wipes her nose on her sleeve. She looks barely fifteen.

"Rivka helped me . . . ," she says between sniffs and sobs. "She . . .

she was my babysitter. She and my sister, Esther . . . And then . . .
when I got married . . . she said, she told me about . . . you know."
She puts her hand on her belly and looks at me through soggy, frightened eyes. "I was so scared that day . . . she . . ." The girl's breathing
starts to speed up; she's sucking in air like she's drowning.

I put my hand on her arm. "I'm so sorry," I say again.

"What happened to her? No one will tell me."

"The police don't really know yet," I say. I'm not going to tell
her her friend was found naked and dumped in a pile of sharp, cold
trash.

"I don't understand," she cries. "Was it a car accident? Rivka
walked a lot. She wore those ear . . . tubes?" she says. "To listen to
music. When she was walking outside. Did she get hit? I worried
she'd walk in front of a bus."

"No," I say. "I don't think so."

Chaya looks puzzled and exhausted. She puts her hand over
her nose and mouth and looks up, like she's trying to see backward
through her tears.

"I asked her boy, Yakov. I said, 'Yakov, where is Mommy?' He
said, 'Mommy is sick.' I asked Miriam, Mr. Mendelssohn's sister?"
I nod. "And Miriam . . ." She pauses. "Miriam is an *akarah*." I try
not to look puzzled at the Yiddish word. If my name is Rivka, I
shouldn't have to ask her to translate. So I write the word down
phonetically and circle it. I'll ask Saul.

Chaya continues: "I said, 'Miriam, where is Rivka? Is she ill?'
Miriam said 'puh-puh.'" The girl makes a spitting sound with her
thin lips. "She said," lowering her voice, "'Rivka is a *zona*.'" Shit, I
think. Another word I don't know. The girl begins to cry again. I
look around the room for a box of Kleenex. There is a roll of paper

towels on the counter near the sink. I get up and tear one off, hand
it to her. She blows her nose and wipes her wet face.

"Rivka was . . . questioning." She says it so quietly, I can barely
hear her above the hum of the refrigerator. "But she would *never,
never* break her vow."

"Questioning?"

Something about my question stops her.

"How do you know Rivka?"

"Oh," I say, stumbling. "I'm . . . I don't . . . I didn't know her.
I'm from the newspaper. We're writing an article."

"I cannot be in the newspaper. My husband is very traditional."

"I understand," I say.

"I thought maybe you were . . ." She doesn't finish her sentence. Her face has changed from sadness to sickness. The corners
of her mouth pull back and for a moment I think she might vomit.
Instead, she gets up and disappears down the hallway toward the
back of the apartment. I hear a door open and close. The state of
the kitchen is pretty bad. The linoleum is cracked in places, and
several cabinets are crooked. There are no magnets or drawings or
photographs stuck to the refrigerator door. I can't imagine what it
must be like to be trapped in such a dingy domestic life at such a
young age. I wonder how old her husband is.

Chaya comes back, carrying something close to her chest. She
sets it down—it's a well-worn copy of *O, The Oprah Magazine*. On
the front, Oprah smiles broadly, offering an Easter-colored cupcake
to her spring reader.

"She gave me this," says the girl. "Take it. You go now. You
cannot be here."

At the front door, the girl peeks out, looking left and right before allowing me to exit. I try again for a little more information. "Do you know Mr. Mendelssohn, Rivka's husband?"

The girl shakes her head. "Go," she says, and pushes me out the door.

I begin to say "Thank you," but before I can finish the phrase, I am talking to the door.

Zona. I walk slowly toward the sidewalk and wonder what it means. A broken vow could be an affair. And an affair is a motive for murder. But I don't know what to do with this information. If it's even true. I wonder if Miriam—or Saul, or Sara—could confirm?

I call in Mrs. Shoenstein's quotes.

"You didn't get anything from the family?" asks Lars.

"No," I say. "They were . . ."

"Go to the house. They'll come home after they bury her. See if you can get something about the gardener. Then you're off."

It takes twenty minutes to walk to the Mendelssohn house. I linger outside, staring, looking for some clue, some evidence of the violence, the sorrow, the trauma, on its façade. But everything is sturdy and stoic. I wonder if she died in there. It's possible. My chest tightens when I think about the way Aron Mendelssohn roared. He is a big man. A big man who owns a dumping ground.

My phone rings. It is Saul.

"Can you meet me?" he asks.

"Where?"

"There is a Starbucks on Flatbush."

"I have to try to get some more quotes at the Mendelssohn house. Can you give me a couple hours?"

"Yes."

I hang up and knock at the front door. No one answers, so I stand on the sidewalk and wait. The little boys are the first people I see. There are several running toward me about two blocks up. They are dressed formally, and several have one hand holding their black hats down, but they are shouting and playful, like little boys anywhere. Behind them are the girls, huddled together, wearing flat shoes on their long preadolescent feet, boxy in their shapeless coats. Most are hatless. I cross the street to avoid, and observe, them. Behind the girls are the mothers, hatted, pushing strollers. They fan out, going down different streets, into different houses. I turn and walk around the corner, toward the back entrance to the Mendelssohns. From there, I can see across the front yard without standing like a guard outside.

After about twenty minutes, I see Yakov, the boy from the bodega, come toward me, escorting two little girls. Yakov sees me, and slows. I smile a little, trying to reconnect; remember me? He opens the back gate for the little girls and tells them to go inside. They do. Yakov walks toward me and points to the iPhone in my hand.

"Is that an iPod?" he asks.

"Actually, it's an iPhone."

"It plays music."

"It does."

"Any music you want?"

"Any music you put on it."

Yakov nods solemnly.

"Do you want to see it?"

"Yes, please."

I hand him the phone. "Slide the bar," I say. "You have to put in the pass code. It's five-six-two-two." Yakov looks up at me. "It's okay," I say. "I trust you."

He cradles the phone in his left hand, carefully wipes his right hand on the side of his pants, then presses his little index finger on the touch pad: *5-6-2-2*. The screen opens and he stares at it.

"The music is here?" he asks, pointing to the iPod icon.

"Yup," I say. "You've used one of these before."

"Mommy showed me," he says.

"Oh really? Your mother had one?"

"It was a secret," says Yakov. He presses the iPod icon and up pops a list of my music. He uses his finger to scroll slowly down, then back up again. Finally, he hands it back.

"You're from the newspaper," he says.

"Yes," I say.

"My mommy is dead," he says, lifting his eyes to me. "Did you know that?"

"I did know. I'm so sorry."

Yakov shakes his head. "She wasn't sick."

"Sick?"

"Tatti says Mommy was sick. He said she was very, very sick. He said we might get sick, too. But she wasn't sick."

I don't know how to respond. Sick could mean a million things.

"Tatti says he is going to send us to the mountains with Meema Miriam and Feter Heshy," Yakov says, his eyes on the sidewalk. *Tatti, does that mean father?* I think.

"Oh? Do you like the mountains?"

He shakes his head. His nose and fingers are red again. I wish somebody would dress this kid better. Maybe when his mom was alive.

"You better go inside," I say. "You look very cold. You don't want to get sick."

Yakov looks up at me. Oops.

"I mean . . . catch a cold." Yakov stays where he is. I rip a page out of my notebook and write my name and phone number on it. "Call me if you need anything, okay?"

The boy takes the paper. "Do you know what happened to my mommy?"

"I don't," I say. "But I'm going to try to find out."

Yakov nods again. He looks at the piece of paper, like he's trying to decide if he should fold it or not.

"Bubby Mendelssohn had cancer before she died. But I asked Tatti if Mommy had cancer, and he said no. And she didn't smell bad like Bubby. And Meema Tova, she coughed all the time before she died. She had a . . . she was connected to a tank. To breathe." He pauses. "If you find out what happened, will you tell me?"

"I will," I say. "I promise."

"Mommy used to tell me lots of things. But nobody tells me anything now."

I see an opening. "What kind of things did she tell you?"

"Last summer she took me to Coney Island and we rode the roller coaster. She told me that she rode it every week, but that it was a secret."

"Did you tell anyone?"

Yakov looks down. "I didn't want to. But Tatti said it was my duty, as a man, to help Mommy get well. He said if I didn't tell, she could get more sick. He already knew, though. He said, 'Has

Mommy been to Coney Island?' What's so bad about Coney Island!"
Yakov starts to cry. I look around. On the other side of the street,
two young mothers push strollers. They gawk at us. I gawk back.

I kneel down and look up at Yakov. "I don't think there's anything bad about Coney Island."

"Me neither!" he wails.

"It's okay," I say. "You're going to be okay. We'll find out what
happened to your mommy."

"Stupid Coney Island! I hate Coney Island!"

"Hey," I say, trying to calm him down. I stand up and push
open the back gate. "Let's go in here." Yakov follows. I close the gate
behind us. Yakov's face is a snotty mess. I give him a tissue from my
pocket. It's probably been used, but he doesn't seem to care.

"Yakov!"

Miriam is suddenly standing three feet from us. "Oh," I say,
startled. "I'm sorry. Yakov seemed very upset. . . ." I should not be
there, obviously.

Miriam says something in Yiddish and Yakov runs inside. I
brace for her to scream at me to leave, but she doesn't. Instead she
motions for me to come with her toward the door to the garage.
She is shivering, but she doesn't seem uncomfortable. The first time
I saw her, Miriam had a wrap covering her head. Today, she is hatless, with a wig a little like Malka's, except that Miriam's is parted
in the middle. The hairline is a little too low on her forehead, and
the part is about half an inch from the center of her nose. The di-
chotomy between her plain, shapeless clothes and the smooth shine
of her hair is a little jarring. The hair has bounce, but Miriam's face
is leaden, her small gray eyes rimmed in red with puffy purple bags
beneath them.

She sees me looking and raises her hand to her head, a little bashful.

"The children are very upset," she says.

"Of course," I say. "How are you?"

Miriam looks surprised that I asked. "It is very hard. Rivka and I were born on the same day. Her mother worked as a secretary in my father's business and when she got sick my father paid for the hospital bills. After she died, he helped with Rivka's upbringing. She lived with us for several years before she and Aron married."

"I'm so sorry," I say again. Rivka Mendelssohn was motherless. "How old was Rivka when her mother died?"

"We were very young. Five years old, perhaps?"

"I lost my mother young, too," I say. I can't help it. I feel like I can tell her. I feel like somehow she'll understand.

"Oh!" she says, putting her hand on my arm. She's not dressed for the cold. "Losing a mother is . . ." She shakes her head, trying to come up with a word, and I think, exactly, it is . . . ? Miriam—like Chaya—seems like a fragile woman. Was Rivka fragile, too? Was she easy prey? At the funeral home, Malka said Rivka was not easy to kill. Miriam, I think, might be easier. Could she be next?

"I wanted to thank you for speaking with me yesterday. I really appreciate your time," I say.

Miriam smiles weakly.

"Do you have any idea what could have happened?" I ask, my voice low, like, you can tell me. "Do you feel safe?"

"Me?"

I nod.

"No, no," she says. I'm not sure if she's answering my first or second question. I have to be better about doubling up on questions.

"I wonder if you know if Rivka was . . . unhappy," I ask. She looks puzzled. "Because I spoke with a woman who said . . ."

"A woman?"

"Just, a woman at the funeral." Another thing I have to be careful of, revealing sources. "I didn't actually get her name."

Miriam's face, if it's possible, becomes sadder. Her chin sinks closer to her neck and she closes her eyes, almost wincing. "There is so much talking," she whispers. "That is how the women are. Their children, they are not enough. Their husbands, they are not enough. They are always talking."

"What kind of talking?"

Miriam shakes her head. "Horrible things. Lies. That is what killed her. The *lies*."

I bring my voice down very low. "What were they saying?"

Miriam puts her finger to her lips. I wait, but she doesn't continue.

"Have you spoken to the police?" I ask her.

"No. I have nothing to say. I do not gossip."

"You never know what might help," I say. "Sometimes little stuff, like the last time you saw her. Or, where she liked to go, that sort of thing." I'm kind of talking out of my ass here. I've never been privy to a murder investigation that wasn't on *Law & Order*. I want to ask again if she's safe, but I stop myself because I wouldn't know what I'd say if she said no.

"The service was very crowded," I say.

"I'm glad," she says.

"Were you there?"

"No," she says. "It was . . . too much."

That's the same thing Mrs. Shoenstein said about why Chaya didn't go. Too much.

"Is there anything else about her you could tell me?" I ask, figuring I should at least try to get a quote I can give the desk. "Was she . . . had she been acting differently at all?"

Miriam's eyes wander toward the back gate.

I repeat my question and Miriam pulls her eyes slowly back to me. But she says nothing.

"Because, you said you hadn't seen her since Tuesday? I just wonder if . . ."

"I am not certain about the dates."

"Oh," I say. "Okay. Well, is there anything you could tell me? What did she like to do? Did she . . ." I'm flailing around for examples of activities, but everything that comes to mind—movies, sports, adventure travel—seems culturally inappropriate. "Did she like to read? Or . . . cook?"

Nothing. It's almost as if she doesn't hear me.

I lower my voice. "I heard . . . I was told she'd lost a baby recently."

Miriam shakes her head. I can't tell if she's indicating that, no, she did not lose a baby, or yes, and it was very sad.

"Thank you," she says finally. She begins walking toward the back gate. "Rivka would have liked you." She opens the gate. Apparently it is time for me to go. "She liked to talk." And with that, Miriam turns and walks back into the house. I stay in the yard for a moment. Once again, I forgot to ask her last name. Maybe Saul can help with that.

·   ·   ·

I get to the Starbucks before Saul and pull out *The Oprah Magazine* while I wait. When I open it, a piece of paper slips out. It is a hand-written note.

Chaya,

I know you are frightened. I was frightened after becoming engaged. I think most of us are frightened. But I cannot answer your questions about whether your marriage will be a happy one. I married because it hadn't seemed possible to do otherwise. I know now that I always had a choice. Had I chosen not to accept Aron's proposal, my life would have become more difficult in many ways. I do not know where I would have lived, but now I know that I would have lived.

What does this life mean to you, Chaya? Why do you pull on your stockings in July? What do you feel when you pray? I wish I had asked myself these questions when I was 18. Hashem can see the truth inside your heart. And I now believe that to defy that truth is to defy Hashem. Your choices may cause pain before they bring joy, but no joy can come from lies. Especially lies you tell yourself.

Yours always,
Rivka

I read the note again. The handwriting is a mix of print and cursive. Flourishes on the *y*'s and *f*'s, but otherwise utilitarian. The paper is thin and pink, the kind of paper I wrote notes to my friends on when I was eleven years old. Not notes like this, though. This note is more honest than any note I've ever written. And judging by its soft, easy crease, Chaya read it often. My dad used to tell me stories about my mom as if she were a character in a fairy tale. Like most suburban girls growing up in the 1990s, I learned about sex young. I was nine when our Girl Scout troop went to Planned Parenthood to learn about ovaries and sperm. I learned the rest sporadically from Madonna songs and Maury Povich and maybe someone's mom's copy of *Our Bodies, Ourselves*. I had several years for the act itself to morph from mildly horrifying to potentially cool, and several years after that to actually get involved in doing it. Not my mother. My mother, my father said, learned about sex only in whispers. And then one day her best friend, a girl named Naomi, became engaged to a man in his twenties. Naomi was seventeen, and my mother was sixteen; neither had ever traveled farther than the Catskills. Her interaction with men was limited to family. And suddenly, Naomi was to be married. Which meant sex. My mother, my father said, stayed with her the night before her wedding. Naomi was sick with dread. She knew not to expect love, but when she'd met her fiance, she told my mother, he made her stomach turn. Your mother, said my father, vowed she would not find herself in Naomi's position. She was not ready to run away then, my father said, but she was planning. She knew that the best way to postpone an engagement was to make herself undesirable to a potential groom's family. That was the word he used, "undesirable." When he came to this part of the story, I always pictured my mother burping in public, or parading around in dirty clothes. That's what undesirable meant to me: ugly, unladylike. But that's not what my mother did. What my mother did was start reading—and asking questions. Word got around, and it bought her some time.

I fold the note back into the magazine. I'm somewhat surprised

I haven't heard from the city desk, which is good because I'm not sure what I should tell them. There is no way I'm turning the letter over. They'd print it.

Saul arrives, and when he sits down I hand him the magazine.

"There's a note inside. It's from Rivka." As he opens it, carefully, I explain. "I met an old woman at the funeral who said her daughter Chaya had been friends with Rivka. So I went and talked to her. She was very pregnant. Her mother knew about the gardener, but Chaya thought maybe Rivka died in a car accident. It seemed weird that the mom knew so much, and Chaya knew so little."

"Not necessarily," says Saul as he opens the note. "Most Hasidim do not watch television or read English newspapers or use the Internet. But there is a lot of talk, especially around something like this. Depending on who they had spoken to, they could have heard completely different stories. Or nothing at all."

He stops talking while he reads the note, which he balances open on one wide palm. After a minute or more, he closes the note and slips it back into the magazine. "This was given to you?"

"Yeah," I say. "We were sitting in the kitchen and she told me that Rivka had been her babysitter and had sort of counseled her before she got married. Then she went into her bedroom or something and came back with this. And then she told me to leave."

"A magazine like this is contraband in an ultra-Orthodox home."

"Really?" I could see *Cosmo* being banned, but *Oprah*?

"Hasidim are taught to fear influences outside their community. They consider most of American culture to be corrupting and much effort is expended to avoid and demonize it. You don't see it, but there are highly subversive ideas in this magazine. Even Oprah herself. Unmarried. Childless. Hasidic girls are taught that having children and bringing them up in a Jewish home is the most important work there is. They are called and blessed by God for this work."

"Right, but . . ."

"There is no 'but.' Not for many people. For many people, this is enough."

I've offended him. "I'm sorry."

Saul shakes his head. "Thank you for this note. This note is very revealing. Have you spoken with your editors at the newspaper about it?"

"No," I say. "They'd probably print it." I chuckle, trying to lighten the moment. Saul doesn't smile. "Seriously. It's yours now."

"Thank you," says Saul.

"I spoke to Miriam again. And the little boy. Yakov."

"Rivka's boy?"

"He was coming home from the service. He said his father told him his mother had been sick."

"Sick?"

"Yeah, but I don't really know what he meant. He said he didn't think she was sick."

Saul considers this. He looks out the window. There is a 1-800-Flowers shop across the street and a narrow pizzeria and a nail salon. I can almost see Saul thinking. The crow's-feet at his eyes twitch. He is squeezing his jaw.

"Also, the old woman at the funeral, Mrs. Shoenstein? She said Rivka had lost a baby recently. Did you know about that?"

"I did."

"What happened?"

"That, I don't know."

My phone rings. It's the desk.

"I'll be right back," I say, and take my notebook outside.

"It's Rebekah."

"Hold for Lars."

Lars comes on.

"Whatchu got?" he asks.

"The funeral was packed."

"How many people?"

"Hundreds?"

"What else?"

"Lots of crying. She was in this plain wooden box and they passed the box back toward the car. The women—it was like, you know at a concert when people crowd surf? They passed the coffin back like that."

"What about quotes? Were people talking about the gardener?"

"Um . . . one woman said she heard the gardener did it."

"Great, what did she say?"

I flip open my notebook and realize I'd never actually written down what Mrs. Shoenstein said, but I remember it clearly. Does that mean I'm getting better at this job? Or just getting used to bending the rules?

"She said . . . 'It's so horrible. She trusted a stranger and look what happened.'"

"Perfect. What else?"

"I mean, she didn't actually *know* anything."

"What's the name."

"Shoenstein. Mrs. Shoenstein." I did write that down.

"First name?"

Shit. I didn't ask, because I wasn't thinking about calling in to the desk during our conversation, I was thinking, how can I be as friendly and gracious as possible so she'll give me her daughter's address. "She wouldn't give it."

"Okay, fine, Mrs. Shoenstein. Was she a neighbor? Relative?"

"She said her daughter had gone to . . ." I can't remember what she'd said. It was something Yiddish. "Her daughter was friends with Rivka."

"Great. What else?"

"I talked to a woman, a social worker; she said Rivka might have been thinking about a divorce."

"Do you have a quote?"

"Not exactly . . ."

"Name?"

"Her name was Sara Wyman."

"Age?"

Again, I didn't ask, because I wasn't thinking about the newspaper. I was thinking about what she could tell me. "She wouldn't give it."

"What else?"

"She said, 'Rivka was a passionate, intelligent woman who cared deeply for her children and her friends.' She also said she ran an organization for new mothers. Boro Park Mommies."

"That all?"

Here we go. "Actually, I talked to a detective, but he didn't want his name used."

"What did he say?"

"He said she was pregnant."

"Great. We can definitely use that."

"He also . . . um, from the funeral home, he said that her body was really, um, beat up. Head wounds."

"Okay. Who's this from?"

"You can say a police official with information about the case."

"Anyone else from the funeral? You said there were hundreds of people there."

"I talked to one woman who said Rivka Mendelssohn used to babysit her and was sort of a confidante."

"Do you have a quote?"

I'm reaching. "She said, 'Rivka liked to walk and listen to music.' She said when she heard she'd died, she thought maybe she'd been hit by a car on one of her walks."

"That's the quote: She liked to walk and listen to music?"

"Yeah." It is, without a doubt, a lame quote. A big part of this job is hearing the quote. People say a lot of shit, and most of what they say is either unprintable or unimportant, or both. At the *Trib*, because the articles are short, they like explanatory quotes—quotes that narrate what happened—instead of supplementary quotes, which add color or context to the action. So, if I was covering, say, an old lady whose geriatric scooter was hit by a garbage truck traveling in the bicycle lane (as I did in September in the West Village), the desk would love me to get someone to say: "She was scooting along toward the Y like she always does after lunch, when this garbage truck came barreling through the light. I don't even think he saw her." If I were working at the *Times*, they would write the information in the first sentence using their own language, then use

"I don't think he even saw her" as the quote. In college, most of my professors said that narrative quotes were lazy, that it was the writer's job to succinctly tell the reader what happened. That quotes should be "gems." But as with much of what I learned in college journalism classes, this does not apply at the *Trib*.

"That's it?" asks Lars.

"She also said Rivka was questioning."

"Questioning? What does that mean?"

"Like, questioning . . . her faith?"

"Is that a quote?"

"No, she didn't exactly explain, but . . ."

"What's the woman's name?"

"She wouldn't give it. You can say a friend."

"Too many unnamed quotes. I can't use them."

"Sorry . . . she also said Rivka Mendelssohn had lost a baby recently, but I couldn't confirm that with the family."

"She lost a baby *and* she was pregnant?"

"According to the people I talked to."

"All right," he says. "The desk wants to run something on the gardener being questioned. Did anybody else say anything about the gardener?"

"No."

"Marisa got some great stuff from his neighbors. Apparently he's a drinker. And he has a couple arrests for fighting, one for exposing himself."

"Do they really think he might have done it?" It doesn't make sense to me that a drunk who doesn't speak English could pull off getting Rivka Mendelssohn alone long enough to tie her up, kill her, and get her dead body into a scrap pile on her family's private property.

"How should I know?" says Lars. "Do you have anything else? How the family is taking the news, maybe?"

"Um . . ." I'm trying to think back. "You can say the family is very shaken up. I talked to her son for a minute on his way home; he was crying. He said the father had told him his mother was sick."

"Sick?"

"That's what he said."

"How old was he?"

"I'm not positive. Around nine or ten."

"That doesn't help me. Did you get a name?"

I'm not going to give them Yakov's name.

"No."

Lars sighs. "Anything else?"

"I guess that's it. Is Cathy around?"

"Greg!" he shouts. "When does Cathy come in?" Pause. "Tomorrow."

Before I can even say thanks, he hangs up.

I look through the glass window at Saul, and suddenly I feel very tired. All I want to do is go to sleep. I can still smell the inside of that room where Rivka's body was. I wonder if I'll still smell it at home. Tomorrow. Forever. Saul is on his phone. I wish I had kept the letter instead of giving it to him.

I go back into Starbucks and sit down across from him.

"The paper is running a story about the gardener tomorrow," I say. "Apparently, he has a record."

Saul does not respond.

"When Yakov told me his father had said Rivka was sick before she died, he got really upset. Oh, and he said they had a big fight about Coney Island. . . ."

"Coney Island?"

"Yakov said his mother had taken him to Coney Island to ride the roller coaster. She told him to keep it a secret. And there was a big fight about it at home. I didn't tell the desk, because . . ." I'm not sure why I didn't, actually. Somehow, it seemed like that might be, I don't know, evidence? I feel like I'm serving two masters here. What goes to Saul and what goes to the *Trib*?

"They had a fight about the roller coaster? Or Coney Island?"

"I don't know. He said . . ." And then it hits me: Coney Island is where the safe house my mom and Saul used to go to was. Could it still be there? "Saul," I say slowly. "How did you know Rivka Mendelssohn?"

Saul looks at his hands.

"Saul," I ask again, my voice louder this time. "How did you know her?"

"Calm down," whispers Saul. "Rivka Mendelssohn knew my son."

"Your son?" What had my dad said about Saul's son? That they were estranged after his divorce.

Saul nods. "He was an instructor at Yakov's yeshiva."

"Oh," I say. "What does he teach?"

"He taught math," says Saul. "But he was let go. Rivka Mendelssohn was one of the only parents who took his side."

"His side?"

"She asked the rebbe to let him stay."

"Did he?"

Saul shakes his head.

"What happened?"

Saul draws and exhales a sharp breath. He seems impatient. I don't think he's going to tell me any more. "That is not really important. What is important is that she helped someone I love at a time he needed help. And I want to help her."

"Did you ever actually meet her?"

"Yes. We met at the house in Coney Island, the same one your mother used to go to. I wanted to thank her and she suggested that would be a good place to talk."

"Did you know she had been going there?"

"No," says Saul. I'm expecting him to explain further, but he does not.

"What about Miriam?" I ask.

"What about her?"

"How do you know her?"

Saul shifts in his seat. Why is this making him so uncomfortable?

"Before Rivka and I met, I made the mistake of going to the Mendelssohn home, uninvited, to express my gratitude. Rivka was not home, but Miriam was. She said Aron did not agree with Rivka's position regarding my son, and that I was not welcome inside."

"Really?"

"She told me she didn't believe it was appropriate for Rivka to speak publicly about my son, either."

"But she let you in last night."

Saul nods. "Last night, well, things had changed." He pauses. "When I saw you at the Mendelssohn house yesterday, Rebekah, I saw an opportunity."

"An opportunity for what?"

"An opportunity to keep this case alive."

"How is it not alive? It's barely been twenty-four hours."

"Yes," says Saul. "And the victim's body is gone."

Right.

"Do you know how many of the murders in this city get solved, Rebekah?"

"No."

"A little more than half."

"Half?"

"Sixty-one percent last year. But it's lower in Brooklyn. Nationally, about four out of every ten murder victims never get justice. Every day, I go to people's homes and businesses who have been robbed. I will work ten hours a day, six days a week, and I will make an arrest for only four of every ten cases. Car theft is worse." He pauses. "I am surprised you don't know this. Your newspaper made a big splash of it last year. I believe the headline was 'New Yorkers Get Away with Murder.'"

"I guess I just don't know what you want," I say quietly.

"I want you to write articles about Rivka Mendelssohn's murder. I want you to keep the pressure on the police and the community."

"And you can't do that? Why aren't you like, bringing a *colleague* to see her body?"

Saul shakes his head. "You talked to Miriam. You talked to Chaya. I guarantee you that Chaya would not have let me—or any other police officer—into her house, or given us that letter."

"But you're the police."

"And?"

"This is what you do."

"I'm telling you that you can do it better than I can."

"So you want to use me."

"Yes," he says slowly. "That is one way to put it. I want you to stay on this story. I want you to do your job as a journalist and try to find out the truth. Do we not, in some respects, have the same goals here? We both seek the truth." Before I can say anything, he says, "I know it's not that simple. I know what I am asking."

"I don't think you do, Saul," I say. "You're asking me to start lying."

"I am not."

"You *are*. I can't tell my editors I spent the afternoon posing as a college student to view a murder victim's body in the basement of a funeral home with a detective from the fucking robbery squad."

"Why not?"

"I just can't!" But the moment I say it, I know I can. I can, but it didn't occur to me, because, up until now, I've never taken any real initiative on any story at the *Trib*. I've done what they've told me—nothing less, and nothing more. I've snuck past doormen to get quotes from tenants in fancy buildings and posed as a customer while stalking some celebrity in a grocery store. I've pretended I was considering enrolling in a city college so I could get a look inside the admissions office a whistleblower claimed was rife with sexual harassment. I've taken chances and pushed limits, but never of my own volition. I can blame it on the fact that the system of the paper is set up to keep me moving, keep my attention focused on something different every day, but that's bullshit. They haven't tried to control my curiosity; they just haven't punished me for not engaging it.

"I would think your editors might be rather impressed by what you accomplished today. You found a source inside the investigation who gave you exclusive information about the case."

"Except you're not exactly inside the investigation, Saul," I say.

"You let me worry about that."

"Okay," I say, "but if you knew Rivka Mendelssohn, I need to know that."

"I did not know her well. I knew she was questioning because I knew she had been to the Coney Island house. I am not involved in the group that runs the house anymore, but I am in contact with those who are. I also know Aron Mendelssohn. Or rather, I know the reach of his influence."

"His influence?"

"He is perhaps the single largest donor to Shomrim, the neighborhood watch group that functions as a kind of quasi-police force. You saw them at the Mendelssohn house. Five years ago, the group was a handful of middle-aged men with cell phones. Now, they have a command center, half a dozen fully equipped former police vehicles, and probably a hundred volunteers."

"What do they do, exactly?"

"They call themselves the eyes and ears of the community. They search for lost seniors and children. You might have seen them driving around. Their cars have an official-looking insignia painted on them. It's designed to look very much like the NYPD's."

"So they're, like, security guards. Pretend police."

This amuses Saul. "Pretend police. Well, some families teach their children to call the Shomrim 800-number before calling 911, if they suspect a break-in. The group encourages that."

"Are they armed?"

"No."

"Are they trained?"

Saul shrugs. "By each other. When there is a problem, something stolen, violence, the community would rather talk to another Jew about it."

"But isn't that what you're for?"

"Yes," he says. "But they have to trust the police enough to call first."

"And they don't trust the police?"

"It's not that, exactly," he says.

"It's *mesirah*." It's the first time I've ever used a Yiddish word in a sentence. It comes out easily.

"Exactly. If they have something bad to say about a Jew, they'd rather say it to another Jew."

"And Aron Mendelssohn is a benefactor to them?"

"Yes. *The* benefactor. For the Borough Park group."

"And you think he could make a murder go away?"

"Well, he already has."

"Has he?"

"Did you see any NYPD at the funeral today? Or at the house?" Saul's voice is getting hoarse. He's got an extra layer pulling at his face and his middle, but in his youth, I'd guess Saul was definitely attractive. He has a strong brow and hazel eyes, and he carries himself with a kind of jittery but confidence-inducing pride. I wonder what my mother thought of him. I wonder what he really thought—thinks—of her.

"You've talked to three people who knew her. None of them have been questioned by police and all of them suggested that Rivka and her husband were having problems. But Aron Mendelssohn has not been brought in."

The employees at the Starbucks are mopping the floor. They've set chairs on tables and turned up the music. It is time to go.

"Would you like a ride somewhere?" he asks.

"Home," I say. "I'd like a ride home."

We cross the street and get into his car in silence. Fifteen minutes later, when Saul pulls up to my building, I take off my seat belt and turn to face him. His yarmulke is made of a thick material that looks more expensive than the sateen loaners they gave men in temple in Orlando. Dad came with me and Anya's family once to Rosh Hashanah services. I snickered at him when he unfolded the "beanie" and placed it so reverently on his head. You know you don't have to wear one if you're not Jewish, I said, like he didn't know. Saul's is black, and he has it secured to what's left of his hair with two bobby pins.

"You'll think about what I said?" he asks.

Which part? I think. The part where there's a dead woman no one cares about except for the two of us? The part where there are two police departments? Or the part where I'm 100 percent in over my fucking head?

I get out of the car without answering.

"Rebekah," he says, "I think your mother would be very proud of you."

Fantastic, I think, as I slam the door shut. Just what I need.

CHAPTER SEVEN

Within ten minutes of walking in the door. I am asleep in my clothes. I wake up sweating at midnight. I turn my face toward the window and look at the street. We face west. It occurs to me that if there were no obstructions, no brick warehouses or apartment buildings or train tracks, I'd be able to see the scrap yard from my bed. The scrap yard that has become the center of my life.

At 2 A.M. I wake up again and see light beneath my bedroom door. I roll out of bed and squint down the hall and into the living room. Iris is on the couch watching *Days of Our Lives,* which she records every day and watches on the weekends. There is a pizza box on the coffee table. I open the box and pick up two slices, then carry them to the microwave on the counter.

"How was your day?" I ask.

"I slept mostly," she says. "Then had dinner with one of the girls from work. How was *your* day?"

"Saul took me to see her body." Iris doesn't say much as I tell her, in disjointedly chronological order, about the funeral and Malka and the pregnant girl with the note, and Yakov and Miriam and Shomrim. She sits cross-legged, looking at me the whole time, her face twisting into an evolving series of *what the fuck* expressions. I do fine recounting everything until I get to Rivka's body, which I leave for last.

"It looked like she'd been attacked by animals," I say, suddenly out of breath. My chest feels like someone is sitting on it. "I guess, where the pieces of scrap got her."

"I can't believe you saw a dead body today."

I shake my head and inhale deeply. Twice. A third time. Iris hands me the glass of water she's been drinking from. I drink. This feels different than the kind of panics I get that make my stomach hurt. This comes from my lungs and my throat, not my intestines. It's hard to breathe.

"You want a pill?" asks Iris.

I nod. Iris goes into my room and brings back the bottle of lorazepam. She fills a glass of water at the sink, shakes out a little white pill, and hands it to me. I drink. When I first consented to be prescribed anxiety meds I noticed that the moment I took a pill I felt a little calmer. My doctor had said that even knowing I had them around if I needed them might help, and she was right.

"So what did he say about your mom?"

"He said her family moved upstate about twenty years ago."

"Wow," whispers Iris. "That's close."

"I know." Iris was pretty crushed after her mom died, and we spent a lot of time crying and talking, mostly while intoxicated, about how helpless we felt, and how screwed up adults were and how we were gonna make our lives better. One of those nights we floated the idea of New York. Back then, I was battling urges to go find my mom. I'm an adult now, I thought. I *could*. Sophomore year, I considered doing a spring-break-long pilgrimage to Brooklyn as the final project for my creative nonfiction seminar. But I chickened out when I realized I'd have to explain what I was doing to my dad, and didn't think I could bear the conversation. Eventually that lack of action hardened into a decision against action. New York, however, remained. I remember telling Iris, as the fantasy became a plan, that being in New York put me in a position where she could find me.

"Did he say anything else?"

"He said she went to Israel for a few years after she left us. He seemed to think she was sort of sent there," I say, realizing I haven't really thought about his story. "He said he'd heard rumors that she, like, had substance issues, but he thought maybe she was mentally unstable. Like, possibly depressed. And obviously getting no treatment."

"Maybe she had anxiety, too," says Iris.

Somehow, it had never occurred to me that her erratic behavior—leaving one life, then leaving another—might have been caused by chemicals misfiring in her brain. Getting help when anxiety started to turn me into a different person was just a matter of walking to student health services. Not so easy in her world.

"Maybe she was just a runner," I say. "Things get bad, you leave. Saul said he thought she was weak. He also said he thinks I'm smarter than she was. And that she'd be proud of me."

"That must be weird."

I love Iris. She may be into makeup and lotions, but when you talk to her, she focuses on the details that matter, and she's quick to put herself in your shoes. I make an ugly face indicating that, yes, it is indeed very weird to suddenly have a direct line to my mom.

"It sounds like he knew her pretty well," she says.

"I know. But when we were talking about it, he was pretty vague."

Iris nods.

"So, I need to figure out what to do here," I say.

"Do you think you could really help?"

"I don't know. I mean, Saul clearly thinks so."

"But who is Saul, exactly?"

"My dad knew him. A little. He seems to vouch for him."

"Do you trust him?"

"I think so."

"You have pretty good instincts about people," says Iris. "But what about the *Trib*?"

"Another problem."

"Do you think they're gonna drop the story?"

"Well, we'll see what tomorrow's issue looks like. Today's story was, like, four inches, and the best part—that she was found naked and bald in a scrap heap—has already happened. So unless something major breaks, yeah, they'll drop the story."

"The best part?" Iris is challenging my crassness. She thinks it's my way of detaching from uncomfortable situations, and she's probably right.

"From their perspective," I say. "I guess I need to talk to Saul again. I don't even really know what he wants me to do, specifically."

"It sounds like he wants you to fight for the story," says Iris. "Stay on it. Tell the paper to stay on it."

"Right," I say. It sounds so simple. "But you know I don't have any control. I could write a story every day and they might never publish it."

"They'll publish it if it's good."

"Define good."

"If it's got new information in it. Inside information. Information the *Ledger* and the *Times* don't have."

"So I've gone from zero to Bob Woodward in twenty-four hours?"

"Pretty much," says Iris, grabbing a slice of pizza.

I don't want to tell her that I'm having a hard time picturing myself being able to pull this off. I don't even really know who makes what decisions at the *Trib*. If the paper has a policy on anonymous sources, I don't know what it is. I was more involved in getting the newspaper put together every day as a summer intern at the *Orlando Sentinel* than I am now, after more than half a year working full-time for the *Trib*. The newsroom buried in the middle floors of that black Midtown high-rise is a machine I don't understand. It's kind of appalling how incurious I've been.

"Here's what I think," says Iris. "Do you want to know what I think?"

I nod.

"Okay." She crosses her legs. "I think there are several things going on here. First, I know this is all very fucked up, but since you started working at the *Trib* you haven't talked about a single story like you cared about it. You're not writing at all." She pauses and puts her hand up defensively. "I'm not saying it's your *fault*. I get that they have people on rewrite. I'm just saying that if you took the initiative and got a source and reported out a story no one was telling, and then wrote it, it seems unlikely they wouldn't publish it, seeing as your name already appears in the paper as if you're writing regularly. And that would be good for you, as a young journalist."

"I know," I say.

"I don't do work like you. I wouldn't have the first clue what to do if a cop told me he suspected a murder was going to go cold, other than say, 'bummer.'"

I roll my eyes—she's exaggerating.

"I choose to work with products. When I get to write, I write about inanimate objects. But you write about people. People with lives way beyond what you see and what they tell you. I get that that's what makes them interesting to you. I totally get that. But you've got a whole bunch of loyalties going on here. You've got the paper and the people you quote and Saul and the dead woman. And you're the only thing connecting all of them. If it weren't for you, they wouldn't come together. So if shit goes wrong—if you write something somebody doesn't like, or write something that isn't true—you're on the hook. And my guess is that none of these people, except maybe Saul, but who the fuck really knows what his deal is, will have your back."

I'm not sure what to say. She's right. This is what I signed up for. This is what being a journalist is: sorting through conflicting information and finding the truth and setting it free. Putting yourself on the line with every word, pissing people off and maybe even fucking with their lives in the name of the truth. In college they talked about journalism as being like sunlight, shining light into darkness; revealing. Sunlight, they said, is the best disinfectant. And it sounded exactly right. It sounded like something I wanted to build my life on. I know a lot of places in the world that could use some sunlight; one of them is Borough Park.

"I don't think I want to talk about this anymore," I say.

"Fair enough," says Iris. "Wanna watch a movie?"

"I think I'm going to go back to bed."

Iris stands up and puts her arms around me. Even after a night of lying around eating pizza, she smells lovely. Like lavender and milk.

SUNDAY

CHAPTER EIGHT

I don't sleep well. I wake up around six and my stomach is going. Rivka Mendelssohn's body was in my dream. I had to carry it somewhere, but I was wearing knit gloves that kept getting caught in the sticky open wounds. My first full thought after I open my eyes is that I have to get out of this. I have to call Saul and make up an excuse and just go back to running where the city desk tells me. I get a pill from my bedside and swallow it. I know, even as I'm trying to figure a way out of it, that my job, or rather, the job I want, the job I've trained for, is exactly what I'm being asked to do. Not solving homicides, but telling true stories. Finding sources other people can't find and using those sources to reveal things other people aren't revealing is exactly what I'm supposed to do. The story of a homicide being overlooked because a powerful, insular community doesn't want attention is a great story. The problem is that one thing I'm very definitely *not* supposed to do is help interested

parties further their agendas. We may not have had much in the way
of ethics training in school, but I definitely remember that. Agendas
are what separate journalists from PR people: they have clients; we
have sources, subjects. And solving this murder, at this point, is Saul's
agenda. I need to figure out how to make it mine, too.

I open my eyes again around noon to a chalky white sky. Rivka
Mendelssohn's body was in my dream again. She was lying on the
metal slab, but this time she was alive, and I said to her, "Wait, I
thought you were dead? How did you survive?" And she said, "It's
all a big mistake, honey." And then she sat up, suddenly fully
dressed, but still bald and bruised and bloody around her face,
hopped off the slab, and knelt down to lace up a pair of sneakers.
"Do you run?" she asked me. And then she took off, without waiting for an answer.

At about 1 P.M., I get out of bed. Iris has left a note saying she's
at yoga, so I make coffee and pull up the *Tribune*'s Web site on my
laptop. Porn mom is splitting the front page with the latest round
of health department raids at city restaurants. Brooklyn's queen of
cannoli, a fifty-year-old steakhouse near Grand Central, two noo-
dle shops on the Upper East Side, and about a dozen other well-
known places were shuttered yesterday for failing inspections. I
scroll down, past an article about a Yankee threatening to pull out
of contract negotiations, another about whether the mayor did or
did not imply he might close sixteen firehouses within the year,
and another about two Child Protective Services workers who say
they were disciplined for "speaking out" about turmoil inside the
agency.

Nine stories down, I find her:

POLICE QUESTION GARDENER IN
SCRAP YARD MURDER
By Marisa Hernandez

An illegal alien with a history of arrests was questioned in the murder of an Hasidic woman found Friday in a scrap pile in Brooklyn.

Miguel Arambula, 41, who does yard maintenance at the Borough Park manse where Rivka Mendelssohn lived, has a rap sheet containing citations for soliciting prostitution, public intoxication, and public urination.

"When he drinks he gets into trouble," said Francine Singer, 54, who lives downstairs from Arambula in Sunset Park. "I hope they send him back to Mexico."

Police declined to comment on whether Arambula is considered a suspect in the grisly death of the mother-of-four. A police official close to the case told the *Tribune* that Mendelssohn sustained massive head trauma and was pregnant at the time of her death.

Mendelssohn's funeral was attended by hundreds of members of her ultra-Orthodox Jewish community.

"It's so horrible," said an elderly attendee whose daughter was friends with Mendelssohn. "She trusted a stranger and look what happened."

—Additional reporting by Rebekah Roberts

A photo of Arambula trying to cover his face as he enters his apartment building runs with the story.

Now I know what Lars meant when he said Marisa got "great stuff" from the neighbors: I hope they send him back to Mexico. Nice. She probably got a whole earful from this lady about her tax dollars and how great people have it in jail. I like to think of New York as a really tolerant, broad-minded place, but sometimes New Yorkers fuck that up.

I'm surprised that the information I gave Lars about Sara Wyman saying she was considering a divorce is absent, but at least her pregnancy made it in. The story makes it seem like an arrest is imminent, but reading between the lines I can see that the only information they actually have is that this man was questioned, and that he has a petty record. My hunch is that Larry Dunn, or whoever was working the Shack, simply got DCPI to tell him that, yes, they'd brought him in for questioning. Being questioned isn't indicative of anything in itself, but it sure does look bad in the paper.

I met Marisa Hernandez once around Christmas when she relieved me on a stakeout of a livery cab driver accused of sexual assault. We hung out together in the lobby of his apartment building near the mall in Elmhurst. Most of the time you can't hang out in people's apartment building lobbies waiting for them to come home, but if the person you're trying to "get" lives in public housing, the rules change. Technically, you're still supposed to be buzzed in, but the doors are almost always open or unlocked. And if not, it's not terribly difficult to find someone to let you in. The men mostly don't care; you can just follow them inside. Women are more suspicious, but if you say something like "I'm going up to 11B," they're likely to let you pass. Best bet is a woman with a stroller; just hold the door for her. Marisa, I found out that evening, was from New Jersey and had been a stringer for a little over two years. She'd gotten married a couple months before and said she went to Sri Lanka for her honeymoon. We chatted for about twenty minutes while I filled her in on which floor the livery driver lived on (five), which entrance he was likely to use (southwest), whether there was any problem with security or ornery maintenance people (no and no).

I call the desk to get Marisa's cell number. She picks up on the first ring.

"Marisa," I say, "it's Rebekah from the *Trib*."

"Hey, how are you?"

"Good, sorry to bug you, but I have a question about the Arambula story."

"Oh God," she says, sounding exasperated.

"What?"

"Did you see the story?"

"Yeah."

"That lady didn't say, 'I hope they send him back to Mexico,' like that. She said, '*If* he did it, I hope they send him back to Mexico.' *If*!"

"That's a big if."

"Exactly," says Marisa. "That's exactly what my husband said."

"Did you get any sense about him? Like, did people seem to think he was capable of something like murder?"

"Not really. Everybody that I talked to who admitted to knowing him—which was only, like, three—said he was a great guy unless he was drinking. But even when he was drinking, they said he'd just get sloppy and, like, take a swing. I asked about the prostitution thing, and nobody wanted to touch that. I don't think it's that uncommon, though. A lot of the guys down there are single, they live in these cramped apartments and work and send money home. It's biology."

"But people weren't saying, like, he's creepy or angry . . ."

"No. Everybody was shocked when I told them what they brought him in for. You were on the body, right?"

"Right. They had me in Borough Park today, at the funeral."

"Did you get that she was pregnant?"

"Yeah," I say.

"Great shit."

"I don't think they were happy about the anonymous source."

"Oh, please, like their standards are so high."

"So are you gonna say anything about the quote?"

"Probably not," she says. "What's the point? I'll just remember I have to be extra fucking clear the next time Lars is on rewrite."

I thank her and hang up, which is when I see that I've missed a couple texts from Tony. Last night he sent: *how'd it go?*

And just a few minutes ago he sent a photo. It's a little grainy, but the image seems to be of a harbor, looking toward the Statue of Liberty.

I text back: *where r u? sry I missed ur txt last night; fell dead asleep early*

red hook; everything go ok with saul?

ish . . .

dinner plans?

not yet:

Tony picks me up at eight. He's wearing cologne, but not too much. I didn't even think of perfume. We drive to Bay Ridge, where his friend Marie, a chef, and her partner are doing a tasting menu to test out some new dishes. The restaurant is a small, glass-front place off the main drag. It's almost absurdly cozy inside, the lights low, candles everywhere. Tony takes my coat and hangs it inside his on a hook at the entrance.

"It's really nice in here," I say.

"Yeah," he says. "They did a great job. Six months ago this was a Chinese takeout."

A woman wearing a tie comes to hug him.

"You forgot parsnips!" she says, like it's the funniest thing in the world.

"Parsnips!" says Tony, slapping his forehead with his hand. "Rebekah, this is Marie. She owns the place."

"It's beautiful," I say.

"Thanks," she says. "We try! This guy spent all afternoon shopping with my sous chef and forgot parsnips."

"I hear," I say, trying to seem as cheerful as she is.

"We actually called a car," she says. "Sent a busboy out for them at five." She shakes her head, amused. "We've got you two by the window," she says, gesturing to a table in the corner. Cops and soldiers, I've been told, like sitting in the back corner of restaurants so they can survey the room and no one can sneak up on them. For a journalist, though, the window is what you always want. Especially in New York—a million stories a minute rush by, and no one faults you for staring out a window.

"I love sitting by the window," I say.

"Good," he says, and smiles.

The moment we sit down, a waitress appears with two flutes of champagne. I'm trying to stay in the moment, but something about drinking champagne seems wrong. Miriam isn't celebrating. Neither is Chaya, or Yakov.

Tony tells me a little about Marie—they grew up on the same block and both their dads died when they were in high school. Marie's dad in a construction accident, Tony's dad of cancer. After a few minutes, the waitress reappears to explain tonight's meal, which will be six courses, paired with wine. Some of the words she says are new to me: amuse, terrine, langoustine, and béchamel.

She sets down the "amuse," which comes in the same kind of spoon they give you with hot-and-sour soup at a Chinese restaurant.

"This is a butternut squash soup with sage and toasted pumpkin seed. Enjoy."

Tony and I slurp our spoonful of soup. It is very, very good.

I drink more champagne and look out the window. It's a busy night in Bay Ridge. Bundled-up couples and groups are hurrying from one place to another, laughing and rowdy.

Tony's phone rings. He looks at it, then silences the call.

"So," I say, because I can't get it out of my mind, "I saw a dead body again yesterday."

"Another one?"

"The same one, actually, but close up. I saw her at the funeral home. There was no autopsy," I say quietly, looking around me. No one is paying attention. "And now she's in the ground."

"No autopsy?"

"I don't think so," I say. "Saul says no. I saw her taken away by the Jewish van, then I saw her in the basement of the funeral home, like, twelve hours later."

Tony considers. "Did Saul know the dead woman?"

"Not well. He said he'd only met her once."

I finish my champagne, and the waitress brings a glass of red wine and the appetizer. It is beef carpaccio, which I know enough to know is raw beef. The wine is warm and bites my tongue like pepper.

Tony's phone rings again. He pulls it out and silences it again.

"You can get it if you want, I won't be offended."

"Thanks," he says. "It's okay."

After the carpaccio, I get up to go to the bathroom. When I come back, Tony is standing up. His face has changed.

"So, I have to go," he says.

"Really?"

"This is obviously embarrassing. . . ."

"Are you okay?" I reach out and put my hand on his arm.

He lowers his voice. "Let's not make a big deal." He gestures toward the entrance. "Can we talk outside?"

Without a word, he gets both our coats, helps me on with mine, and opens the door for me to go outside.

"What's going on?" I say again.

"It's my mom," he says. The color has left his cheeks entirely. "She's . . . I have to go home."

"Okay," I say. "I'll come with you."

Five minutes later, we pull up to a two-story house. An ambulance and two police cars, one marked and one unmarked, are parked outside. A medic stands over a woman sitting in the back of the ambulance. He appears to be bandaging her arm. Another woman, younger, maybe the ambulance lady's daughter, is standing in front of the open doors talking on a cell phone.

Tony skips up the steps and through the front door. I follow, slowly. Inside, two uniformed officers are pointing their guns at a wild-haired woman standing on a sofa wielding a hammer. She is wearing a pair of pink sweatpants and a Bruce Springsteen T-shirt. My appearance causes her to turn her head toward the door, her eyes sparkling with a combination of menace and elation. Everyone else in the room is tense—but she's having a ball.

"She has to drop the hammer, that's number one," says one of the plainclothed cops.

"Mom! Drop the hammer!"

"I was hanging a picture," she says defiantly.

"Drop the hammer, ma'am," says the one of the uniformed cops, shifting his balance, his gun still trained on her. "Nobody has to get hurt here."

"Drop it, Mom!" screams Tony, his voice cracking.

She drops it.

The two uniforms rush to her and place her in handcuffs. She sits on the sofa.

"Was anybody here?" Tony asks the cop in plainclothes, who seems to be the ranking officer. "Who called?"

The cop jerks his head toward the street. "Neighbors. She was banging and they came over. She went at them."

"Are they pressing charges?"

"I don't think so." The cop looks exhausted. He is wearing a blazer and pants that don't match. His tie is brown; he probably keeps it in his car. "But they could. She's gonna need stitches."

"I don't even know what to say, man," says Tony. "I'm sorry."

Tony's mom, who fifteen seconds ago resembled a character in a horror movie, is now sitting on the couch, looking totally bored. She sees me; I am a stranger in her home, but she does not ask me a question. She does not even really acknowledge me. I decide to step outside. Neighbors, some at their windows, some in coats on the sidewalk, are all gawking. I know that if the same thing were happening on my block, I'd be the first one at the window with my binoculars, disdaining and enjoying the dysfunction simultaneously. I catch the eye of one of a trio of women two doors down. One is on her phone, probably narrating the scene for some relative. She sees me and I make an aggressive face, like, mind your business, bitch. She reacts only slightly, then turns and faces the other way. Nothing like straddling the moral fence, Rebekah, I think.

The uniformed officers come outside first. One talks into the radio on his shoulder; the other unlocks the cruiser and gets in the driver's seat. They start up the car after a minute and drive off. The medics shut the ambulance doors and idle in their cab. I go back to the front door and see that Tony and his mom have both disappeared from the living room. Brown tie is sitting on the sofa, while his partner talks on the phone.

"Come on in," says brown tie. "Tony'll be out in a minute."

"I'm Rebekah," I say, extending my hand.

"Darin," he says. "All your dates end like this?"

"You'd be surprised," I say, referring to nothing, trying to sound nonchalant.

"Me and Tony went to school together. Mrs. Caputo wasn't always like this. Tony's great with her, but eventually something's gonna happen we can't fudge on the write-up."

"You're a detective?"

"Just since Halloween," he says. "Third grade."

"Do you like it?"

He shrugs. Perhaps "like" was the wrong word. His partner snaps closed his phone with finality.

"We're gonna write it up as an EDP," the man says. He's older than Darin, could be forty. Could be fifty. "I'll double-check with the neighbors that they aren't pressing charges again. But next time, she's gonna have to go in. He's on top of the meds?"

Darin nods. "I'll make sure."

The partner leaves, and Tony reappears, looking exhausted. There are sweat stains on his crisp white oxford. Darin gets up and Tony shakes his hand. "Thanks, man," he says.

"Don't," says Darin. He's a good-looking guy, sort of. Broad shoulders, trim. Too trim, maybe. He's got ginger-colored hair, cut short and thinning.

Tony looks at me. He's embarrassed.

"Are you okay?" I ask.

"I think the question is, are *you* okay."

"I'm fine," I say.

Darin sighs. "You got any beer, man? I could use a beer."

Two hours later, Tony and Darin and I are half-drunk on cans of light beer. My stomach is so bloated, I can barely bring myself to rise and pee. Tony lives in the basement of his mom's house. It's nice, actually. There's no mildew smell or draft like you usually get in a basement. It's warm and wood-paneled, with a flat-screen TV and carpet. There's even a fireplace. Tony didn't have any cut wood, but there was a peat log upstairs. He lights both sides and after a while the two flames meet in the middle. It burns silently, odor-lessly. The bathroom is tiny; not more than a closet, really. When I sit on the toilet, my knees are inches from the shower door. It is re-markably clean for a bachelor pad.

"So," says Darin when I sit back down next to Tony on the sofa, "you've got a source in the department who's taking you to see dead bodies?"

I look at Tony—like, *what the fuck?*

"I told him about Saul," he says.

"What precinct is he in?" asks Darin.

"I'm not going to tell you that," I say. The pleasant light-headedness I'd had just before going to the bathroom is gone. How could Tony have thought it was okay to talk to his friend—a *cop*—about what I'd told him?

"I didn't know there were Orthodox cops," says Tony. He can tell I'm pissed, and now he's trying to be casual.

"Sure," says Darin. "There are a few. How do you know him?"

"He knew my mom," I say. My tongue is heavy in my mouth.

"I know some cops work with reporters," says Darin, "but sneaking you into a funeral home to look at a homicide victim is . . ." He's looking for a word.

"Unorthodox," offers Tony.

"That's one way of putting it."

I'm about to say that he didn't *sneak* me in, although, I suppose, he did. I can't believe Tony has put me in this position.

Darin shrugs. "Why would he trust you, though? I mean, no offense. I'm sure you're a very nice person. But you're a reporter. Not trusting reporters is part of the job."

"The question is," says Tony, "is she safe?"

"That's not the question," I say. I love it. He betrayed my trust because he's worried about my well-being.

"It is, kind of, right?" He looks to Darin to back him up.

"I dunno, yeah. I mean, he's not gonna *hurt* her," says Darin. "But I'd guess you're getting used. He needs you for some reason."

I roll my eyes. He's right, which infuriates me further.

Darin leans forward. "I don't know this case well, but I know a little. The lady's Jewish. Hasidic. They got weight. Could they discourage a full autopsy? Yes. Absolutely. Especially if one of their guys has a medical examiner's license. But that doesn't mean the department isn't working the case."

"They haven't brought the husband in," I blurt out.

"You sure about that?"

I'm not sure; it's just what Saul told me. And I believe him. Still, I should ask the desk about that. I bet Larry Dunn at the Shack could confirm. I stand up and start putting on my coat.

"I'll call you a car," says Tony. I barely look at him.

"I didn't mean to piss you off," says Darin, finishing his beer. "I'm just saying it's possible you're not seeing everything he's seeing. Maybe he's got an ax to grind. Maybe he's hoping a story about a bungled investigation or whatever stirs up some shit. It will."

"Why would he want to stir up shit?" I say, sounding more antagonistic than I meant to—probably because I know, even as I'm asking it, that it's a stupid question. There are a million possible reasons. "Nevermind."

Tony follows me to the door and has the good sense not to try to kiss or hug me good-bye.

"I'm sorry," he says quietly. "I was thinking maybe he could help you out. But I knew as soon as I said it that I should have kept my mouth shut."

I'm not super-interested in his apology, but I don't want to get into it. I just want to go home.

MONDAY

CHAPTER NINE

My alarm rings at eight. I roll over and call the city desk. The woman on the phone tells me Mike isn't ready for me yet. I ask for Cathy.

"Hold."

"Rebekah!" says Cathy when she gets on the line. "I never called you back. Sorry. The desk was short so I had to chase down porn dad's ex-wife in New Jersey. What was it you said on your message? You had some new info on crane lady? Was it about the gardener?"

"No, I talked to a woman who knew her who said she had talked to a rabbi about getting a divorce. And another friend said Rivka Mendelssohn was, like, questioning? You know, sort of rebelling against the rules." I've been rehearsing. "Which is sort of a big deal."

"I know," says Cathy. She's typing. "Go on, I'm listening."

"And I have a source, in the NYPD, at the funeral home, that says that what was done to her was pretty brutal, and it would have taken a lot of organization and access to a car *and* access to the yard, which is private property. . . ."

"Which is it, NYPD or the funeral home?"

"Um . . ." Shit. "Well, both. The cop has a source in the funeral home."

"So, your source says the killer was organized and had a car. Is he on the record with that?"

"Yes, but he wants to stay anonymous."

"Who's this source?"

I'm not technically supposed to have to tell her this. "He'd rather me not say. For now. He's a detective, though."

"Have you talked to Larry about this?"

"No," I say. I've never met the *Trib*'s longtime police bureau chief. I'm actually not sure I've even spoken to him. "I wanted to see what you thought first. If there might be a story there."

"If you've got a source, work it. But talk to Larry first. I'm here all day, so call me. Wait, are you on today?"

"Yeah, but I haven't heard from Mike."

"They may want you on porn dad. Apparently he's getting out of Rikers."

Shit. "Well, I could follow up on the Mendelssohn story if nobody else is on it. Make a few calls. See if it leads anywhere."

"Talk to Larry."

I hang up and call the desk again for Larry's number.

He picks up after the first ring.

"Larry," I say. "It's Rebekah from the *Trib*. I was going to make some calls on the Rivka Mendelsson murder. . . .

"I've been meaning to call you," says Larry. "Did you get that info on her being pregnant and the head trauma?"

"Yeah . . ."

"Who'd that come from? They're freaking out about it down here."

"Really?" My heart rate speeds up. Already: consequences. "Um, a detective, but he needed to remain anonymous."

"Well, you pissed some people off with that, and I'm the one they're squawking at. Next time you use an anonymous police source, run it by me. Lars should know that, but he's an asshole."

"Sorry, I just called in what I . . ."

"I know. It just makes me look bad."

"Got it."

"If you hear anything else from your detective, let me know. I'll be working porn dad all day."

We hang up. I'm sitting on the edge of my bed and I can hear Iris in the bathroom.

The phone rings again.

"Hold for Mike."

I hold.

After about a minute, Mike gets on the line. "Rebekah, hang tight. I'll call you back after the meeting."

He hangs up. "The meeting" is when the editors in the office decide what stories to cover for tomorrow's paper. There are typically half a dozen or so stringers per shift, and at this meeting editors decide which event needs a live body to get information and which can be written with a couple phone calls. There are several more meetings as the day goes on, to adjust as necessary. When the plane landed in the Hudson, I heard every single stringer was pulled to go to the West Side. And of course, 9/11. There hasn't been a story like that since I got here.

Ten minutes later, Mike calls back.

"Okay," says Mike, "I need you in Park Slope to relieve Ericka. She's been staking out porn mom's apartment. They released porn dad last night. She visited him at Rikers yesterday. We wanna know if she's gonna take him back."

"Why'd they let him out?"

"Some sort of evidence fuckup. Larry is on that angle. I just need you to sit on the building and make sure you don't miss her coming or going. Ericka's been there since midnight. Lisa was there yesterday and saw her go in, without the kids. She has to come out sometime."

"Hey, so, I actually have some new information about crane lady. I just told Cathy . . ."

"Is it about the gardener?"

"No . . ."

"I need you on porn mom. We're getting national interest on this."

He gives me the address, then clicks off.

Iris is brushing her teeth, and I shoo her out so I can pee.

"So," she says from behind the door, "where are you going today?"

"I'm supposed to go to porn mom."

"Supposed to?"

"Well, I've got leads on Rivka Mendelssohn."

"Can you do both?"

I flush; Iris comes back to spit.

"I can call the social worker I met at the funeral while I'm standing outside porn mom's," I say. "But I really want to go try to talk to Miriam again in Borough Park. And I should talk to Saul again. See what he's got."

Iris is silent, but I can tell she has something else to say. I look at her in the dirty medicine cabinet mirror and her eyebrows are pressed together.

"What?" I ask.

"You have to be honest with yourself about why you're doing this. Don't follow this story because you think it'll lead to your mom somehow. Saul will probably tell you about her either way."

I look down. She's right; I've conflated the two.

"I know," I say.

"Do you?"

I nod, but I can't bring my eyes back up to hers.

"Hey," says Iris, putting her arm around me. "I love you. This is it. This is *your* story. It's about your people. It's about what you care about. No one else is going to keep this woman's death alive but you, right? That means something."

I look at the two of us in the mirror. Her with dark eyes and sleek new bangs and a faded chicken pox mark on her nose not yet hidden with foundation. Me with my wild red hair and too pink cheeks. Iris is the closest thing I'll ever have to a sister and she looks nothing like me.

"You can do this," she says. "Just be careful. Be smart."

Porn mom lives in a pretty prewar apartment building on the corner of Third Street and Eighth Avenue. From a block away I can see the scene has turned into a celebrity-style clusterfuck. Two photogs are camped out in folding chairs at the corner. A van from the local Fox station idles in front of the fire hydrant, and a half dozen other reporters, bundled like Arctic explorers, linger near the building's front door.

Ericka is leaning back in the front seat of her Honda Civic, reading today's paper. I knock on the window and she motions for me to come around and sit inside. She's got a police scanner on the dashboard and a pile of McDonald's bags behind the passenger seat.

"What's the scoop?" I ask.

"Same shit. She's up there. Lisa saw her go in. I did a door-knock around ten last night but she didn't answer. Nothing since. There's no doorman, but there's a biddy on the first floor who keeps screaming she's gonna call the cops if we try to come in again. Of course, they'll still make you go."

"Of course," I say.

"You don't have a car?"

I shake my head.

"It's fucking brutal out there. I burned a tank of gas not freezing last night."

"Is photo here?"

"The German guy with the point-and-shoot."

I sigh. I've been on several assignments with Henrik, who is Austrian, and he always manages to get in the way. In December, we were at a press junket in Midtown for a treadmill-workstation that was supposed to revolutionize the cubicle, and he wouldn't get off the thing. There were four PR chicks in black all standing around giving him the evil eye as he trotted in place asking questions about balance and liability and calories. I tried to pretend he wasn't with me by gorging on the free sushi and crudités until I could pull a black dress aside and ask her some questions, the answers to which, I knew, would never make the paper. Half the "stories" I get sent on don't make the paper. Stringers are cheap and the editors are frightened they'll miss something. It was cold that day, too, I remember, and Henrik was in shorts—with socks held up by tiny garters. And instead of a proper SLR like every other professional photographer I've ever seen, Henrik carries a Canon point-and-shoot on a string around his wrist.

"How long's he been here?"

"Since about eight. He's in the red Mazda." She points up the block to Henrik's car. He has a bumper sticker that says SAVE THE HUMANS.

"Okay," I say, readying myself to return to the cold. "Anything else? What did porn mom say when she went in?"

"Nothing. Lisa said she just kept her head down."

"Have you seen the kids?"

"Nope. Probably with Grandma or something."

"What apartment is it?"

"3E. There's a window—two, actually—one's frosted, like it's a bathroom. But she's got the curtains closed."

"Did you talk to any neighbors?"

"I got one coming in last night with his dog. He said the usual, she seemed nice, kids are nice. Blah blah. He gave me a good quote about the guy, though. Something about how porn dad was always in the lobby without a shirt on."

"Nice."

"Did you ever see that show she was on?"

"I think it was before my time."

"Me, too—but I watched one of the *Melrose* episodes on You-Tube. She played a hostess at a club. Maybe they'll replay the porn on Cinemax now that she's famous again."

"So she's blond?" I need to make sure I recognize her if she leaves.

"Tom got a picture of her yesterday. Have photo e-mail it to you. She was all bundled up, but she looks blond. She's still thin, too. She was wearing a red coat."

"If she's smart, she'll change it to black."

"She can't be that smart if she's living with porn dad."

"True."

"TMZ's here somewhere. And *The Insider*."

"Fantastic." I know most of the other reporters at the *Ledger*, and a couple from the *Times*. We're used to competing for quotes on stories. But the celebrity press frightens me. At the *Trib* we're still rewarded for good leads and the occasional social service story (often involving how the MTA is scheming to fuck riders, or how the teachers unions are scheming to fuck students); all the celebrity press does is stalk. And they're good at it.

I get out of Ericka's car and watch her pull away. I knock on Henrik's window and he leans over to unlock the door. 1010 WINS is playing two notches louder than my ears are prepared for.

"Good morning!" he says.

"Seen anything yet?"

He shakes his head. "No, no. She's not coming out."

"I wouldn't if I were her." My phone rings. It's the desk.

"Hold for Mike," says the receptionist.

I hold. Mike picks up. "What's going on out there?"

"Nothing. She hasn't been outside since Lisa saw her last night."

"What about neighbors?"

"Ericka said she got one. I just got here. I'll look for some more."

"Talk to merchants. Deli, nail salon, whatever. See if you can get someone who saw him with the kids. Or her with him. She's been at that address six years, so people know her. Maybe somebody's got her headshot on the wall, like at the cleaners." Right. Jerry Seinfeld, Bernadette Peters, Sarah Jessica Parker—these people get asked for personalized photos, not the forty-something former soft-porn sitcom sweetheart. "This is tomorrow's wood, so get as much as you can."

"I will." The wood, in tabloid newspaper language, means the lead story, the story that's going to get everybody excited. That's going to, presumably, give them wood. When one of the editors first said it to me, I thought, he can't mean what I think he means. But I've never had the balls to ask. "You know TMZ's here, right?"

"Yeah. They've got an old shot of mom and dad at the beach. He's in Speedos. Photo's having a shit-fit. Jaime wants a family portrait. Is photo with you?"

"Yeah."

"Who is it?"

"Henrik."

"Fuck. Hold on. Jaime!" I can picture Mike, standing up, shouting over his cubicle to the photo desk. I hope Henrik can't hear. "You've got Henrik on porn mom? Yes! . . . Rebekah, they're gonna pull him. Photo will call you."

"Okay."

"Quotes," he says. "Have you done a door-knock?"

"No, I just got here. Ericka says there's a lady downstairs who . . ."

Mike cuts me off. "Is there a doorman?"

"No."

"Good. Do another door-knock. Ask her if she suspected. Ask her if she's seen the pictures. See if we can hang out until he gets home. Get the reunion."

"Okay."

Mike hangs up. Henrik's phone rings. He listens, nods, hangs up.

"They are taking me off."

"Oh yeah?"

"To Queens. To courthouse."

"Okay, well, drive safe."

"Say hi to porn mom," he says, snickering.

I climb back out into the cold. My phone rings again. It's a 917 number I don't recognize. Probably the photographer. When you're a stringer, strangers are always calling and you have to pick up.

"Hi, it's Rebekah," I say.

"It's Bill from the *Trib*." I know Bill. He's thirtyish and claims to have been a war photographer. Apparently he shot "conflicts" in Africa. He's got long wavy black hair that he usually wears in a ponytail. Once, while we were on a story, he said he knew a cute café for lunch nearby. But when we got to the restaurant, one of those tiny French bistros with thin iron chairs and the menu written in gold cursive on a mirror, a tall woman with short hair and chandelier earrings was waiting for him. We ate at separate tables.

"Hi, Bill."

If he remembers me, he doesn't say so. "I'm in Manhattan. I'll be there in about an hour. Don't do anything without me. Is the *Ledger* there?"

"Yup. And TMZ."

"Fuck. I'm on my way."

I stick my phone in my pocket and walk across the street, into the group of reporters in front of the building. I recognize the *Ledger* reporter, a girl about my age whose name I always forget. We smile and walk toward each other.

"Did you just get here?" she asks. Like me, she's so bundled, she has to move her entire upper body if she wants to turn her head. Half her face is covered with a scarf, so I can't see her lips move.

I nod.

"I was on this yesterday, too. It's fucking horrible out here. I think I'm getting a cold."

"I was in Chinatown Friday. Then Gowanus, by the canal."

She shivers. "There was a body, right?"

"Yeah, a woman. You guys had Pete Calloway on it."

"Figures. He probably ferreted it out before the desk even."

"Did you run anything?"

"I think it went in the blotter. You guys got the gardener angle before us."

"Ah."

"Well, porn mom's a fucking hoot. Everybody got a shot of her going in yesterday, but nobody's seen her since."

"Did you do a door-knock?"

"No, but if you do, I'll come with."

"I have to wait for photo," I say.

"Mine's here," she says, motioning toward one of the two men on fold-out camping chairs.

"Have you talked to anybody, like, in the neighborhood?"

"I stopped a couple people leaving for work, but everybody's just pissed that we're here. One lady actually pushed the TMZ kid. He loved it."

"I'm gonna go get some tea. I'll find you before I go in. Do you want anything?"

"I'm good. Thanks." She pulls two tiny beanbag-sized hand-warmers from her coat pockets. "Got these." Smart girl.

I head up Eighth Avenue into the wind. I get tea at a bodega and look through the *Ledger*. Porn mom and dad are on the front page. The *Ledger* ran with a courtroom sketch of dad at his arraignment and a twenty-year-old glamour shot of mom, plus a fuzzy still from her *Melrose* appearance. I scoot into the corner by the beer and dial Sara Wyman.

"This is Sara," she answers.

"Sara, hi, my name is Rebekah Roberts. I'm a reporter for the *Tribune*."

"Hello, Rebekah," she says. "I'm pleased to hear from you."

I'm not used to hearing that.

"Oh? Great. Well, like I said, I'm interested in learning a little about Rivka Mendelssohn. We'd like . . ."

"Are you in Brooklyn?" she asks, interupting me.

"Yeah," I say. "I'm in Park Slope right now."

"Wonderful. I'm downtown. Are you free?"

"I'm actually on another story assignment," I say, hoping she's flexible. "How about twelve thirty?"

She tells me to meet her at a Starbucks on Atlantic near the R train stop. I put my phone in my pocket and almost smile.

I linger by the door of the bodega, scrolling through news on my phone. I should be interviewing the guy behind the counter. I should at least ask if he recognizes either porn mom or dad. But I just don't care. Instead I think about Sara Wyman, and what I should ask her. The information I gave Lars yesterday, that Sara had said Rivka Mendessohn was considering a divorce, didn't make the gardener story, but if I can get more details, it might be enough for a short feature, especially if Larry can add confirmation that the police haven't yet questioned her husband. I need to ask how many people knew she was unhappy in her marriage, and if Sara thinks that could have had something to do with her death.

Eventually, Bill calls.

"Where are you?" he asks.

"I'm a couple blocks up."

"The *Ledger*'s going to do a door-knock," he says. "We can't miss it."

"I'll be right there."

Back at the building, the *Ledger* chick is standing with Bill and the seated photogs. Bill is a douche. She wouldn't have done the door-knock without me.

"Mara said there's a biddy downstairs . . ." says Bill.

"Maya," says the *Ledger* reporter. Right, Maya.

"Okay," says Bill, not looking at her. "The desk wants a studio of the big happy family." A studio is where we take a picture of a picture. We use studios a lot for dead people—school portraits, church bulletin, weddings. "And nobody has her full-face yet, right?" The *Ledger* photographer shakes his head. He's short and wide. I think his name is Mac, or Bo. Something with one syllable.

"If she opens the door, we might not have much time," I say, turning to Maya. "I'm thinking the first question is whether she's gonna take him back."

"Definitely. Then ask if she's seen the photos."

I nod. "Does anybody know where the kids are? I haven't heard anything about Child Protective Services being involved, but it seems like that's a possibility."

"Our overnight said they heard there's a grandparent."

"Okay," I say. "So if she's taking him back, if she's seen the photos, where the kids are."

Maya nods and jumps up the front step to peek into the lobby. "No sign of biddy. Let's do this."

The four of us enter through the heavy metal and glass front doors into the white-painted lobby. The floor is a mosaic of little octagonal black and white tiles. A giant nonworking fireplace and mantel stands stark and empty, a reminder of a time when some sort of butler stood stoking the flames, ready to greet residents with warmth and cheer and a whole bunch of pampering shit that doesn't exist anymore, at least in Brooklyn. We won't all fit in the elevator, so we start to climb the stairs, and as we do, the front door opens and TMZ, *The Insider,* and Fox come shuffling in, video cameras perched on their shoulders, microphones in their fists.

"Fabulous," I say to Maya.

She rolls her eyes. "Let's just get up there first."

We pick up the pace and make it to the landing with Mac huffing behind us. It's a narrow hallway, maybe four feet wide and long, six apartments per floor. Maya and I stand in front of the door. 3E. Bill is practically on top of me, the long lens of his Canon scratching my neck. I knock. Nothing. The TV people have piled into the elevator and I can hear them laughing as they rise slowly toward us. I knock again. Nothing. "Ms. Dryden? Ms. Dryden my name is Rebekah and I'm from the *New York Tribune.* I know you don't want us here and I don't blame you, but if you could just give us a minute of your time, a couple of questions, we'll leave you alone."

"Look," Maya says quietly, pointing to the glass peephole. "I think I just saw her move."

"Ms. Dryden," I say, my voice a little louder. "We'd really like to hear your side of the story. People are saying some pretty awful things and we'd really like to give you a chance to . . ." TMZ and the rest come galloping out of the elevator, pushing up behind us.

"Did you get her?" says the girl from *The Insider*. She's dressed for a stand-up: lipstick and foundation, no hat. I try to ignore her and knock again, more softly. "Ms. Dryden, could you just tell us if Frank is planning to come home?"

I hear a lock turn—everyone does—and like dogs sensing a squirrel, we all point our noses and notebooks and camera lenses toward 3E. But the door stays closed. And behind it, a woman's voice.

"Please," she says softly. "Can't you please just leave me alone?"

"What's she saying!" yells the kid from TMZ.

"Shut the fuck up, asshole!" shouts Bill, but he doesn't move from his pose, so he not only practically shatters my eardrum, but spits in my hair, too.

"I'm sorry, Ms. Dryden," I say again, putting my hand on the door. I look at Maya and she nods. Keep going. "Are you planning to take Frank back?"

"Please, can't you just go?"

"I'm really sorry, but none of our bosses will let us leave until we talk to you. It won't be long, we just want to know if Frank is coming home. If you could just open the door for a minute . . ."

"Missy!" shouts TMZ. "Have you seen the photos? Ask her if she's gonna do another soft core."

Bill whips around to yell at TMZ, but he moves so fast, he forgets to lower his lens and smacks the chick from *The Insider* right in the face.

"Oooooh!" yells TMZ, sounding like a middle school boy witnessing a playground dis. "You okay, Chrissy?"

Chrissy is not okay. Chrissy is bleeding. She's got her pretty leather glove pressed to her mouth. Bill's kneeling, tending to his lens, which appears intact. He looks up at TMZ and hisses, "If you fucked up my lens, I'm gonna fucking kill you, motherfucker."

TMZ puts his hands up, like in surrender. "Tell your fucking reporter to tell porn mom if she don't come out, we're gonna be on her and her kids and her fucking whatever all day every day until she jumps out the window."

"Hey!" I say. I look at Chrissy and I look at 3E and I'm not sure which to attend to. Chrissy's lip is split. She's done for the day—you can see it in the tired, blank sheen that's fallen over her eyes. I'm done, too.

CHAPTER TEN

Sara Wyman arrives at the Starbucks a few minutes late. She has the rumpled, distracted look of a librarian, with ruby red–rimmed eyeglasses and half-gray hair cut in a shapeless bob.

"I saw the article about the gardener," she says after we sit down. Up close, her face is much softer than it seemed at the funeral. She's probably forty-five, and has very few wrinkles. "Not much real information there."

Touché.

"Yeah," I say, pulling out my notebook and pen. I'm going to get this right. "I'm hoping to round that out. Fill it in, rather. I spoke with a young woman she used to babysit. And her sister-in-law."

"Miriam," says Sara. "You mentioned that."

"You said you knew her, too?"

Sara nods. "First," she says, "I need to set some ground rules.

I will tell you what I know, but my words do not appear in the newspaper unless I approve the language."

Letting sources approve their quotes is frowned upon. But I'm not really in a position to be picky. At least I can use her name.

"Absolutely," I say.

"Rivka began coming to my gatherings about a year ago. I host a weekly group at an apartment near the United Nations. We have an open door policy. People hear of us through friends. Those who come are unhappy in their Orthodox identity somehow. They come to have a supportive, positive place to think and question. To sort things out with the help of others."

"Do you know why Rivka started coming?"

"She had just lost a child," says Sara.

"Yes," I say. "Someone else mentioned that. A miscarriage?"

"No. The baby was nearly eight months old. A little girl named Shoshanna. She was devastated. Rivka said it was asthma. The little girl had a breathing attack. She was devastated, and I think it changed her."

"How did she change, do you think?"

Sara sighs. "I didn't know her before, but she was angry. And she talked about feeling that she had just woken up to the anger. At the group meetings, she kept things close to her chest, but when we met separately she was less circumspect. You said you'd met Miriam?"

"Yes."

"Rivka spoke often of Miriam. You know she'd been away for many years."

"Away?"

"Yes. Miriam had problems. Mental health issues, we call them now. Rivka said that starting around age eleven she just couldn't act like everyone else. She wouldn't always wash herself, things like that. Seemingly purposeless defiance. And she had rages. Rivka said she gave herself a concussion banging her head against the kitchen wall when she was barely thirteen. Rivka and Miriam had been friends since they were very young, and Rivka went to live with the family after her mother died and her father was unable to care for her."

"Miriam said Rivka's mother had worked for their family," I say.

"Yes, I believe that was the background. She died of cancer and the Mendelssohns took Rivka in. Her brothers went upstate, to the grandparents, I think. Rivka remembered Miriam being punished a lot. Locked in a bedroom. Made to miss meals. The parents didn't know what to do. And she got worse as she got older. She was expelled from school."

"What happened?"

"Rivka said that Miriam pulled her hair out. It's a nervous habit, of course, and now we know it's somewhat common for young women with certain kinds of mental disorders. The other girls made fun of her. One day the class was in the kitchen, and Miriam . . . well, something happened with a kettle. Rivka said Miriam poured the boiling water on one of the girls. Right down the back of her neck. The girl was in the hospital for weeks and her family made a big stink. You can't blame them, of course. I believe that was when Miriam was sent away—the first time, at least. To some sort of hospital."

"But Rivka stayed?"

Sara nods. "She said she felt terribly guilty about the way the family reacted to Miriam's . . . departure. She told me that they didn't speak of her at all in the years she was gone. It was as if she hadn't ever been there."

"Rivka didn't want to go back with her father?"

Sara shakes her head. "Rivka's father was not much of a presence in her life, even before her mother died. She told me that now she could see he had mental problems, too. He spent his time at work—I believe he was a clerk of some kind—or shul, or his bedroom. He jumped off the Tappan Zee Bridge when Rivka was sixteen."

"Oh my God."

"It was considered a great blessing in the family when Aron proposed to Rivka."

"Really?"

"You seem surprised."

"He's much older. . . ."

"Almost twenty years, I think. But that isn't terribly unusual. He was away in Israel most of her childhood."

"I've met him a couple times. Honestly, he kind of scared me."

"You met him, I assume, just after the violent death of his wife."

I nod.

"Aron is a generous man, from what I can tell. He helped find a match for Miriam, which was not an easy task, despite their wealth."

"And Miriam never had children."

"As if things weren't bad enough for Miriam, yes, Rivka told me she was infertile."

I flip back through my notebook to find the word Chaya used. "I talked to a girl who said Miriam was . . . akarah?"

"*Akarah*, yes. That means barren. Who said that?"

"Um, just a woman who knew her. A young woman. She was very pregnant."

Sara shakes her head. "Miriam does not need more scrutiny from the community. I'm sure her infertility is a great sorrow for her. She and Aron were two of eleven in their family."

"Jesus."

Sara laughs. It's the first time I've seen her smile. She has dimples in both cheeks. "They were fruitful and they multiplied. Heshy, Miriam's husband, I believe has health issues as well. Couples without children do not fit into Hasidic society easily. They are suspicious. Something must be wrong, people think. And of course something *is* wrong. But something is always wrong, isn't it?

"I think that when she came to me, Rivka had been very unhappy for a very long time. She told me she'd never felt right about the way the family—and everyone else—treated Miriam. From what Rivka said, Miriam was a wonderful, sensitive friend to her, especially throughout the tragedies of her childhood. But what could she do?" Sara pauses. "Rivka started reading. Secretly, of course. She spent time in bookstores, in Manhattan, away from the community." The Strand, I think. Like my mom. "She started reading religious philosophy, but quickly began reading about mental illness. She believed Miriam was very definitely bipolar, with borderline traits as well."

"But she was never diagnosed? Or medicated?"

"That's unclear. A few months ago Rivka mentioned she was considering a trip upstate to the hospital where Miriam had stayed. I think she suspected it wasn't actually a hospital."

"What would it be?"

"Some sort of home for inconvenient family members, perhaps. Run by a rebbe. Where she was kept but not really treated."

"Do things like that exist?"

"Oh yes," says Sara. "It's informal, of course. Money is donated from the community."

"Are they locked in?"

"I don't know. I've never been to one. It can't be much worse than some of the state-run homes for the disabled. You've read about those, right?"

I have. Tales of violence and neglect; lots of hand-wringing, not much corrective action.

"Rivka was angry when she learned that what made Miriam act the way she did was something that was so out of her control. 'Miriam wasn't bad,' she told me. It had been a revelation to her. She said it took several years, but that she finally convinced Aron to bring Miriam home to Borough Park. She'd felt pain about her friend as long as she could remember. The way the community dealt with Miriam's illness—and Rivka's father's, probably—terrified Rivka. I remember her saying that it interfered with her love of Hashem. You're Jewish?"

I nod.

"Then you know. Jews, we are all sons and daughters of Hashem, God. He is accessible to us through how we live our lives. Where I grew up, where Rivka Mendelssohn grew up, everything is about Hashem. From our hairstyles to our clothing to when we rise and where we go and what we eat and when we eat and what we do and do not have in our homes. It is very difficult to live this life without an abiding devotion to Hashem. And to the community itself. To the idea of living apart. To creating more Jews here and living our values."

"What are the values, exactly?"

"What I described. Exalting Hashem, modesty, family, prayer, tradition."

"And Rivka Mendelssohn rejected those values?"

"No, I wouldn't say that. But she was beginning to reject how she felt she was forced to express them. And then she fell in love."

Aha.

"And that changed everything that hadn't already changed inside her. I think. She told me she didn't mean for it to happen—and I knew that. I watched it! They were just drawn to each other. From the moment they met."

"You saw them?"

She sighs again. "They met at one of my gatherings. Both were new. I never saw them alone together, but I could tell. When she told me, I knew who she was talking about."

"When was this?"

"Last spring. It was just warm."

"And when was the last time you saw her?"

Sara pauses. "It was . . . more than two weeks ago. We had coffee. Here, actually. She met me at lunchtime."

"Did she seem . . . ?" I don't even know what to ask. I wonder if Rivka sat in this very Starbucks chair. I wonder what she ordered.

"Like she was worried she'd be murdered? No. She seemed relatively happy. She told me that her son had been chosen to sing in shul. Apparently he has a beautiful voice."

"Did you know she was pregnant?"

Sara shakes her head. "Not until I read it in your newspaper. It is true, then?"

I nod. "So she didn't tell you?"

Sara shakes her head.

"Is it possible the baby was . . . out of wedlock?"

"Anything is possible, of course," says Sara. "But Rivka would know that sexual intimacy out of her marriage would mean . . . Well, it would mean the end of her marriage. Her husband would ask for a divorce immediately. The rebbe would grant it quickly and she would be out of her home. I doubt very much that her brothers would take her in. She would be considered a very bad influence, especially if they have children, which I'm certain they do. I don't know if Rivka would be willing to risk all that could come from an affair. She was a cautious woman. She cherished her children, and she would lose custody in a divorce."

"Automatically?"

Sara nods. "In Brooklyn and other Hasidic enclaves, family court judges are influenced by the wishes of the community. In a custody case, a rebbe and other powerful members of the community will testify that the children will be confused if they are exposed to a parent who is less religious. And even if they are granted some kind of visitation, very often the children are poisoned against the parent who left. Their family—even the family of the absent parent—will talk about that person as if she is dangerous. Children, especially young children like Rivka's, become frightened. They do not want to upset their primary caregivers and so many begin refusing to see the less religious parent. I know many, many people who have lost all contact with their children after a divorce."

I stare at Sara. I knew my mom came from an insular world; a world of rules with no easy path out. I knew how her world had fucked her up, and through her, me. But what I hadn't known—what I hadn't even suspected—was how the tentacles of that world reached into the secular systems that are supposed to be our great equalizers. Blind justice, my ass.

"Do you think her husband knew?" I ask.

"About Baruch?"

"Baruch?"

Sara purses her lips. "I did not mean to tell you his name. Do not put his name in the newspaper."

"I won't," I say.

She is silent a moment, and I can tell she's considering whether she should go on. I wait, and then ask another question.

"But the baby could have been her husband's, right?"

"Yes," she says "And Aron would have no reason to suspect it was not his. . . . Unless."

"Unless?"

"Unless he did have a reason." Sara is considering something. "If you don't mind my asking, how did you find out about the pregnancy?"

"A source in the police department saw the body." I'm not sure why I'm not telling her the whole truth.

"There was an autopsy?"

"Not officially," I say. Sara looks puzzled: there either is or isn't an autopsy, obviously. "No. The person in the department had gotten the information from someone at the funeral home."

"Ah," says Sara. "That makes sense."

"How did you hear she had died?" I ask.

"I got a call that evening from . . . someone else in the group." She's talking about Baruch. "He said she was dead. He wasn't making much sense. I called around and found out that a woman's body had been taken from the scrap yard her husband owns. I prayed it wasn't true. That it was just a coincidence. But . . ." She shakes her head.

"Were you surprised?"

"Of course! It was so . . . violent. So shocking."

"Is murder unusual in the Hasidic community?"

"I've never known anyone who was murdered."

"What was your first thought?"

"You mean about who might have killed her?"

I nod.

Sara is quiet for several seconds. She turns her teacup in her hands. "This is off the record." I nod. She lowers her voice. "When I heard she was found in the yard, I did think of Aron. For no real reason other than, well, when a married woman dies, isn't it often her husband who killed her?"

"Did you ever get the sense that Rivka was the victim of domestic violence?"

Sara shakes her head. "She rarely spoke about her husband. Except to say that she never loved him."

"Do you think he knew that?"

"I have no idea."

I look at my notebook. I should have written down my questions before I got here. Sara doesn't seem impatient, though. I flip back a couple pages and see my note about the fight Yakov said his mother and father had about Coney Island.

"Have you ever heard about a house in Coney Island, where people sometimes go who are questioning?" I ask.

"Oh course," says Sara. "Menachem Goldberg's house. I don't know that he lives there anymore, but it's been open for, decades, I think. Since the eighties, anyway."

"Have you been there?"

Sara nods.

"Do you think you might be willing to give me the address? I think Rivka spent time there, and I'd love to maybe learn a little more about her from the people there. I won't use names if they don't want."

"I suppose that's fine." She scrolls through her phone and finds the address, then sends it to me in a text.

"Do you still consider yourself part of the community?" I ask.

Sara smiles. "I don't think I'll ever escape it. And so much of my work is with people in the community. It is who I am. I choose to live apart, but I am never really . . . apart."

I haven't been writing down much, but I scribble *I don't think I'll ever escape it* into my notebook. That, I think, is a good quote.

"Now," says Sara, "let's talk about what you're going to write."

I take the bus back to Park Slope and manage to get a couple pieces of usable information from the clerk at the bodega where I got tea near porn mom's apartment. Apparently, porn dad came in for energy drinks and gum after jogging.

"He always buy gum," said the clerk.

The desk, as I predicted, loves this.

"Gum!" says Mike, taking my notes. "For the kids."

"I guess," I say. Who cares.

It's only three, so Mike tells me to stick around until someone can relieve me.

"Make sure you get anyone coming in or out," he says. "Neighbors."

"Sure," I say, but as soon as I hang up, I slip into a sushi restaurant where I can sip green tea and call Cathy.

I tell her that I've got a source, a woman with a name, who says Rivka Mendelssohn had been grieving the loss of a daughter, might have been having an affair, and was considering a divorce before she died.

"And the police haven't questioned the husband?" she asks.

"I don't think so," I say.

"We need that," she says. "Call Larry. I'll pitch this at the meeting, but I'm not sure they'll want it."

I call Larry.

"I can't confirm for sure," he says, "but I don't think they've brought him in."

"They made a big deal about bringing the gardener in, right? If they'd brought the husband in, you think you'd know."

"Not necessarily," he says. "I'll see what I can find out."

When I hang up, I take out my notebook and start scribbling a draft.

The Hasidic woman found dead in a Brooklyn scrap yard Friday was no stranger to tragedy. [cliché?]

Less than a year before she was murdered, Rivka Mendelssohn, 30, lost a child, according to Sara Wyman, a social worker who runs an informal group for "questioning" ultra-Orthodox. Wyman says Mendelssohn told her that her daughter died of an asthma attack last spring when she was less than a year old. [get second source—Miriam?]

"Rivka was devastated," said Wyman, who grew up in

*Borough Park and has since left the ultra-Orthodox commu-
nity. "I believe it led her to question her faith."*

*Wyman said that as a teen, Mendelssohn lost her father to
suicide, and several members of her extended family struggled
with mental illness. [check? death records?]*

*"The Orthodox do not typically seek medical help for psy-
chological problems," explained Wyman.*

*Wyman said Mendelssohn had been coming to her weekly
meetings for nearly a year and told her that she was considering
a divorce, but was worried about losing access to her four young
children.*

*Wyman said the last time she saw Mendelssohn was two
weeks ago.*

*"Rivka said her son had been chosen to sing in shul," she
said. "She was very proud."*

*Wyman said she had "no idea" how Mendelssohn could
have met such a gruesome end.*

*"I just hope the police find who did this—she didn't de-
serve to die so young."*

*Police have questioned and released the family gardener, but
refused to comment on the case, citing an ongoing investigation.*

I make the last bit up, figuring I'll fill in whatever Larry finds,
or doesn't find.

I read over what I've written and decide it's not bad, but it's
definitely what my professors would call a "one-source story," which
isn't ideal. I need Miriam in here. I need somebody at 1PP. I need
Baruch.

Back at the porn mom scene, Bill is sharing a cigarette with a tall woman wearing Pan-Cake makeup and an *Entertainment Tonight* badge around her neck.

"Where the fuck have you been?" he asks.

"Did I miss anything?"

ET shakes her head. "Neighbors are like Nazis," she says, blowing smoke out her nostrils. "Biddy's on patrol, too." I look past her into the lobby and see that, indeed, biddy is manning the door in her housecoat and snow boots. Maya is across the street, so I cross and ask her if she's gotten anything.

"Nothing," she says. "Total bust. I followed one woman around the corner and she started running, *literally*. Where'd you go?"

I shrug. "Coffee."

"Smart. If they have me back here tomorrow, I'll do the same."

I call Mike and tell him the biddy has the place locked down.

"The *Ledger* has nothing either. Nobody does," I say.

"All right," he says. "You can take off."

CHAPTER ELEVEN

I first heard about the house at Coney Island from my dad. It figured briefly in "the story of Mom." They hatched the plan to run back to Orlando together in Coney Island. It was their hideaway. Where they could meet in private. As a child, I imagined "Coney Island" as a tiny island, like the ones that cartoon characters get marooned on. With a single palm tree in the center. Later, when I saw a picture of the boardwalk and the roller coaster, I pictured them walking hand in hand together down the shoreline. By high school, when I understood a little about sex, and experienced its connection to what I'd always been told was love, I realized that Coney Island was where my parents went to have sex. I might even have been conceived there.

But Coney Island was just one line in the story. A story that was communicated to me in pieces as I was deemed ready. Mom isn't dead, but she's not here, at three. She's not here because she had to go take care of her family in New York, at five. We didn't go with her because Mommy and Daddy were divorced, like so-and-so's parents, at seven. Mommy and Daddy were divorced because Mommy grew up a certain way, at nine. Actually, Mommy and Daddy weren't exactly divorced, because they never got married, at eleven. From there it started getting muddy. They weren't ever really lies, and I can see now that it was not a story that easily lent itself to a child's comprehension, but it always felt to me like another big secret was coming—another piece of the picture dangling above my life like a piano. Ready to drop and force me to climb over it. For years I hated my father as much as I hated my mother. And in some ways I still do, but now I also have sympathy for him. And respect for how he handled the situation. Twenty years old with a baby girl and a thoroughly appalled family can't have been easy, and he made it work for us. He might not be as in touch with his actual emotions or, to some extent, reality, as I wish he was, but he's a good guy. To the core. And even at twenty-two years old I know that's rare. One parent who would protect you at all costs is more than a lot of people get. But he doesn't want to understand who I really am inside. He thinks I've turned away from God. Those were his actual words. I called him to say how bad I'd been feeling sophomore year in college. I told him how I was scared all the time but I didn't exactly know what of. Well, he said with a kind of sadness, You've turned away from God. His words infuriated me. I've never seen or heard or felt this "God," but my life is basically a mess made by people twisting themselves into knots, trying to please him. My parents were both looking for God in a bookstore when they met. Oh wow, they must have thought. Someone I can obsess over God with who I also want to fuck! And why did my mother leave?

God. All the good I've ever seen in this world, all the beauty and joy, comes from people, or from the earth. An evening sky, music. Did God make it all? Maybe. But we don't look at a Picasso and worship his father, I said to my dad. And he responded, sounding both smug and sad, But see, we have to worship something. Fuck you, I said. And fuck God. And that was the last time we talked about it.

I get off the F train at the last stop. The track is elevated here, and I can see the Cyclone and the Wonder Wheel. I can see the icy cold Atlantic slapping the empty beach. I shuffle down what feels like fifteen flights of stairs to the street, the wind coming from everywhere at once, tiny specks of ocean water and grains of sand like needles on my exposed face. People are all around me ending their day, beginning their day, heads down, encased in wool and nylon and fur and fleece. It's a terrible time to try to get people to talk, the winter. As bad as in the pouring rain.

Snow left over from the big storm a couple weeks ago is still taking up parking spaces, slate-colored and frozen into walls by the passing plow. The dedicated pedestrian walkway and bike lane is impassable, though it's hard to imagine too many leisure riders rolling to the beach today. The address Sara gave me is six blocks from the station. Nathan's hot dogs and the souvenir shops on Mermaid Avenue are closed up tight. The faded color murals remembering strong men and sword swallowers of yore look hopelessly one-dimensional. A right and a left and I'm in front of 331 Sand Street. It's a narrow two-story house with dingy vinyl siding on a block of the same. I open the knee-high white-painted metal gate, and when I reach the base of the concrete steps the front door opens and two young women come out. They're both within five years of my age, give or take. The older one has close-cropped brown hair and wears shoulder-grazing feather earrings. The younger one is blond, with her long hair in a ponytail. Both are in coats, but they don't appear to be leaving. Judging by the sofa on the porch and the pint glass of butts beside it, I'd say they're out for a smoke.

"Hi," says the blonde.

"Hi," I say, pausing at the bottom of the steps. The brunette pulls out a pack of Merit cigarettes and lights one. She passes a cigarette to the blonde and then holds her pack out to me.

"Thanks," I say, stepping onto the landing. "My name's Rebekah."

The brunette hands me a lighter and sucks on her cigarette.

"I'm Suri, that's Dev," says the blonde. "Are you from Williamsburg?"

"No," I say. "I live in Gowanus."

"You're *frum*?"

Frum. It's a Yiddish word and I don't know what it means.

I shake my head and shrug at the same time.

"You're Jewish?" asks the brunette. Her face is unnervingly angular. Cheekbones and chin and a tiny mouth no wider than her nose. Her eyes are jade green, rimmed in thick black liner and clumpy mascara. Half a dozen tiny silver hoops climb up her ear.

I nod. "I'm actually a reporter," I say slowly, lighting my cigarette.

The two girls look at me, and then each other.

"Really?" says Suri. Unlike Dev, Suri is dressed in the female Orthodox uniform: long skirt, tights, and flat shoes. Her sweater covers her collarbone, and her face is colored only by the cold. They are, apparently, in different stages of rebellion.

"Yeah," I say. "I write for the *Trib*."

"Wow!" says Suri.

"What do you write about?" asks Dev.

"All different stuff," I say. "But I'm actually doing a story about a woman who was murdered. I think she might have come here."

"She's writing about Rivka," says Suri softly.

"Rivka Mendelssohn," I say. "Did you know her?"

Both girls nod solemnly.

"Did you write the article that said she was pregnant?" asks Dev.

"I did, yeah. Did you know?"

Dev shakes her head.

"I don't think anyone did," says Suri. "The article said the gardener killed her. Is that true?"

"The police aren't sure, actually," I say. "I was hoping maybe I could learn a little more about her."

"She was definitely having sex with Baruch," says Dev.

"Dev!" says Suri. She says something in Yiddish to her friend.

"I'm just saying, if she really was pregnant, it could have been his."

"Or it could have been her husband's," says Suri.

"Do you guys know Baruch?" I ask. "I'd love to talk to him if I can."

"He's been staying here," says Dev. "But I haven't seen him in a couple days."

"Me neither," says Suri. "I can't believe she's really dead."

"When was the last time you saw her?" I ask.

Suri thinks a moment. "The week before last. It was right before the big storm and she was rushing to get home before it got really bad. She'd come over to make some food so there'd be something in the house if the city shut down. She was always doing stuff like that. She never stayed here overnight, but she wanted to make it nice for whoever did."

"Who usually stays here?" I ask.

"Well, Moses," says Suri, "he's sort of the landlord. He's Menachem's grandson. Menachem owns the house, but he's not here. Then it's sort of ever-changing. How long have you been here, Dev?"

"About a month. Since I got back from Montreal. Baruch's been here, too, for a few weeks."

Dev finishes her cigarette and drops the butt into the pint glass. "It's fucking freezing. Let's go in."

"Do you mind if I ask you a few more questions?" I say. "I won't be too long, but I'd really like to write something about what she was like and I haven't gotten very much from her family."

Suri rolls her eyes. "That's not surprising."

"I don't have to use your names, if you don't want."

"You can use my name," says Dev. "Suri might get in trouble at school."

"I don't care," says Suri. "I've missed so many days, they'll probably kick me out for that first. And Rivka is dead. She was *murdered*. Somebody has to say something. Somebody has to help."

Dev opens the front door. "Come in," she says.

I hold my breath as I cross into the house, imagining for a moment that once I enter, the floor will collapse and I'll fall through time back to 1988, crashing atop my parents holding hands as they scurry toward a bedroom. *I am where Aviva was.* But the ground beneath me is steady, and though I'm prepared for the house to lay some heavy emotional burden on my back, I don't feel much of anything except warmer once Suri shuts the door behind us. The foyer and hallway are cramped. Faded floral wallpaper curls away where the first-floor ceiling meets the staircase. I smell mold. We squeeze past the stairs to the back of the house, which is an open room that is one-third kitchen, and two-thirds living-dining room. The TV is tuned to CNN, but the only person in the room, a fat man bent over an old PC at the table, isn't watching.

"Moses will be back soon," says the man, his back to us.

Both girls ignore him. Dev opens a cupboard above the sink and grabs a half-empty bag of Doritos. Suri takes a liter bottle of Coke from the fridge.

The man turns around. I've seen him before. He was with Aron Mendelssohn in the gas station convenience store by the scrap yard. He does not recognize me. One of his eyes is wild, or lazy. He is sweating.

Dev leads us upstairs. I put my hand on the old, white-painted banister. Every step squeaks in several places. I am here, I think again. Aviva could be brushing her hair around the corner. Napping behind the next door. Dev and Suri walk to a room at the end of the hall, where there's a bunk bed set and a futon. Everything seems damp. The carpet is a mess of crumbs and hair. A duffel bag spilling clothes sits on the floor. I assume this is the room Dev is occupying. It doesn't feel like much of a refuge, though I suppose it isn't creature comforts Suri and Dev and Baruch and Rivka and Aviva came here seeking.

The two girls plop on the futon, and I sit stiff on the edge of the bottom bunk. Suri leans down and digs through a backpack, her hands emerging with a tiny metal pipe and a plastic bag of pot.

"You won't write about this, right?"

I shake my head.

"So did Baruch actually file for divorce?" Suri asks as she packs her pipe.

Dev nods. "The week before last. I heard *all* about it. They were gonna do it, like, at the same time, but Rivka didn't. She was supposed to at least ask for a *get*. They had a big fight about it. He was crying. She made him cry. He stormed out and Heshy, of course, was all over her."

"Heshy?" I ask. Where have I heard that name before?

"The guy downstairs," says Dev. "He's obsessed with Rivka."

"No, he's not," says Suri. She turns to me. Their willingness to invite me immediately into their world is surprising, given what I thought I knew about this clan. But these girls seem almost hungry, or at least eager, to share themselves, and eager to learn. Perhaps, I think, they are more open and trusting with someone like me, who they imagine won't judge them the way their Orthodox peers will. Do they know that, technically, everything they say to me once they learn I am a reporter can be considered on the record? Everything they say I can keep in my head and type into a computer and render it public, on paper and online forever.

"Heshy is Rivka's brother-in-law," says Suri.

"Really?" I say. And then I remember: Sara Wyman said Miriam married someone named Heshy.

"He's weird," says Suri. "And slow. But she's nice to him."

"And he's obsessed with her."

"Stop it, Dev," says Suri. She lights her pipe and takes a pull, holds it in her lungs, then exhales. It seems a little odd that they smoke pot inside but go out to smoke cigarettes. She holds the pipe to me, offering. I smile and shake my head. She hands it to Dev, who lights it and smokes. They pass it between each other one more time; then Suri taps the ash onto the windowsill. I wait for one of them to say something, mulling the ethics—and efficacy—of stoned sources.

Dev leans forward. "Promise this won't be in the paper?" she asks me.

"Sure," I say.

"I'll be right back." She slides off the futon and runs out of the room.

"Dev is in love with Baruch," says Suri once Dev is gone. "Their families know each other from Montreal. They're related, somehow. I think he might be married to her cousin. But clearly, that's not working out." She lowers her voice. "Baruch is *fucked up* over what happened to Rivka. Does anybody know anything?"

I wish I had something I could tell her. "I think the police are still trying to figure it out. Has anyone been here to ask questions?"

"You mean the police? I don't think so. Dev didn't say anything."

"Would you mind telling me a little about her, for my article?"

"What do you want to know?"

"Well, what was she like? How did you meet?"

"Rivka's great. She was great." Suri puts her hand over her mouth, catching a sob. "We met at Sara Wyman's. She leads a group for people leaving the community. Rivka takes all this stuff really seriously. I mean, yes, I come here to smoke pot and like, get away, but I also come because I know I can't live like my mother and my sisters and cousins do. I just can't. I can't marry some awful boy I've barely met. I can't pretend I think it's really God's will that boys can study Torah and travel and all I'm good for is having babies."

I nod.

"Rivka lived like that a lot longer than I could," Suri continues. "I think she was really . . . conflicted. I mean, we all are. A lot of people fall off the deep end trying to get out. Once you get it in your head that everything you've been taught is bullshit, like, that the earth isn't just five thousand years old, or that you can eat shrimp or wear pants or touch a man while you're on your period and Hashem won't strike you down, it's a little bit of a shock. And if those rules don't count, maybe none of them do, you know? Maybe heroin and stealing and prostitution and shit are okay, too. I know a girl— well, I heard about a girl—who started living with some black guys in Crown Heights. She started having sex, for money. And they were like, her pimps."

"Wow."

"Yeah. There are a lot of stories like that. Like Dev—if you want a good story, you should write about her. They took her daughter away when she left. She can't even see her now. Seriously. Which is why this place is great. And Rivka knew that. She was all about making this a sacred space. That's what she called it. She wasn't here a lot. She had kids and a whole big family. But in the last few months I bet I saw her here a couple times a week. Eating lunch with Baruch, or on the computer. She spent a lot of time on the computer. I'm pretty sure they didn't have one at her house. Even though they were rich. We don't have one at my house either. There used to be some at the Borough Park library, but they broke and never got fixed."

It's a relief to talk to Suri. She knows I'm a reporter and she doesn't care. She sees me as a person first, a peer. At Chaya's apartment, I felt like an intruder, afraid her husband would come home and chase me out like Aron Mendelssohn had. But here, I am welcome. Suri might be hiding out here in Coney Island, but she is not afraid. She has made decisions about how she will live her life and she trusts herself enough to follow through on them. Even if they mean that her only sanctuary is a dingy row house with filthy carpet and strangers standing in for family. She and Dev seem to have a kind of friendship, but even I can tell that at the core, they are very different young women brought together by the accident of their birth and the curse of a restless spirit.

Aviva had to make the same decisions. So did Rivka Mendelssohn, but Rivka had so much more to lose. Suri is just a girl. Aviva was just a girl. But Rivka was a married woman, a mother. She knew that continuing to come to Coney Island, to see Baruch, to deceive her husband and expose her children to her rapidly unraveling faith was not behavior that came without consequences. Could she have imagined she'd pay with her life? Could anyone?

"Rivka told me once that she was jealous of me," says Suri. "I offered her some pot and she said no. She said she wanted to try it—Baruch smokes—but she was too frightened. She said coming here, uncovering her hair, and being with Baruch, that these were things she could explain to her children once they got older. But not drugs. She was very afraid of things like that. Things that she thought would make her look like a bad mother. Sara Wyman asked her to speak at a *chulent* over the summer, but she wouldn't do it. She said that if her husband found out she was speaking in public, in front of men, that he would not tolerate it."

I pull out my notebook.

"Is it okay if I take notes?" I ask.

Suri nods.

"What do you mean, he would not tolerate it?"

Suri shrugs. "He would take her children away. And her home. Which is pretty much all she had."

Suri pauses and looks out the window. "I can't believe she's dead. Maybe she was right to be afraid. Do you think her husband could have killed her?"

"I really don't know," I say.

"She didn't love him, but I don't think he ever beat her or raped her. . . ."

"Raped her?"

"Forced her to have sex, I mean. In a *frum* home, a wife is expected to be available for sex at any moment—unless she's on her period. It's really jarring because, when you're a girl, they tell you that you have to cover yourself from head to toe so you don't tempt or distract boys. You don't speak to males you are not related to, and you certainly don't touch them. Then you get married and it's like, virgin to farm animal overnight. And if you don't actually like your husband, let alone love him . . ." Suri shudders.

"Did Rivka ever love her husband?"

"I don't know," says Suri. "Maybe once. But she was definitely thinking about leaving him. She used to go online and look at apartments. She showed me pictures of one in Queens. Or maybe Long Island. She said it had three bedrooms."

"She and Baruch were always looking at places to live," says Dev, coming back into the room, carrying an envelope. "She showed me an apartment in Miami once."

"Miami!" says Suri.

"She was just pretending," says Dev.

"Pretending?" I ask.

"She was never going to leave," says Dev. "She was stringing Baruch along."

"I don't think that's true," says Suri. "Just because she's not the same as you doesn't mean she's not serious."

"She was too serious, that's what I'm saying. She could be a bitch."

"Dev!" Suri looks at me. "She doesn't mean that. Dev, why are you saying that?"

"She pretended to be nice to me," says Dev. "But she said shit about me behind my back to Baruch."

"She was *worried* about you!" Suri looks at me again. "Please don't write this down. Dev disappeared for, like, two weeks."

"I didn't disappear. I just didn't tell Rivka and Baruch where I was. Anyway, here." She hands me the envelope full of photographs. "Those are pictures of Rivka."

I stretch open the envelope and there she is. Alive. Laughing as she sits at a picnic table in the woods. Her eyes are squeezed closed and her head is thrown back. A baby is in her lap and it's done something she thinks is hysterical. Her smile is enormous. She has a long neck and rosy cheeks. Her hair is pulled up beneath a wrap like the one Miriam was wearing Friday night. In another, she is unsmiling in a frilly wedding dress; a lace collar brushes her chin. In another, she is a student; a teenager. Buttoned up and posed; a shy, crooked smile. She is wearing a black headband with a tiny black satin bow holding back her dark brown hair. It isn't until I see her here that I realize I had been picturing her with red hair. Like me and Aviva.

"She's pretty," I say. I want to burn this face into my brain and use it to replace the chalky, bruised Rivka lying naked in the funeral home basement. They are nothing—and everything—alike. Full eyebrows growing together, never plucked. Delicate hands. The *Trib* loves photos of victims. Especially attractive victims. If I can get Dev to give me these photos, I can get a story in the paper.

"Where'd you get these?" asks Suri, now standing over me.

"Heshy's drawer."

"You went in his drawer? It's not locked?"

"If it was locked, I couldn't get in it," says Dev.

Suri is not happy. "We have drawers, lockers sort of, in the mudroom downstairs," she tells me. "Just to put stuff you need, like a toothbrush, or money, or whatever. Do you go in mine?"

"You lock yours," says Dev. "Anyway, do you think that's normal? Having your sister-in-law's photos tucked in a little stash so you can look at them whenever you want?"

"How long have you been going in there?" ask Suri.

Dev shrugs. "Does it matter?"

Suri sits down next to me to look at the photos. "Maybe Heshy killed her," she says softly.

My hands feel clammy and hot. Heshy is downstairs. Is anyone else in the house?

"Does anyone else know about these?" I ask Dev.

She shrugs and goes into Suri's bag for her pipe and pot. As she's lighting another hit, my phone rings. It's Tony. I silence it.

"How long did you know Rivka?" I ask Dev.

"As long as she's been coming here, I guess. A year? Less? I don't know."

"Did you know she'd lost a child?" I ask. Both girls nod. "Do you know what happened?"

"She said it was asthma or something," says Suri. "She said Shoshanna—that was the little girl's name—had weak lungs. I thought it was kind of weird. Rivka's husband is rich. I *know* there's medicine for asthma. My little brother has it. Anyway, we only talked about it once. She kept saying it was preventable."

"Do you know what she meant by that?"

"Not really. I mean, I figured she meant that, like, she felt guilty. Maybe she'd missed some medication or something. But she said it really angry. That was weird, too, actually."

"Why was it weird?"

"It felt like she wasn't saying everything. It was like she blamed something, or someone."

"Did either of you ever meet her husband?"

Suri shakes her head.

"I did," says Dev. "About two weeks ago. He came here. He was fucking pissed."

"She didn't think he knew she'd been coming here," says Suri.

"We were in the kitchen. Fucking Moses let them in."

"Them?" I ask.

"Him and Heshy and Heshy's wife."

Heshy's wife. "Miriam?" I ask.

Dev shrugs. "She was Rivka's age, but she was uglier." That could be Miriam, I think.

"Heshy was with them?" asks Suri.

"Yeah. He's such a fucking putz. He was, like, pretending he'd never been here. The husband came in and *grabbed* Rivka. He shook her really hard. She dropped a plate and it broke on the floor but nobody even noticed. He was shouting and his face was so close, he was totally spitting on her. And she didn't say a word."

"What did he say?" I ask.

"He said what you'd expect. He said she had betrayed her community and her family and Hashem and everything. He said he'd divorce her and shun her and she'd never see her children again. I thought she'd, like, yell back. Tell him off, or at least try to *explain*, but she didn't. She just sort of zoned out. It was like someone turned her off. Baruch came running from upstairs and I thought they'd, like, announce their love, but she basically ignored him. I don't think he knew what to do. And then Heshy's wife fainted."

Suri looks skeptical.

"I'm serious. She took one look at Baruch and keeled over. It was super dramatic. Aron and Heshy carried her out to the car. Rivka refused to go with them, but afterward she was, like, catatonic. Baruch was pacing and muttering about the laws and what countries would give them asylum with their kids."

"Asylum?" asks Suri.

"He was saying they were being oppressed because of their religion, or lack of religion, and that the judicial system was corrupt— which it is—and that Rivka should be able to keep her children because she'd always been their primary caregiver. I asked him what happened with the sister-in-law, and he said she must have recognized him from the grocery store. He said once when he and Rivka were shopping—that's how they used to meet at first, before they started fucking, at the grocery store. He'd, like, shop with her and they'd talk. They ran into her and Rivka pretended she didn't know him, but Baruch said the lady looked suspicious."

"So she *fainted*?" asks Suri. "That's weird. You're sure that's why?"

"Who fucking knows? The whole thing was weird."

"Do you remember the woman's name?" I ask. "Was it Miriam?"

"Maybe," says Dev. "You can ask Heshy."

My phone rings. It's Tony again. I decline the call just as we all hear the front door slam and someone come in.

"Suri, before I forget, can I get your last name? And your age?"

"Goldblatt," she says. "I'm seventeen."

"You can use mine, too, if you want," says Dev. "Devorah Kletzky. I'm twenty-two."

Whoever is coming up the stairs shakes the house. A man appears at the bedroom door. He is breathing heavily, and he is drunk. Pickled. The alcohol has a sweet-and-sour smell as it seeps as sweat out of his pores. He looks at Dev and Suri and then he looks at me. I've got my notebook out but he doesn't seem to notice. Just another Jew girl in the house at Coney Island.

"I need to take a nap," he says.

"You stink, Baruch," says Dev.

Baruch does stink, but he is nonetheless incredibly attractive. He has olive skin and dark wavy hair. He's months past a haircut and thick curls fall in front of his eyes. He is lean, but seems powerful. The veins in his hands are thick with blood. I don't really know anything about how Rivka Mendelssohn felt about her husband, but looking at the man she was considering leaving him for, I can't help but wonder if sheer chemistry wasn't part of it. Baruch is fucking hot.

"Moses wants to talk to you," he says. I'm not sure which of them he's talking to.

"Tell Moses he can come get me if he wants to talk to me," says Dev.

"He wants to talk to you, too," says Baruch, looking at Suri. "He doesn't think we're taking it well."

"What?" says Suri.

"He doesn't think we're taking it well," he says, louder.

"Clearly *you're* not taking it well," says Dev.

"How could I take it well!"

"He seriously wants to talk to us?" asks Suri. Her eyes are darting between Dev and Baruch.

"Fine," says Dev. "We want to talk to him, too. We've got something to show him."

"Dev . . . ," says Suri.

"Look!" Dev says, grabbing the photographs from me and shoving them at Baruch. He doesn't catch them all and several fall to the floor. He fumbles for a moment with the photographs, then, recognizing their subject, straightens up. His breathing slows.

"This is Baruch," says Dev, introducing him to me.

"Where did you get these?" asks Baruch, his voice quiet now.

"Heshy's drawer," says Dev.

Baruch looks at Dev. His eyes are liquid with drink. Bloodshot and cloudy.

"Yank material starring your girlfriend," she says, enjoying her crude explanation.

Baruch frowns. He's trying to put the pieces together with a spinning mind.

"I think Moses should know about these," says Dev. "I mean, if he's going to make us talk about our feelings . . ."

"Moses knows about this?" says Baruch.

"No," says Suri, standing up. She's a smart girl. This conversation is about to get ugly. "Moses doesn't. . . ."

"Why don't you just ask Heshy? He's right downstairs," says Dev.

This gets Baruch's attention. "He's here?"

Dev shrugs. "You didn't see him? He's been here all day."

Baruch turns and runs down the hall. Suri and Dev follow. I bend down and grab one of the photos he dropped, sliding it under my coat as I go after them.

Downstairs, Baruch is shouting in Yiddish, and Dev and Suri are standing in the doorway between the hallway and the kitchen. A tall man whom I take to be Moses is standing inches from Baruch, trying to keep him away from Heshy, who is cowering on the sofa. Next to him sits Saul.

He doesn't see me at first; like everyone else in the room, he is focused on Baruch. But I see him, in a moment unguarded, and something seems wrong. Why didn't he tell me he was coming here?

"Who's that?" says Dev, pointing at Saul.

Saul looks at Dev and sees me standing behind her. He stands up, leaving Heshy to sink farther into the sofa.

Baruch shakes the pictures at Heshy. "What did you do to her!" he shouts.

"Baruch," says Saul, stepping toward him. "Heshy is . . ."

Baruch runs at Saul, his hands up like he wants to fight. But Saul, twice his age and several inches shorter, is ready. In a swift, easy motion he grabs Baruch's left wrist and twists his arm down and back, hard. Baruch screams in pain, falling to his knees.

"You're hurting him!" shouts Dev. "Let go!"

Saul does not let go. Dev runs at Saul, and he pushes her aside. She stumbles back, then falls on her ass with a thud.

"Saul . . ." I say, stepping forward.

"Rebekah, I have this under control," he says.

"I'm calling the cops," says Suri.

"I am the cops," says Saul, glaring at her.

Suri looks at me. I don't know what to say. Saul looks like a different person. The dumpy, tired cop I met on Friday is gone. In his place is a man confident with his physical strength. Baruch is no longer fighting and Saul lets him go, but Baruch stays on the floor, slumping to the side. He brings his hands to his face and begins to weep.

"Everybody needs to calm down," Saul says. He looks down at Baruch. "Do you understand?"

Baruch grunts an affirmative. Dev crawls to sit beside him. Heshy is still half-sitting half-lying down on the sofa, and Suri and Moses are standing, looking at Saul.

"I know you're all very upset about Rivka," says Saul. "I'm here to ask some questions. That's all."

My phone rings again. It's Tony again. I silence it and see I've missed a text from him:

saul katz is not a cop

CHAPTER TWELVE

"He's on indefinite suspension from the NYPD," says Tony. I'm halfway to the F train station with the phone to my ear.

"Oh," I say, stopping to catch my breath beneath some scaffolding across the street from a housing project. "So he *is* a cop."

"No! Rebekah. If he's pretending to be on the job when he isn't, you need to stay away from him. He's off the rails."

I bolted from the house the moment I got Tony's text, hoping, as I ran down the steps and around the corner that maybe everyone in that living room would just forget I'd ever been there. I've got three people on the record now. I've got a photograph of Rivka Mendelssohn. I have a story even without Saul. What I don't have is any fucking answers.

"I assume Darin told you this," I say. Obviously, the information that Saul—whom I've been quoting as a source inside the NYPD—has been suspended from the force is important, but I'm still unhappy with Tony for getting Darin involved in my life. I feel like a child and I'm going to kick. "I'm glad he's so concerned with my welfare."

"I'm the one that's concerned for your welfare, okay?" says Tony. "This guy's been lying to you, Rebekah. He might be a bad guy."

"What do you mean, a bad guy?"

"I don't know," he says. "But Darin says they want you to come in."

"Come in?"

"To the station," says Tony. "They want to ask you some questions."

"Questions about what?"

"About Saul. I think they think he might have been involved in the murder. Apparently, he has a history of violence."

I need to sit down somewhere and think. Other than lying about his employment status, everything Saul has told me so far has been true. No one from the police department has been to the Coney Island house to ask Rivka's friends—or lover—any questions. No one has talked to her sister-in-law or her brother-in-law or her husband or her son. No one but Malka and Saul and me and, presumably, her killer, has seen her injuries up close. I'd like to hear Darin explain how all that adds up to a proper homicide investigation.

"Where's Darin's precinct?" I say. "I'll take the train."

"I can pick you up," he says. I almost feel sorry for him.

"I'll call you after," I say, and hang up. I know I'm being a bitch, but I don't want his worry and guilt clouding my judgment any more than the situation with Saul and my now possibly in-jeopardy job already are.

I turn around and start walking back toward the house. At the end of the block, I see Saul.

"Rebekah," he says, jogging toward me. "Are you all right?"

I step back. "Why have you been lying to me, Saul?"

"Lying?" His yarmulke is askew, his coat unbuttoned.

"You're not a cop anymore."

Saul closes his eyes for a moment. "Rebekah . . ."

"What are you doing here that you don't want me to know about?"

"Rebekah, I understand you're upset," he says. "I hope you know I'm only trying to work . . ."

"What were you talking to Heshy about?"

Saul takes a breath. "Heshy is a troubled man."

For some reason this makes me laugh. My teeth are chattering but I'm not cold anymore. I feel like I'm on speed. "Every single person in there is troubled, Saul. That doesn't mean shit. What did he say? Did he tell you Aron and Miriam were here? Did he tell you Aron threatened Rivka?"

"Moses asked me to come to the house to speak with Heshy," says Saul slowly. "He felt perhaps Heshy knew something about what had happened to Rivka. I didn't call you, because I knew he wouldn't talk to a woman."

"Do you have any idea what kind of situation you've put me in? I'm going to *lose my job* when they find out my source is a fucking suspended . . ."

"Rebekah . . ."

"And I assume the NYPD has no idea you're currently acting as a homicide detective?"

"I don't think so," says Saul. There is no apology in his voice. He doesn't think he's done anything wrong.

"What did you do to get suspended?" I ask.

Saul hesitates.

"Tell me or I'm going to go back in there and tell them all you're a fucking fraud and that they should report you to the police."

Saul lowers his voice. "I was suspended because I assaulted a man." He pauses, then continues. "I told you that Rivka Mendelssohn stood up for my son when he was fired from his teaching position? He was fired, in part, because of what this man had done."

"In part?"

"Can we please go back inside?" asks Saul. "I can explain."

"I'm supposed to go to talk to the cops," I say. "They think you're . . . involved."

Saul nods sadly. "Do you think I'm involved?"

"No," I say, and it's the truth. I've been thinking about it since getting Tony's text. If Saul had been involved in killing Rivka Mendelssohn, there is no way he would have taken me to see her body. It was a desperate, dangerous move on his part, the only way he could think of to force me to care enough to keep her death in the paper. It hadn't been difficult to reel me in: You look just like your mother, he had said. That was all it took. I've spent twenty years battling the ghost of Aviva Kagan. Fighting to extinguish any emotion involving her. Tamping down anger and longing. Talking myself out of curiosity. My brain and stomach and heart engaged in a fucking war of attrition against any trace of her. And it hasn't worked at all. I've never been without her for a moment—and I've never really wanted to be. The moment Saul said her name, I knew there was nothing on earth I wanted more than to see her; for her to see me. That he lied about his position and that I didn't think to question it infuriates me. But that shit is about me, not Saul. Saul is not the bad guy here.

"Good," he says. "Then let me tell you what happened before they do. At least then you'll have both sides."

I follow Saul back down the block and into the house. Saul opens a door just off the tiny foyer and we enter a den slash storage closet. Navy blue sheets function as curtains, and two futons are the only furniture. There are boxes and bicycles. An old acoustic guitar leans against one wall, a folded-up crib leans against another.

"Would you like to sit?" asks Saul.

"I think I'll stand."

Saul takes a deep breath. "My son, Binyamin, was abused as a child. Sexually." He looks me in the eyes as he speaks. "Do you understand?" I nod. "After his mother and I separated, she and Binyamin moved back in with her mother and father in Crown Heights. The abuse took place at his yeshiva. I knew something was wrong with him. He was angry and defiant and unhappy, but I blamed the divorce. He did not have a father."

"My dad said you weren't allowed to see him," I say.

"I could have handled the situation better," he says. "The man who abused my son, and many other boys, was a rebbe. It went on for years—decades—until someone finally spoke to law enforcement. The man was indicted, eventually, but the case fell apart last year. The DA was unable to secure enough witnesses." Saul pauses. "I argued with one of the men who was involved in silencing the victims, and it got physical."

"When was this?"

"December. It was a mistake. I allowed myself to be provoked."

"Who was this man?"

"His name is Leiby Bronner. He was the director of Crown Heights Shomrim."

"Shomrim, really?"

"If you have not physically witnessed the act of abuse, you are not permitted to go to secular authorities with your suspicions. Most families would go to their rebbe. But if the rebbe is the one you suspect . . ." Saul pauses. "Parents called Shomrim. But they were directed to keep their stories to themselves. And the man continued to abuse."

"Is this why your son was fired from his job?" I ask.

"Not exactly," says Saul, looking away.

There is a soft knock at the door and then Suri peeks inside.

"I'm sorry to interrupt," she says.

"Come in," says Saul. I decide to let the last non-answer be; he's explained enough for now.

"Baruch went upstairs to lay down and Dev went with him," says Suri. She has her backpack on her shoulder like she is getting ready to leave. "Moses took Heshy home."

"I'm sorry for the commotion," says Saul.

"Are you going to find out who killed Rivka?" she asks.

I look at Saul. "That's what we're trying to do," he says.

"It's hard to imagine anyone wanting to hurt her," says Suri. "There's always a lot of drama around here. Everybody is so unhappy and afraid all the time, you know? Rivka was unhappy, too, I guess, but she never seemed that way. She seemed like she'd found some kind of peace, somehow."

Suri takes off her backpack and opens it. I pull out my note-book; that was a great quote: *She seemed like she'd found some kind of peace.*

"She was helping me study for my GED. She was really smart, you know. She read a lot. She would give me books she thought I'd like," says Suri, showing us a paperback book called *The God Delusion*.

"Baruch is big into atheism, so he read a lot about that. Rivka still believed in Hashem, but she gave me this one book because he talks about how people who grew up with religious parents and in a religious community like ours don't even know they *can* think dif-ferently. And it's totally true. I didn't know I had a choice. Rivka was big on choice. She used to agonize over how her husband was raising their children. She wanted them to know that the world was bigger than Brooklyn. And that it wasn't all scary."

"Do you know if there was anyone she was afraid of?" Saul asks.

Suri shakes her head. "Rivka wasn't afraid of much. Except losing her kids. She was really afraid of that. If it turned out she was pregnant with Baruch's baby, that would have been really bad. She would have lost custody for sure."

"Do you think Baruch could have killed her?" asks Saul.

Suri looks at the ground. "I don't think so. They were so in love. It was really cute. Rivka said being in love had changed her. She said she couldn't help but think Hashem wanted her to be with Baruch."

"But Dev said he filed for divorce and she didn't," I say.

Suri shrugs. "I guess. But honestly, Dev could be making that up. She lies a lot."

Saul takes a business card out of his pocket and gives it to Suri. "I appreciate your honesty," he says. "Call me if you think of anything. Or if you have any more questions."

Suri says she will, and then leaves. I turn to Saul. "I assume that's an NYPD card."

"Yes, but it has my cell phone number on it," says Saul, almost smiling. "Now, do you mind my asking how you learned about my suspension?"

"This guy I've been seeing, he's friends with a detective. I told the guy about you because I thought I could trust him. He told his friend. And now they want to talk to me."

"They?"

"The detective, I guess. His bosses? I don't think his precinct is responsible for the case, but presumably he contacted whoever is."

"Well," he says, "I'm sure they'll be calling me, too. I have my car here. Why don't we turn ourselves in together?"

We pull up in front of the precinct just before six. The station is inside a neat brick building, probably built in the 1960s. The area it serves encompasses several neighborhoods, including my own, where Rivka Mendelssohn was found—nearly carried away forever on the Gowanus canal. Also in this precinct are several upscale residential and commercial neighborhoods. Single-family brownstones with tasteful, low, wrought-iron fences around their yards. A movie-star couple lives two blocks away. I sat outside their house for two nights just before Christmas for a story about celebrities on Broadway, but I never saw either of them. There are several bakeries and Thai restaurants, an artisanal ice cream shop, that sort of thing.

And the scrap yard at the very end. I wonder if they've ever found a body on the canal before this.

Saul and I approach the desk sergeant.

"My name is Rebekah Roberts," I say. "I'm here to see—"

Before I can finish, the officer, a petite woman with elaborately braided hair, picks up the phone and dials an extension: "She's here."

A moment later, Darin comes through a side door, flanked by four other men in ill-fitting suits with badges clipped to their waists. They see me, and then Saul.

"Katz," says the tallest of the group. "Come with me."

Saul obliges. The tall man holds open the side door, and two others follow Saul through it.

"You're okay," says Darin. It is a statement, not a question. His face is stiff.

"I'm fine," I say.

"We need to ask you some questions," he says. Then: "Please."

I nod and am ushered out of the reception area, through a waist-high door, and past a row of lockers. Uniformed officers, with their guns on their hips, seem to be lurking around every corner, staring. Everyone is tense. We pass a series of doors with tiny windows—interrogation rooms—and I see Saul and the three men in one. Is that where I'm going? My lower intestines ignite, sending what feels like blue fire through my bloodstream. It's a funny condition, acute anxiety. It can murmur low in your stomach for days, weeks even, with no apparent cause. Am I worried about school? My boyfriend? Paying rent? I used to lie in bed and try to identify the source, but the feeling defied logic or categorization. My stepmom, also a worrier, maintains that anxiety is our body's way of keeping us from danger. It's telling you something, she'd say. Which sounds logical, but breaks down when the feeling buzzes on and off constantly and seems to have little to do with what's actually happening. I roll my mind back over the last three days. I don't think I've done anything illegal, but I am alone in here. If I am not brave, they will devour me.

Darin opens a door and motions for me to enter a small breakroom kitchen.

"Please sit down," he says, gesturing to a folding table and chairs set. The room smells like burnt popcorn and hand soap.

One of the men stays outside and the other enters with Darin, who shuts the door behind him and then sits down next to me.

"This is Captain Weber," says Darin. "This is his station house. He is working the Mendelssohn case."

I nod.

"I'd like you to tell me and Detective Spinelli exactly how you met Saul Katz," says the captain.

"I met him Friday, the day they found Rivka Mendelssohn. I had been assigned to go to the Mendelssohn house to get quotes and he was there."

"Had you ever met him before?" The captain is leaning toward me. I can see the tiny black hairs growing out of his nose. He has a deeply wrinkled face.

"No. Why would you ask that?"

"I'll ask the questions for now, all right, young lady?"

Oh boy.

"Had you ever met him before?"

"No," I say. "I said that."

The captain looks at Darin.

"You're saying you had no connection to Saul Katz before you just 'ran into him' at a murder victim's house on Friday?"

Now I look at Darin. "What the fuck?" I say. "You're the ones with a rogue cop. I'm a reporter. I was doing my job."

"I'm running a murder investigation, ma'am." Ha. Young lady to ma'am in less than a minute.

"Are you?"

"Is that what Saul Katz told you? That we're not running an investigation? Did you ask anyone at my department anything about this case at all? Because none of my people have heard of you."

"I've spoken to DCPI . . ."

"Have you? Who, exactly, have you spoken to?"

I didn't get the name of the tall man at the scene. Then, he was nothing more to me than DCPI.

"I'm sorry," I say as earnestly as I can muster. "I'm not sure what Darin told you, but I met Saul Katz on Friday night. He said he had been called in as a liaison to the Orthodox community on this case. He told me he usually worked in property crimes. Is that true?"

"Yes," says the captain.

"But he's not a liaison?"

"He's not anything anymore," says the captain. "Except a suspect."

"Why is he a suspect?"

The captain sighs. He is sick of me. "He is a suspect because he is attempting to manipulate the investigation. He is a suspect because he knew the victim. And because if not for the miracle of modern medicine, Saul Katz would be in prison for murder."

On cue, Darin hands the captain a folder. "Would you like to

see what Saul Katz did to a sixty-year-old man?" He doesn't wait
for me to answer, and of course, I don't get up. He opens the file
and with his fingertips spreads out four 8 × 10 glossy close-up photos
of a man in a hospital bed. The man's face is almost unrecognizable
as a face. Both eyes are purple and swollen shut. There are metal rods
that look like scaffolding attached to either side of his head, which
is shaved; a fresh red surgery scar runs like train tracks up his skull.

"He'll never walk again," says the captain. "Severe brain damage. Saul beat him into unconsciousness. With his bare hands."

I'm not sure what to say. Protesting that the man in the pictures may have intimidated witnesses in a felony case seems impru-
dent.

"Tell me the truth about your relationship with Saul Katz,"
says the captain.

"My relationship?" And then I realize: he's talking about my
mother.

"Saul Katz knew my mother before I was born," I say. "She
grew up in Borough Park. Her family was—is—Hasidic. I'm not
sure how they knew each other, but they did. But then my mother
met my father, and they moved to Florida, where I was born. So I
never met him."

"I'll check all this out," says the captain. "I'd like to talk to
your mother."

"Can't help you with that."

"You're not in touch?"

"We are not in touch."

"Is she deceased?"

"Could be. I have no idea. She left us when I was six months
old. I haven't heard from her since."

The captain pauses a moment. "I see," he says. "I assume Saul Katz will tell me the same story."

"It's the truth," I say.

"Something Katz seems to have trouble with," says Darin.

The captain gets up.

"Before you go," I say, "could you tell me where you are in the investigation into the Mendelssohn murder?"

The captain raises a bushy salt-and-pepper eyebrow.

"Have you interviewed her husband? Or her boyfriend?"

"Her . . . ?" The captain catches himself before finishing his sentence and positively revealing that he had no idea the woman whose death he is supposedly investigating had been having an affair. I don't even try to hide my smile.

"Maybe you should ask Saul Katz," I say.

I peek at Darin, who is looking down, shaking his head.

"No comment, then?" I say, leaning down to my bag and taking out my notebook and pen.

The captain opens his mouth then closes it. Then opens it again. "You know I can't comment on an ongoing investigation."

I scribble *no comment—ongoing invest* into my notebook.

"And just so I'm clear, you *haven't* interviewed the victim's lover or husband?"

The captain is losing patience. "Like I said, I cannot comment on an ongoing investigation." He gathers the photographs of the man Saul assaulted and tucks them under his arm. "You are free to go for now. But we may have questions for you later."

"I can't wait," I say, feeling mildly triumphant.

"Your friend Saul Katz is in a lot of trouble, miss." This guy really loves his diminutives. "From where I'm sitting, he has at the very least interfered with a police investigation. And if I discover you and he so much as stood in line for coffee together before last Friday, you may have, too. We take obstruction seriously, and I have no problem indicting a reporter. Your paper doesn't hold nearly the weight it thinks it does. And you can feel free to tell your bosses I said so."

"Will do," I say.

The captain leaves, and for a moment, Darin and I sit in silence.

"Don't blame Tony," he says finally. "I didn't really give him a choice."

"You're worried about your friend," I say. "That's a nice quality."

"Are you being sarcastic?" he asks, sounding exhausted. "I can't tell. I thought you'd take it better from him than me."

"Take it?"

Darin exhales and shakes his head. "Look, I don't feel bad about this. What Tony told me about a detective taking you to the funeral home was a red fucking flag. No two ways about it. And it took one phone call to confirm he was who he was."

A phone call I never made.

"Can I ask you a question, off the record?" I say.

"You can ask," he says.

"Do you really think Saul Katz murdered Rivka Mendelssohn?"

"I'm not going to answer that," he says, standing up.

"I don't remember reading anything in the newspaper about an NYPD detective who nearly killed a man," I say. "I'm guessing that somebody convinced that man's family not to press charges. Most people don't just get suspended from their jobs when they commit what looks to me like aggravated assault." I'm out on a limb here, but if I'm not in legal trouble—which I can see now that I am not—then I have a real story. About a police cover-up and a compromised murder investigation. And maybe another story about Shomrim's relationship with the NYPD. And maybe another about witness intimidation in the community.

But Darin doesn't bite.

"Here's my card," he says instead. "We are investigating this murder now, Rebekah. That I can assure you."

"Now?" I say. "So you weren't before."

Darin doesn't respond. He holds open the swinging door for me to leave, then follows me to the exit and opens the door to the cold.

I'm not outside a minute when my phone rings. It is UNKNOWN

"It's Rebekah," I say.

"Rebekah! What the fuck is going on?"

It's Larry.

"Where are you?" he asks.

"I'm in Brooklyn."

"You need to get to Midtown. They want us both in the office."

"Why?"

"Because somebody high up in the department told Albert Morgan that he had a reporter trying to pass off the ramblings of a suspended cop as inside information. You can think of how to explain it on the subway."

CHAPTER THIRTEEN

The newsroom is quieter now at nearly eight thirty at night than it is in the middle of the day. The desks in the gossip and Sunday sections are empty. All but one of the five TVs above the spiral of cubicles that makes up the "city desk" are tuned to sports. Mike sees me as soon as I walk through the heavy glass doors from the elevator bay. He is very unhappy.

"We need to talk," he says quite a bit louder than he needs to. He is red-faced and his breathing is shallow. "Albert Morgan has a reservation at Eleven Madison Park with his family tonight, but he is coming here before to personally ask you what the fuck."

Mike always struck me as the gentle giant type. Big and soft and harmless. He's never even raised his voice at me, unlike Lars, who barks and insults with glee. But clearly, he is shaken by Morgan's summons. He hired me and he runs the day shift stringers, so he's probably concerned Morgan will blame him for not supervising me properly.

"Sorry," I say, just as Larry Dunn walks in.

Larry is in his fifties and his thin blond hair is turning white. He is wearing black orthopedic shoes and a yellow Livestrong bracelet around one wrist. Marisa told me a couple months ago that one of the editors had cancer. Maybe it's Larry.

"We're supposed to wait in his office," says Mike.

"You first, boss," says Larry.

Mike ushers us past sports and art to a part of the twelfth floor where I've never been. Albert Morgan's office is smaller than I'd imagined the managing editor would get. There are two windows that face the building next door, but the rest is unremarkable. Standard, sturdy dark wood executive desk; leather wingback with all the ergonomic details you pay an extra grand for. Albert Morgan is the first black managing editor of the *New York Tribune*. He won a Pulitzer in the early 1990s—the *Trib*'s first and only—for a series of reports and columns about race relations and the Clarence Thomas nomination hearings. There is a plaque on the wall commemorating the award, next to a photograph of him holding a giant fish beneath a banner reading, MARTHA'S VINEYARD STRIPED BASS AND BLUE FISH DERBY, 2001. On the wall behind his desk is an antique map of China.

There are only two chairs in the room, other than Morgan's behind the desk. Mike and Larry and I all stand, waiting.

Albert Morgan enters the room and immediately orders that we "sit down."

Mike sits. Larry hesitates, gesturing to me. I appreciate the courtesy but nod for him to sit. I need to stay standing; I think it will make me seem more in control.

"Sir," I say, before he's even got his coat off, "let me tell you what happened."

"Wonderful! Someone who gets to the point. Go."

I take a deep breath; I've been practicing a succinct version of the last three days on the train. The quicker I get it out, the quicker I know if I still have a job. And, if I'm lucky, the quicker the brick in my stomach begins to dissolve.

"Mike sent me to a crime scene on Friday. A dead body in a scrap metal yard in Brooklyn. I talked to DCPI and workers and even to the victim's son—though I didn't know he was her son at the time. Later that night, Cathy had me go to the victim's house in Borough Park. There were several police cars out front, including the Shomrim."

Albert has thrown his coat over the back of his enormous leather chair. He is standing with his arms crossed over his chest, his face expressionless. I wait for him to ask me what the Shomrim is, but he does not. "Keep going," he says.

"One of the cars had uniformed officers in it, one had plain-clothes. They were detectives. I asked them about the case but they wouldn't talk to me."

Larry sits down. We make eye contact and he nods, like, you're doing okay. Mike is biting at his cuticles and looking at the carpet. I continue.

"Then another detective arrived. He had a badge. At least it looked like a badge. And he went directly to the uniformed officers and spoke with them. And they spoke with him. So I assumed he was a detective. I went to question him and . . . he recognized me."

"Excuse me?" Morgan's tone is teetering on exasperation.

"He knew my mother. I look like her."

"Get to the part where you explain quickly, please."

"He said he was in property crimes but that because he was Orthodox and had grown up in the community he was sometimes called in as a liaison. The problem is that he wasn't actually working the case at all, because he'd been suspended from the force in December for . . . assaulting a man."

Mike shakes his head. "Jesus."

"But everything he told me has been right on," I say. "Are the police actually denying she was pregnant?"

"No," says Larry. "In fact, I've been told off the record that it's true."

"Off the record?" asks Morgan.

"Brooklyn South commander gave it to me an hour ago."

Morgan turns to me. "What else did this . . . What's his name?"

"Saul Katz."

"What else did Saul Katz tell you?"

"He told me he didn't think the police were going to do a real investigation."

"What made him think this?"

"He said the community was obsessed with keeping unpleasant things under wraps. He said there was a kind of don't-ask-don't-tell thing going on between them and the police. He said Aron Mendelssohn, the dead woman's husband, was a major benefactor of Shomrim and that he would make sure they pinned this on someone outside the community, or just let people forget about it."

"Didn't they bring in a gardener?" Morgan asks.

"They questioned a gardener and released him," I say.

"No arrests?"

"No," I say. "And at the scene the M.E.'s office let the Jewish van take the body straight to the funeral home."

"Larry, there was no autopsy?"

Larry shakes his head. "The funeral home might make a report."

"Has anyone seen a report?" asks Morgan.

"I've seen the body," I say.

Everyone looks at me.

"You mean at the crime scene," says Mike.

"No," I say, "I got into the funeral home on Saturday. I saw her after they'd . . . prepared her."

"Let me guess," says Larry, "Saul Katz got you in."

I nod again. Larry looks impressed. Mike looks annoyed. Morgan is still wearing a poker face.

"She was savagely beaten," I say, trying to impart the graveness of her injuries with my inflection. "Someone hit her in the face and the head and the neck repeatedly with something. They shaved her head and stripped her and dumped her in the scrap pile. She'd be on her way to China if not for dumb luck."

"Okay," says Morgan. "Ms . . . ?"

"Roberts. Rebekah Roberts."

"Ms. Roberts. You've obviously done some good work on this. You've also made some pretty major fucking mistakes. Are you a New Yorker?"

"No," I say. "I'm from Florida."

"Well, if you were a New Yorker, you might know that the Orthodox community does, in fact, have some clout with the department and the city. That's not a story."

"Exactly," says Mike.

"But," he says, leaning forward on his desk, "a rogue NYPD detective and the slow-footing of the investigation into the brutal murder of a pregnant woman because the department doesn't want to upset a population of voters *is*."

"I agree," says Larry. "And the investigation isn't following normal avenues. It's been three days and they haven't questioned the husband. He owns the yard where she was dumped. He's at least worth questioning to figure out who has access."

"They also don't know about the victim's boyfriend," I say. "And we do."

Morgan raises his eyebrows; I've impressed him.

"What about this Saul Katz character?" asks Morgan. "Is he a suspect?"

Larry's phone rings. He answers quietly.

"They're sort of acting like he might be, but I think they're just pissed he's talking to the press."

Morgan considers this.

I am not dressed to meet the boss. My dirty hair is twisted up in a plastic clip and I'm a month overdue for a lip and eyebrow wax. Albert Morgan is in a hand-cut navy suit. Cuff links on Monday night. I must look like a child: no makeup, chipped purple nail polish, old red Doc Martens on my feet.

"Ms. Roberts," he says. "What are you hoping will happen after we leave this meeting?"

"Well," I say, "I'm hoping you don't fire me."

"Go on."

"I know I've fucked up the sourcing, but I've got a ton of information on Rivka Mendelssohn. She had a daughter who died about a year ago. And she was considering a divorce. She had looked at apartments with her boyfriend. And her husband had threatened her recently."

"This is on the record?"

"Yes."

"From Saul Katz?" asks Mike. Why is he being such a dick?

"No," I say. "From a social worker who knew her. And two girls—young women—who were friends with her. They're all part of this group of ultra-Orthodox who are, like, questioning. On the margins. I have a picture, too."

I take the snapshot out of my pocket. I hadn't even looked at which one I'd gotten. It's the one of her in the wedding dress. I hand it to Morgan.

He looks at the photo and nods.

"Write that up for tomorrow," says Morgan, handing the photo to Mike. "Friends talk about her, say she was rebelling, the boy-friend, the dead child, whatever you have. But we can only milk the victim for a day. There are about five hundred murders in the city every year. This is a corruption story. We need to connect the hus-band to the Jewish patrol. I have a very angry commissioner on my ass, but from what I can tell, it's his people he should be angry at, not mine. You let a source use you. Don't do it again."

"I won't," I say.

"Background your sources. Ask the library."

"I will," I say.

Larry gets off his call. "That was my source in Brooklyn hom-icide. They just arrested Saul Katz."

"For what?" I ask.

"Impersonating a police officer and obstruction," says Larry. "They say they're looking at him for the murder."

"On the record?" says Morgan.

Larry nods. "They called him a 'person of interest.'"

Morgan rubs his hand over his mouth. "Okay," he says. "We need two stories. Larry, you write up the arrest. I don't want Rebekah near that. She's compromised. I don't think you need to get too detailed about his relationship with the paper. Maybe just that Katz had been speaking to a *Trib* reporter about the case. Rebekah, we'll have to name you."

I don't bother arguing. Hopefully, Larry will gloss over the fact that I failed to realize Saul was no longer an active member of the force when I used him as an NYPD source. After all, it makes the paper look bad, too.

Morgan turns to me. "You write up the story about the boyfriend and the divorce. Mike, make sure photo gets the image. Rebekah is on the family and the Shomrim tomorrow. Confirm a financial connection. Have the NYPD comment on their relationship with the group. Do they train them? What's the deal? And get the family on the record about the murder investigation. Who do they think did it? Are they worried it won't get solved?"

I pull out my notebook to scribble his directions. He continues.

"Ms. Roberts, you have not yet lost your position here. But consider yourself on probation. Larry, you're lead on this. Update me tomorrow."

After Morgan leaves, Larry and I follow Mike back to the city desk and we sit down at two computers no one is using. I flip through my notes as I wait for the machine to boot up. These PCs were out of date when I started college.

"So," says Larry, "who do you think did it?"

I hesitate. "I've been thinking the husband. She was dumped

in his yard. She was cheating. These people don't take stepping out of line lightly. And infidelity is totally unacceptable in women, from what I can tell. Like, automatic loss of custody of the kids. I tried to talk to the husband, and he scared the shit out of me. He looked desperate. And the people I talked to, the other outsiders, they said he threatened her. Said he'd take her kids away, shun her, that sort of thing. They said he was really angry. And this was, like, a week or two before she died."

"What did Saul think?" asks Larry. "Did he say anything? He was feeding you information, but was it to send you in the wrong direction?"

"I didn't feel like he had a direction," I say. It's nice to be able to bounce what I've learned off Larry. Unlike some of the old-timers I've met, he seems genuinely interested in his work, despite the fact that he's probably been doing it for more than three decades. I bet I can learn a lot from him. "He never speculated on who might have killed her. Just that he was sure the department was fucking it up. Not interviewing people. Kowtowing to the community." I tell Larry who the man Saul assaulted was, and why he said he did what he did. "Obviously, the assault didn't make the papers, but I don't remember reading anything about a rabbi sex scandal either," I say. "Did we cover it?"

"We wrote a short piece on the initial arrest," he says. "And another when the charges were dropped. I'll see if I can get confirmation on the name of the man he assaulted, though I doubt I'll be able to connect the two cases tonight. What's your plan for tomorrow?"

"I think I can get some good information from Miriam, Aron Mendelssohn's sister. She and her husband live in the same house as

the Mendelssohns. And she was there when the husband threatened Rivka. Apparently she got really upset about the whole thing."

"Will she talk to you?"

"She's already talked to me a little," I say. "Now I have more
information to go at her with. Even if she doesn't give me details,
maybe she'll confirm stuff."

"Okay," says Larry. "You go to Borough Park tomorrow. But
everything has to be on the record. First and last names. The department is embarrassed and they're going to be on everything you
say. If you give them a chance to make you look bad, they'll take it.
Get it on tape if you can. Start small. Be accurate. That's the most
important thing. If all this shit you think is true is true, you've got
weeks of stories on this. Maybe more. You're going to write up what
you got from her friends now, but what's the story for tomorrow?
What can you get by four P.M.?"

"I can talk to the family. Get their take on the investigation.
And ask about their connection to Shomrim."

"Okay. I'll work on Saul, and getting an official cause of death
for Rivka. If the cops don't have that, they don't have anything. So
we're set?"

I nod.

"Good," he says, and stands up. "You've got everybody's attention here, Rebekah. Yesterday I didn't know who you were. Neither
did Albert Morgan. Personally, I think you've done some great
work. But this could still turn out pretty bad for you. Could turn out
good, too. Real good. A big story like this will impress people. Just
get it right. And get it on the record."

Larry leaves. I take out my notebook and type my earlier draft into the system. To what I already have from Sara Wyman about Rivka's dead child and the fact that she was questioning her marriage and the rules of the community, I add the bits about Aron Mendelssohn threatening Rivka and Suri's comments about how Rivka wanted Coney Island to be a "sacred space." I send the draft to Mike.

"Rebekah!" he shouts moments later from behind his cloth cubicle wall. I jog over. "It's way too long. We only have seven inches."

I watch as he hacks the story to pieces with the DELETE key.

The woman whose body was found naked in a Brooklyn scrap pile Friday wanted to divorce her wealthy husband, but was afraid she'd lose her children, according to multiple friends.

"Even if she was granted a divorce by the rabbi, Hasidic women rarely retain custody," said Sara Wyman, a social worker and former member of the Hasidic community to which Rivka Mendelssohn belonged.

Two weeks before the 30-year-old mother-of-four's death, friends say that her older husband, Aron Mendelssohn, confronted her about an affair and physically assaulted her in a "safe" house for ultra-Orthodox Jews in Coney Island.

"He grabbed her," says Devorah Kletzky, 22. "He was yelling in her face. He said he'd see her shunned."

Wyman and Kletzky both told the Tribune *exclusively that Mendelssohn had begun "questioning" her rigid Orthodox life after the tragic death of her infant daughter, Shoshanna, last year.*

Wyman said she had "no idea" how Mendelssohn could have met such a gruesome end. "I just hope the police find who did this—she didn't deserve to die so young."

Police have made no arrests in Mendelssohn's murder. A gardener for the family was questioned and released over the weekend.

It's all technically accurate, but lacks any context or background. Mike presses a button and sends the story to the copy desk.

"Call in with what you have on the family and the Jewish cops before four tomorrow," he says. And then, without looking at me: "Good luck."

CHAPTER FOURTEEN

By the time I walk out of the *Trib* building, it is nearly ten o'clock, but just as I'm walking down into the F train to go home, Sara Wyman calls.

"Can you meet?" she asks.

"Now? Where?"

"There's an all-night diner on Flatbush. I'm bringing someone I think you should meet."

I walk across Fiftieth Street to the 1 train, and forty minutes later I'm back in Brooklyn. Sara Wyman is already at the diner when I arrive. Sitting beside her is Malka, from the funeral home.

"Thank you for meeting us," says Sara. Her hair is a wild, rumbled mess of hat-head and her eyeglasses are hanging on a beaded chain around her neck. Malka looks polished and prim, just like she did in the basement of the funeral home.

"You are the reporter?" asks Malka as I sit down. She looks uncomfortable.

"You two know each other?" Sara is surprised.

"I met Malka the day of the funeral," I say.

"You did not say you were a reporter," says Malka.

"I know," I say. "I should have. I apologize."

This seems, oddly enough, to satisfy her. Or else she is simply distracted. "Is it true Saul Katz has been arrested?" she asks.

"Yes," I say.

"I suppose it was inevitable," says Sara. "I'm no fan of Leiby Bronner, but . . ."

"You know about that?" I ask.

Sara smiles. "Word travels. And the community is very divided over the issue of sexual abuse."

"There is not division over the issue of sexual abuse," says Malka, looking cross. "Everyone agrees it is *averah*. A sin. There is division over the proper response."

"Yes," says Sara. "Of course."

"He wasn't arrested for the assault, though," I say. "They're saying he obstructed the investigation into Rivka Mendelssohn's murder by talking to me."

Sara shakes her head. "Poor man. He's always been solemn. Navigating the worlds he lives in, so many years of not belonging anywhere. No real family. And then when his son, Binyamin, died . . ."

"His son died?" I ask. Saul didn't say that. "When?"

"Recently," says Sara. "During the fall. October, I think."

"What happened?"

Sara lowers her voice. "It was suicide. He had a wife and three children, but . . . he was gay. And when it was discovered, he was forced to leave his teaching job. He rented an apartment in Kensington and that's where he was found. Hanging from the ceiling. He'd been for days. Neighbors called the super because of the smell."

"Oh my God," I say. I cross my arms over my stomach and wince. "Saul told me he'd been molested."

Sara nods. "Yes," she says. "That is what I was told as well."

"Binyamin Katz went to yeshiva with my brothers," says Malka.

"Oh!" says Sara.

Malka is staring into the middle distance.

"Saul said it was a rabbi," I say. "And that the indictment failed because people wouldn't speak out."

Malka's eyes return to the table. "That is accurate," she says.

I've never seen a woman quite like Malka before. Her features are tiny and her white skin smooth, like a porcelain doll. And like a doll, she is completely expressionless. The most her face has moved since I sat down is to blink. It occurs to me that she would make a great soldier or spy. Not even Al Qaeda could get her to talk if she didn't want to say anything.

"But this isn't why I asked you to meet us," says Sara. "Remember when we talked I told you that the reason Rivka Mendelssohn came to me was she had endured the death of a child? After we talked I called Malka. Malka?"

Malka looks me in the eyes for the first time since I've met her. "The baby was murdered," she says. "She was hit on the head. Like her mother."

The way she says it, it seems almost as if she is posing a challenge. I take out my notebook. It's now or never.

"I need this on the record," I say.

She nods, her gaze steady. "My name is Malka Grossman," she says, looking at my pen. "Two *s*'s. I prepared the bodies of Rivka Mendelssohn and her infant daughter for burial. I believe both died of massive head wounds."

It takes me a moment to start writing, and then I begin to scribble: *m grossman prep R and inf d 'massive h wounds'*

"Sara, you said Rivka told you the girl had an asthma attack?"

"She did tell me that. Apparently she was not telling the truth."

"Do you have any idea why she lied?"

"I suppose it's possible she didn't know for certain," Sara says slowly. "Or she wanted to keep the details to herself."

Or, I think, she was hiding something. Or in denial.

"Did anyone else see the bodies?" I ask Malka. "I'm just wondering if I can confirm . . ."

Without a word, Malka pulls two neat manila envelopes out of her bag and places them in front of me on the tiny round table. "These are copies of my notes."

"Do the police have these?" I ask.

"No."

"Have you ever been interviewed by the police?"

Malka shakes her head. "I thought my notes were going to the police when I handed them over."

"Handed them over?"

"To Joel Yazbek. Of Borough Park Shomrim."

"And he was supposed to give it to the police?"

Malka nods. "But I have since learned he did not."

"Were you alone when you prepared their bodies?"

"In Rivka's case, I had an assistant. But I will not allow her name to be used. Absolutely not. I made a decision to come forward. She did not and I must protect her."

"Fine," I say. "I won't even ask her name. But if I need to check something later, can you put me in touch?"

Malka considers this. "I can. As long as she remains anonymous."

That works. I unfold the top of one of the manila envelopes and finger through the contents. Paper and photos.

"So you prepared these yourself? What exactly is your . . . title?"

"My family owns the Mandel Memorial Funeral Home and my husband is the manager," says Malka. "I am the bookkeeper and volunteer preparing bodies. You are Jewish?"

I nod. She's about to tell me something I should "know"—but of course I don't know.

"So you know. A woman must prepare a woman for burial. So she can rest with dignity."

"Tell me about the little girl," I say.

"Shoshanna was brought in by Shomrim. I was told she was dead when they arrived at the home. It's all in the report."

"What about Rivka. Did you give those notes to anyone?"

"I'm giving them to you," says Malka. She pauses, then speaks again. "This is not a decision I came to lightly. I'm sure you find our way of life strange, perhaps even repellent. But there are many things you do not know. And many people who tell lies about the way we live. Most Haredi in Brooklyn are descended from Holocaust survivors. My mother's entire family—six brothers and sisters, her parents and grandparents—were murdered by the Nazis in Poland. We know intimately how quickly our goyish neighbors can turn on us. We know that to survive we must rely on one another, we must support and protect our fellow Jews. We do not do this because we do not believe that sin should be punished. We do this because the strength of the community is vital to our survival. You look at us and you see black hats and wigs and you think we are to be pitied. You think you know better. But you do not see more than you see. You think the prohibition against men and women touching is misogynist. You don't see the tenderness, or passion, with which a husband touches his wife after she is *niddah*. You think that clothing that exposes your flesh makes you free. But in my modest clothing I am free from the leering stares of men. I am free to be judged by my intellect and my actions, not my body."

Malka pauses, then continues.

"Did you know that in Borough Park and Williamsburg and Crown Heights, Orthodox shopkeepers allow many of their customers to shop on credit?" asks Malka. "They fill their baskets with what they need and their purchases are simply logged in an account. It is called *aufschraben*. No Jew goes hungry in Brooklyn. No child goes without clothing or formula, because families like the Mendelssohns pay the grocery bills of those who are less financially fortunate. If the community were more integrated with those outside, such a system would not be possible."

"I didn't know that," I say. "That's really interesting." Maybe, I think, I could write about that, once this is all done.

"It is important to me that you understand all this," says Malka. "I do not wish to invite scrutiny by people who do not respect our way of life, but the secrets have to stop. The community can heal, but individual people, boys and girls, they cannot. They need protection. Someone murdered Rivka Mendelssohn and her daughter. That person did more damage to the strength of the community than a thousand newspaper articles."

It's after one in the morning when I get back, but Iris is up watching TV.

"I hadn't heard from you," she says. "I was worried."

As she makes tea, I tell her about Coney Island and Albert Morgan and Saul's arrest and meeting Sara and Malka. We spread the contents of the two manila envelopes on the kitchen table. I start reading Malka's notes, and Iris pulls out the photographs.

"Jesus, Rebekah," she says. "Have you seen these?"

I lean over. The first picture is of the baby, taken maybe six inches from her face: Her eyes are slightly open. Her pudgy cheeks are red with webs of broken capillaries. There is a bloodless cut on her bottom lip. The next is the child's head from the back. It looks like someone hit her with a bat. A bruise extends across her skull. When I was standing above this little girl's mother's body on Saturday, I was too shocked to empathize. I knew I needed to remain standing, so I didn't look at the black skin surrounding each wound and think about the pain. But Shoshanna's bruise, glossy in a picture, looks like it *hurt.* How do you do that to a baby?

"According to Malka's notes, there were two points of impact on the baby's head," I say.

"*Two?* Fuck. Who are these people?"

"I only see this one," I say, pointing to the dark center of the wound. "But I guess I don't really know what I'm looking for."

Iris gets up. "Yeah, I can't look at that." She goes to the couch but doesn't sit down. "And the police don't have any of this?"

"I don't think so. But I have to figure that out for sure tomorrow."

"Do you think the husband killed them both?"

"I don't know," I say. "I can see him maybe killing Rivka. But bashing a fucking baby's head in is different. And children are really important in the community, too. It doesn't make sense that he'd kill his own child. Unless he was fucking evil."

"Maybe it's like in China, where they kill the girls because they want a boy."

"I don't think it's like that," I say, but who the fuck knows?

That night, I sleep—or rather don't sleep—like I'm drunk. When I close my eyes, I feel dizzy. I dream of lying in bed and feeling dizzy. And I dream of Shoshanna. I'm sitting at Starbucks and she's in a high chair beside me. Her nose is bleeding.

TUESDAY

CHAPTER FIFTEEN

My alarm rings at seven thirty, and though I've barely slept, I have little trouble getting out of bed. I log on to the *Trib*'s Web site and find my article about Rivka Mendelssohn—including her photo. Larry's item about Saul's arrest is listed below it. No picture illustrates his story.

I call Larry's cell to tell him about my meeting last night.

"I've got today's story," I say. "Last night I met with the woman who prepared Rivka Mendelssohn's body for burial. The same woman also prepared her daughter's body."

"Her daughter?"

"She had a daughter, an infant, who died last year. My source is a woman whose family owns the funeral home. She prepares Jewish women for burial. She says they both had massive head trauma. She says both were homicides."

"You've got her name?"

"Yes," I say. "And her notes."

"Autopsy?"

"No. She said it's against Jewish law to cut open the body. But she made notes from what she saw. And there are pictures."

"Great work," says Larry. "Give me the name, I'll run her background."

I do, and we agree to meet at the office to look at the reports. When I get in, Larry is sitting at the same computer that I wrote my story on last night. I pull up a chair and show him the reports. I also fill him in on what Malka and Sara told me about Leiby Bronner and the rabbi. Mike comes over to get an update. We tell him what we have.

"Okay," he says, "I'm going to the meeting with exclusive postmortem reports on crane lady and her infant daughter. We need official comment on all this. Where are police on crane lady's killer? Do they think she was killed at the yard or just dumped there? What did they know about the baby? *Did* they know? Do they think the two are connected?"

"I can work that," says Larry. "I'm gonna try to get someone at the M.E.'s office to look at these, too."

"Great. So, Rebekah, you're back in Borough Park. We really need a picture of the baby." I flash to the dead girl's face. Alive. He means we need a picture of her alive. "You've spoken to the sister-in-law? Maybe you can get one from her."

I tell him I'll try. Larry and I leave together; we both get on the N headed downtown.

"Saul Katz is at the courthouse in Brooklyn," Larry tells me after we sit down. The Caribbean island of St. Lucia has purchased advertising throughout the entire subway car. All around me are color photos of pristine beaches: white sand and blue water. "He's got a bail hearing this afternoon. My guess is that the judge will let him out."

"What about Leiby Bronner? Do they have an explanation for why he was never charged for that?"

"I'm waiting on that. They know I know. I need to get the Bronner family's number from the library."

Larry transfers to the R at Union Square, and I continue on, into Brooklyn, aboveground and back below. I get off at New Utrecht, just a block from the building that I first saw Aron Mendelssohn come out of. I walk over, and as I lean in to peek into the ground-floor window, the door in the building beside 5510 opens and a haggard, dumpy-looking woman dressed in black pulls open the door with her foot, struggling to squeeze a double-wide stroller outside. Three other small children run in front of her; boys with sidecurls, girls in matching skirts. I hold open the door to try to help her and glance up the narrow stairs where she came from. There are six different buzzers in the doorway. How do they all fit in what must be a tiny apartment? My mother was not from a wealthy family like the Mendelssohns; my grandfather managed a livery cab company. My father told me that he mostly employed Jewish immigrants, many of them from Russia, and that the Kagans assisted the families in their transition to American life. Little Aviva showed the Russian girls how to ride the bus to school; she read with them, gave them her old skirts and sweaters and winter coats. My father said that Aviva first got the idea that not every Jew in the world followed the same strict laws of living as her family did from the immigrant girls. He said they were confused about the rules governing stocking thickness, and about not being able to sing in public. Once

my mother got it in her mind that maybe God wasn't the one making the rules, as Suri had said, it all turned into bullshit. And the
fact that her life was built on bullshit—and that nobody else saw
the truth—made her angry.

But here on the main drag in Borough Park, and in houses and
apartments as far as I can see, there are thousands of men and
women for whom, ostensibly, none of it is bullshit. It is God's will,
as natural as breathing, as common as writing a rent check. It is the
foundation of life. The meaning, the reason, the tools. It is how sorrow and disappointment and frustration are overcome. Do these
things and you will know God. Do these things and he will reward
your devotion. The ridicule of the outside world is meaningless. But
inside the fold, in the family, in the home, doubt is a cancer. A
blooming menace; poison.

I'm standing on the corner of Fifty-ninth Street when I see
Miriam. She emerges from a corner deli with her head down. She
lights a cigarette and then starts walking quickly down New Utrecht
toward the Mendelssohn home. I have to jog to catch up with her.

"Miriam," I say, when I am two paces behind. "Excuse me,
Miriam?"

She turns sharply, her eyes wide.

"We cannot talk here," says Miriam. "Come." She resumes her
pace. I follow, two blocks and then a left, and another block and a
right. She stays ahead of me, sucking on her cigarette. Across the
street from the house, she stops.

"They do not know I have gone," she says. "We are sitting shiva
and we cannot leave the house. Aron and the children are in the
living room on their chairs and I went to lie down in my room. But
it is too much in that house. There are too many children. Do you

understand? I had to get out. My brother. He expects me to be their mother. But I am not their mother. Do you understand?"

"I understand," I say. "Do you have a minute for me to ask you some questions? We could do it inside."

Miriam shakes her head. "No." A woman and her children come up the block. Miriam turns her back to them. They pass us by without a glance.

"Come," says Miriam. She drops her cigarette on the sidewalk and crosses the street. When we get to the edge of the Mendelssohn lot, she stops and peers around a leafless shrub. "Go to the side. See if the window shades are open."

"What?"

"Go!" she says. "They cannot see me outside. Go! Through the gate. See if they are looking."

I go. I walk up to the gate and slowly lift the latch, running through the words I'll say if I encounter Aron Mendelssohn. Hello, sir. Trespassing? Oh no, your sister asked me to stop by. If I could even get the words out before I just turn and run. The backyard is empty and quiet. Snow is frozen in dunes beside the shoveled brick walk between the house and the garage. The window in the back door, the door I went through last time, is covered with a curtain. I take two more steps and see a row of windows; the kitchen, perhaps. They are not covered with curtains, but inside the room seems dark.

"See?" Miriam is suddenly behind me. "There are many windows. Come. I need one more cigarette." She crouches down and scurries behind the house, underneath the row of windows. She turns and motions for me to follow, then darts across the yard and disappears inside the garage. I look around. It's an overcast morning. Cold, but less windy than the past few days. A man in a black hat walks by the house. Does Miriam really have to hide in the garage to smoke? My heart is starting to flutter unpleasantly. There are so many fucking secrets in this world. I can feel my armpits slick and the skin on my neck burn. Should I not be following Miriam? My body is screaming at me. But it screams so often that it's easy to ignore. And I have a story to get, so fuck you, body. I'm going to get it.

The door at the side of the garage is open and I let myself in. Miriam is pacing, smoking. There is a minivan in one space, but the rest of the garage seems to be used for storage. There are half a dozen card table chairs folded up and leaning against one wall. Along the wall by the door are a couple of deep plastic bins full of discarded objects—old cookware, broken desktop filing systems, dirt-caked garden tools, a table lamp without a shade. And more bins full of empty water and juice bottles, presumably ready to recycle. Beside the bins is a wobbly plastic shelving unit holding canned food.

"In here it is safe," says Miriam, closing the door behind me. "You see? My brother, he does not want anyone to know about Rivka. But I will tell you. What would you like to know?"

"I actually wanted to ask you about . . . Shoshanna," I say.

This surprises her. Her face doesn't change—it's still pinched and pale, her eyes half hidden beneath the thick bangs of her wig—but her body does. She jumps slightly.

"I thought you wanted to talk about Rivka?"

"I do," I say. "I was hoping you could tell me how she handled the death. I spoke with some people who said she was very . . . affected. That it was very difficult for her."

Miriam scratches at her wig.

"Could you tell me when she died?" Miriam shakes her head.

She seems to have forgotten her cigarette, which is burning down slowly, ash dropping onto the concrete floor. "Were you here? Do you remember what happened? It must have been horrible."

Miriam says nothing. I take my notebook out of my bag and ask again, "Do you remember anything about that . . . ?"

"I do not want to talk about Shoshanna."

"Okay . . ."

"Shoshanna was just a baby. Babies die. Sometimes we don't know how. Sometimes they die inside their mothers. It is the will of Hashem. We must accept it."

"But she was a bit older, right?"

Miriam glares at me. "She was a little *momzer*. Her mother was a *zona*."

"Her mother . . . you mean, Rivka?"

"You want to know about Rivka. Rivka was weak. She turned her back on Hashem and on her family. *My* family. My family that took her in. Rivka had everything, but she always wanted more. She thought she deserved more." Miriam's face is flushed. "What do you think of this?" she asks. "What do you think of what I am telling you?"

"I'm not sure," I say. "I'm sorry, I didn't mean to upset you. . . ."

"You said you wanted to write a story about Rivka," she says. "I am telling you about Rivka."

"I know," I say, "but maybe we could go into the house?"

Miriam shakes her head slowly. Before I saw her on the street this morning, I hadn't spent more than five minutes interacting with Miriam. I'd never encountered her alone and I hadn't spent much time thinking about her personality, just her situation. Dead sister-in-law; frightened, seemingly, of her domineering brother, yet willing to talk to me in her grief. Which, come to think of it, was unlike most of the grief I've encountered getting quotes from the relatives of homicide victims over the past few months. Usually, they beg me to leave them alone. They hold their hands out and squint, like they're trying to find shade from a hot, horrible sun. Please, we can't, they say. Not now. Some sizable minority get angry; they call me a sicko, a vulture, a parasite; they slam doors. In October, I was chased off a tiny Staten Island front lawn by the aunt of a girl who was found buried in a shallow grave in New Jersey.

But Miriam, it occurs to me, was not at all emotional. Not until now. And now it's the wrong emotion. Miriam is not sad—she is seething.

"What do you think of this?" she asks, breathing heavily. She comes closer to me. "What do you think of a mother who betrays her family? For *sex*."

"Sex? . . ."

"When she told me, she was happy. Happy to be shaming her family and her husband. Her children."

Her face changes again, now to an expression of extreme distaste, like she's just eaten a mouthful of shit.

"'Miriam,' she said"—her voice is thick with sarcasm—"'Miriam, I wish you could find this love. You would understand that it must be Hashem speaking to me. It must.'"

"You were close, then . . . ," I stammer. "She trusted you?"

"Why are you not writing this down?" She flicks her cigarette at my face. It's just a butt now, but it hits below my right eye and stings. "Rivka betrayed her family. She was greedy and she was a *zona* and she deserved to die."

I am afraid that if I turn away, I will provoke her. This is a woman with a mental illness, I remind myself. A woman who has been mistreated. Like the men and women who mutter and pace and shout in the subway late at night, she is unpredictable. One wrong look, and suddenly I become a demon to be slain. I need to say the right thing, I need to remain calm, and I need to leave the garage.

"Miriam," I say, stepping backward toward the door, "I think maybe . . ."

Miriam grabs a card table chair and swings it at me. I turn toward the door, but before I can take two steps the sharp end of one of the chair's aluminum legs connects with the side of my skull. I stumble sideways and land on my hands and knees.

"What do you think, *Rivka*?" hisses Miriam, standing over me as I try to get up, her voice an echo in my ears. My head is sparkling with pain. "Don't you think that is a good story?"

I look up and see she is holding something else. The table lamp from the plastic bin. I lift my hand to her, and just as the base end comes down on my head, I think, this is gonna hurt.

CHAPTER SIXTEEN

When I come to, I am sitting, and the first sensation I recognize is great thirst. Something is stuffed in my mouth, holding it wide open. I try to swallow and I start to choke. It feels like my tongue might fall back down my throat. My jaw is sore, the corners of my mouth pulled taut. There is something cold and wet itching in my left ear. I try to lift my hand to wipe it away, but my hand—both my hands—are tied behind my back with something coarse that is digging into my skin. Twine, maybe. My feet are tied, too, each to one leg of the chair I'm sitting in. Miriam is sitting cross-legged on the concrete floor. She has the contents of my purse laid out in front of her and she is browsing through my wallet, sliding my debit card, my Visa, my Florida driver's license, out of their little pockets. I have no idea how long I've been in this garage. There are no windows.

I watch Miriam for what seems like at least a few minutes before she looks up.

"Rebekah," she says, turning my license toward me. "Rebekah is Rivka. Rivka is a pretty name. Prettier than Miriam."

She picks up my plastic bottle of anti-anxiety pills and shakes it, smiling.

"I know this," she says. "This is for when you get too upset. Too . . ." She waves her hands around. "I have lots of this. I have other pills, too. All kinds. Blue and pink and white and yellow. Big ones and little ones and sometimes I take them when I'm not supposed to. Do you ever do that?" She is talking very fast. "Sometimes I take too many. Rivka always counts my pills. 'Miriam, Miriam.' She likes to say my name because it makes her prettier. We are not sisters, you know. I was the one who asked Tatti to take her in, when her mommy died and her crazy father was crazy. Then we were like sisters. We did things girls do. Silly things. What did we know? She did not really know me, Rivka." She giggles. "You are Rivka."

Miriam bows her head forward and pulls off her wig. What is underneath looks much like what was above, but messier, frizzier, streaked with gray. She puts the wig on the ground and fluffs up her hair.

"Itchy," she says.

She is still holding the pill bottle. She is also holding a pair of scissors.

I try to say "Miriam," but the sound that comes out is just a grunt. A quiet grunt. The sidewalk isn't fifteen feet from the wall of the garage, but grunts at that pitch aren't going to bring anybody running.

Miriam twists open the cap of the pill bottle and shakes the ten or twelve pills that are left into her palm.

"I can take some?" she asks. But she's not really asking. She smiles and then nods, and says, "Yes. I feel very anxious. Do you know that word? That is the word they call it. My mind is spinning. I should take some."

Miriam takes an empty plastic bottle from the recycle bin and goes to the far corner to fill it at the slop sink. I need to get the scissors away from her. Without those scissors I can survive. The weak spot is my feet. They're tied, but not as well as my hands. She used electrical cord. If I can slip one leg out, I can probably use my foot to push the cord off the other leg, and then I have motion.

"Rivka was very devout when we were girls," says Miriam once she's filled the bottle. "We used to talk about our wedding day. And our husbands. We hoped we would marry a man who studied Torah all day. A man who devoted his life to Hashem."

She rolls her eyes and then tosses my pills—all of them—into her mouth and takes a long drink of water. Ten of those pills probably won't kill her, but if I can keep things calm for twenty minutes, they might knock her out. After she swallows the pills, she stands up and starts walking toward me.

"And we would show him our devoutness by shaving our heads. We practiced putting on my mother's snood, and her wigs. Rivka's mother did not wear a wig and Rivka wanted to wear one, like my mother." She is standing behind me now, her hand stroking my hair.

"But Rivka was a liar. She was not devout at all. She was too vain to shave after her wedding."

Miriam gathers my hair into her hand and pulls my head back. Her face is inches from mine. I can communicate only with my eyes and I know that all they show is fear.

"Rivka was afraid, too," she says, looking down at me. She pulls tight and then she starts to cut. I can hear my hair rip, and I can feel the way the blade tears through it, nicking the base of my scalp. Rivka Mendelssohn was bald when she died. Freshly shorn. Getting all that hair off with scissors would have taken a long time. I wonder if she died in this garage. I wonder if, someday, Miriam will look back and it will seem like one time in her mind.

"After Shoshanna died, Rivka became like everyone else. They think I don't notice. They think that they can send me away and that I will return and I will forget. They think I can't see what they think of me. But I can always see. I can see inside them all. Rivka said that she forgave me. She said that she knew it must have been an accident. That she shouldn't have burdened me with her child's care. She said she should have been more sensitive about how I might feel about all her children. Because she was blessed with so many, and poor Miriam couldn't even get Hashem to give her one. But she did not understand. She did not deserve her children. When I saw what she was doing—the shame she was bringing to my family, to my brother—I could not bear the whispers anymore. Everywhere I went, they were looking at me. Talking about the *zona* in the Mendelssohn home. As if it was my fault. I must have infected her. But I was never unfaithful. I am not as pretty as Rivka but I had my chances. And then I saw that Heshy had fallen under her spell. How could I be expected to bear that? In the same house?"

My phone rings, and Miriam stops talking. It rings again.

"Who is that?" she demands. She runs to where she's dumped my purse out and picks up my phone. She does not answer, just stares at it as it rings. "Who is this? It is a blocked number." It is also, I decide, my chance. I tighten my stomach muscles and throw my weight backward. My head hits the floor and I twist sideways. I'm still tied to the chair but I try to whip around. If I'm a moving target, it's harder for Miriam to just pull her arm back and stab the shit out of me. I am *not* going to die in this fucking garage. Miriam hurls my phone at my head, but misses. I tense my stomach again and swing my hips forward. My thighs collide with her calves, knocking her off her feet. We're both on the ground now. I turn my head and she's right there, her pale, ugly face, her yellow finger-nails. I've startled her. She looks down at her hand, and then presses it to a spot on her lip that's broken and bleeding. The scissors are on the floor just above both of our heads.

I toss my weight counterclockwise, knocking my knees into her head. She grunts and curls forward into a ball while I push back-ward, scooting toward the scissors to try to kick them away and put the chairback between myself and Miriam. Did I tell anyone I was coming here? I forgot to call photo. Larry knows. But he's not going to worry soon enough. I focus my mind on my right foot. If I point my toes inside my boot and pull up with my ankle, I can wiggle some room in the loop holding my foot to the chair leg. I point and point and it feels like the muscle holding my foot onto my leg might snap. I point and push, hearing Miriam next to me crawling toward the scissors. And then finally I feel a give. I kick at what I now see is a simple double knot around my left ankle. Four, five, six kicks and then there's enough space to push the loop to the end of the chair and off. Miriam stands up. She holds the scissors in front of her, pointing at me.

My legs are free, but I'm still tethered to the chair so I can't actually stand. I scoot backward along the floor. Miriam is gripping the scissors with both hands, pointing them at me like she's protecting herself.

My phone rings again; again, Miriam is startled.

"Who is that!" she screams, and begins backing into the opposite corner, toward the sink.

"Don't come any closer," she says.

And then I hear it: footsteps. Boots.

"Miriam!" calls a male voice.

"Get away!" screams Miriam.

"We're coming in!" shouts the man. A kick, and the door swings open.

It's Aron Mendelssohn. Behind him is Detective Darin Spinelli, holding a gun.

"Drop the weapon!" Darin shouts at Miriam.

But if Miriam hears him, she doesn't act like it. She wipes her eyes with her bloody hand and charges forward with the scissors in front of her. She takes less than three steps before Darin blasts her. One, two shots to the chest and she falls like a bag of bricks.

Aron Mendelssohn runs to me and kneels down, frantically untying my hands. "Are you all right?" he asks, grabbing my arms, turning me, examining me, and then suddenly, pulling me to him. Holding me, and murmuring, *"Baruch Hashem. Baruch Hashem."*

CHAPTER SEVENTEEN

Miriam does not get taken away by the Chesed Shel Emes. Aron Mendelssohn objects, but he is handcuffed on his own sofa and he doesn't seem to have much energy. The police, not the Shomrim, take custody of the body of the second woman to die at the Mendelssohn house in a week.

Darin gets his gun taken away, and I am wrapped in a blanket and put in an ambulance. I have lacerations, a concussion, and possibly a broken bone and some torn ligaments in my right foot. My hair is mostly gone.

Tony and Iris are at the hospital within hours. My dad and Maria get on an airplane.

It is dark outside when Captain Weber and another detective come to question me. They say that the police found Rivka Mendelssohn's blood and hair in the garage. They say they want to exhume

her body, but Aron Mendelssohn, who is in custody, is refusing to
give his permission.

"We'll get around him," says Weber. "It'll just take a few days."

"Why is he in custody?" I ask.

"For now, we've booked him on illegal disposal of a body," says
the detective. "We have surveillance video of his car going into the
scrap yard the night Rivka Mendelssohn's body was dumped."

"What is he saying?"

"He's not saying anything. He lawyered up. But he's got a lot of
explaining to do before he sees sky."

"I don't think he killed her," I say.

"We'll be the judge of that," says Weber. At least he's dropped
the diminutives.

"How did you know I was in there?" I ask.

"The little boy noticed the aunt was missing."

"Yakov?" I cringe thinking of what that little boy knows.
What's he's seen in just the past year.

Captain Weber nods. "He told his father and the father called
Shomrim. It was just luck that Detective Spinelli was at their mis-
sion control interviewing the leader when the call came in."

I sleep through most of the first twenty-four hours. My head
feels huge and delicate, and my dreams are throbbing cascades of
faces and hard surfaces and fear: Aviva holding a knife; Miriam
trying to dial out from my phone; Rivka Mendelssohn rubbing her
pregnant belly.

Iris brings a purple scarf and ties it over my head. She holds up
a mirror for me to see, and the reflection is unfamiliar. The white of
my left eye is blood red. Black stitches hold my bottom lip together.

I am lopsided and swollen everywhere else. I feel weak in my unattractiveness.

Tony does a lot of pacing. Maria spends hours on her phone just outside my room, arguing with their insurance company, which may or may not cover me in New York State. Larry shows up with the paper. There is a short item about a police-involved shooting in Borough Park. My name isn't mentioned. He tells me they're going forward with the story about the murdered baby and the cover-up. I'll have a byline, he says, but Albert Morgan doesn't want to wait.

"He's thinks Pete Calloway could scoop us," he says. "We're calling it the "'Hasidic House of Horrors.'"

I close my eyes. All I want to know about the *Trib* is whether they're going to help with my hospital bills. Larry says he'll ask.

When Iris leaves for her office, my dad takes her place by my side, sitting forward, hands ready to hold. The second evening, as the sky goes purple in the window behind him, I catch him murmuring to himself.

"Dad?" I say. "Are you okay?"

He smiles weakly, and puts his hand on mine. My dad is a young man compared to the fathers of most of my friends; he was still in his thirties when I started college. He wears his sand-colored hair a little bit long; it curls around his ears and falls over his forehead. He was just a boy when he became a dad.

"How are you feeling, sweetheart?" he asks.

"I think I'm okay, Dad," I say. I'm glad you're here, I think. I'm glad you're mine.

"What were you doing?" he whispers. "Why were you all *alone*?"

I close my eyes. "I made a mistake, Dad. I didn't see what was happening. I just . . ." I just wanted the story. I wanted to *know*. But I don't say that; he won't understand.

"I feel like this is my fault," he says. "All the questions you have, about your mother. And I could never really answer them, could I?"

"I don't even know if there are answers, Dad," I say. But even as I say it, I know that I don't believe it. If I believe in anything, I believe that there are always answers. You just have to ask the right question of the right person at the right time. And my dad, loving and incurious and satisfied in his life with Maria and his children and his church, was never the right person. But the Orthodox women who knew Rivka Mendelssohn, they are. All week, I've looked at each of them and asked myself: Is this Aviva? Is she frumpy and kindhearted like Sara Wyman? Guiding others on the path out of the community that suffocates them. Is she timid and unhappy, like Chaya? Married now, bearing babies—grandbabies, even. Accomplished and content like Malka? I want her to be like Rivka: responsible, admired, agonizing over how to balance her long-held beliefs with newfound ideas and emotions. But I don't think she was. Or is. I think that if she's like any of them, she might be like Miriam. Beset by an inconvenient, undesirable illness. And in way over her head. I want to tell my father about all these women. About all the things I've learned about them. About the new perspective I have. But the stories seem too long to tell now, and so I say this: "I think maybe I forgive her, Dad."

He looks at me with soggy, hopeful eyes. "Oh, Rebekah," he says, reaching for me, clumsily wrapping his arms around my bed-bound body. "I'm so glad." And then we both start to cry. I'm not sure what he's crying about, or whom he's crying for—his injured only daughter, or the woman who left us both behind—but me,

I'm crying because I've finally seen a little bit of the world as Aviva saw it, and it nearly killed me.

I stay in the hospital a few more days while they monitor me for a possible blood clot. When I leave, Dad and Maria and Iris and I all pile into a livery car and go back to Gowanus. After they get me in bed and my dad and Maria go back to their hotel, I tell Iris to bring in the newspaper. I avoided the article I knew they'd published while I was in the hospital because I knew it would stress me out, but I told Iris to get a copy so I could read it when I got home.

The story about the cover-up is teased on the front page ("Hasidic House of Horrors" in white letters on a red banner) and gets three-quarters of page seven:

INSIDE THE "HASIDIC HOUSE OF HORRORS": NYPD TURNED A BLIND EYE AS JEWISH "COPS" COVERED UP MURDER
By Rebekah Roberts and Larry Dunn

Who you gonna call? Not the NYPD.

A private security force made of members of the ultra-Orthodox Jewish community tried to keep the murder of both the infant daughter and the wife of the group's primary benefactor under wraps—with the help of New York's Finest.

The *Tribune* has learned that instead of calling 911, relatives of eight-month-old Shoshanna Mendelssohn turned to a group known as Shomrim, which means "guards" in Hebrew, to whisk the child's body away to a

Jewish funeral home and avoid an official police inquiry last year.

The child's father, Aron Mendelssohn, 49, has donated tens of thousands of dollars to the Borough Park Shomrim. Mendelssohn's wife, Rivka, was found dead in the family's scrap yard along the Gowanus canal last week.

The NYPD allowed a group affiliated with Shomrim to take Rivka Mendelssohn's body from the scene without examining it for evidence.

"It's time for the secrets to stop," says Malka Grossman of Mandel Memorial Funeral Home in Borough Park.

Grossman prepared both Shoshanna and Rivka Mendelssohn's bodies for burial. In the Jewish tradition, bodies must be cleansed by a member of the same sex.

According to Grossman's notes, obtained exclusively by the *Tribune*, both Shoshanna and Rivka Mendelssohn sustained blunt force trauma to the head.

Grossman says she handed her notes to Shomrim with the belief that they would be turned over to police.

But the NYPD says they never saw her notes.

"For years, top brass have let the Orthodox police themselves," says a department official. "It's all political. They vote in a bloc. They contribute to campaigns. They want to be left alone."

The Borough Park Shomrim declined to speak with the *Tribune*.

Last year, the group received more than $25,000 in funding from the City Council.

Aron Mendelssohn has been charged with improper

disposal of a body. Mendelssohn's sister, Miriam Basya, 30, was shot by police on Tuesday after threatening an officer with a pair of scissors. Police tell the *Tribune* that they believe it was Basya who murdered both Shoshanna and Rivka Mendelssohn.

"There is violence in the Orthodox community, just like any community," says Sara Wyman, founder of a Manhattan-based support group for the ex-Orthodox.

"Many would rather keep this unpleasant side from the outside world."

Police Commissioner Donald Evans told the *Tribune* that, in light of the Mendelssohn case, the department planned to "clarify" the relationship between the NYPD and Shomrim.

"It's a good story," says Iris.

"Not exactly thorough," I say. I'd like to write some follow-ups. Look into the "hospital" where Miriam was sent. Interview Baruch. Maybe profile Dev and Suri, and Sara Wyman. But not now.

I go to bed early, and the next morning when Iris goes to work, Tony comes over with coffee and bagels.

"How's Darin?" I ask. "Have you seen him?"

Tony nods. "He's okay. He's on desk duty, but he says that's normal after a shooting."

"Had he ever shot anyone before?"

Tony shakes his head. I take his hand and squeeze it.

"I know you were looking out for me when you told him about Saul," I say. "I'm sorry I got so angry."

"Thanks," he says. "I'm glad I did it, considering. But I'm sorry. I broke your trust."

I smile. "Your big mouth probably saved my life."

"Listen," he says, "I wanted to explain about my mom."

I almost object, but I'd like to get to know him better, and what's going on with his mom is clearly a major part of his life.

"She isn't always like that. She has Alzheimer's."

"Really? But she's only like . . ."

"She's fifty-five. It can hit you young. And she had it for two years before she told me or my sister. But she's only been violent like that once before." He sighs. "I'm sorry you had to see it. Once should have been enough."

"What are you gonna do?" I ask.

"My sister's coming down for the weekend. I don't know. If we can do it, we might hire a part-time nurse or something. I know eventually she'll have to go . . . somewhere."

He's looking at our hands as he talks, embarrassed.

"I'm really sorry," I say. He looks up. "Please don't worry about me. Let's just call it even on mama drama, okay?"

This makes him smile. Oh Rebekah, she's so funny.

"You have a sister?" I ask.

"I do," he says, leaning back. "Her name Meredith. She lives in Delaware."

My dad and Maria return to cook dinner for me and Iris. While we're eating, my dad asks about Saul.

"Have you spoken to him?"

"I haven't," I say.

"He called your phone," says Iris.

"When?" I ask.

"The first couple hours. I think I sounded kind of hysterical. I meant to tell you—I'm sorry. I just forgot."

"It's okay," I say. "So he's not in jail?"

"He's not," says my dad. "He called me, too. He wanted to explain."

"Why did no one tell me this?"

"I didn't know how you'd feel," says my dad. "I haven't heard your side of the story."

My side of the story. They mean, do I blame Saul for what happened. What could have happened.

"I don't blame him," I say. "I mean, I don't think he thought he was putting me in danger. Maybe he should have, a little, but he was . . . desperate." And he wanted to do the right thing.

After dinner, my dad asks how I would feel about him meeting up with Saul.

"Maybe just for a coffee," he says. "I'd like him to meet Maria."

I tell him I would feel just fine about that, and that evening, after they leave, I call Saul.

"How are you?" he asks. I can hear a bus backfire wherever he is.

"I'm okay," I say. "I'm alive. I'm bald."

"Bald?"

"It's a long story," I say. "Saul, I'm sorry about Binyamin. Sara told me. I wish I'd known."

"Thank you, Rebekah," he says. "Can I see you?"

"Yes," I say, "my dad wanted to see you, too."

"I'd like that."

"But first I want you to do something for me," I say.

"Tell me."

"I want you to get me in to see Aron Mendelssohn."

Silence.

"I think they're still holding him. Disposing of a body."

"Yes," says Saul.

"Do you know anybody at the detention center?"

"I do," he says.

SATURDAY

CHAPTER EIGHTEEN

It takes almost an hour of ID checks and waving electronic wands to get into the visiting room at the detention center in Downtown Brooklyn. Aron Mendelssohn is wearing plastic slippers and jailhouse orange. He is allowed a yarmulke, but his sidecurls are straight and hang low, grazing his shoulders.

I sit across from him at a long plastic picnic table.

"Thanks for seeing me," I say.

"You are welcome," he says. "How are you?"

"I'm fine," I say, my hand going automatically to my head. I am still wearing the scarf.

"It will grow back," he says.

"It will," I say. "I hear you're not talking to the police."

He nods. "I read your article in the newspaper."

"It doesn't really tell the whole story," I say.

He shrugs. "How can it?"

Good point.

"Did Miriam kill Rivka?" I ask.

Aron nods, almost imperceptibly.

"And Shoshanna?"

Again. Yes.

"Why?"

"I have no idea," he says. He pulls on the end of his black and gray beard, which crawls over most of his long face. Without his big black hat and heavy coat, he seems smaller. His voice is soft. "Shoshanna, of course, I thought that was an accident. A tragedy. I came home and Rivka and Miriam were in the living room. Rivka was shivering. She'd left the children with Miriam while she went to run errands. Miriam and Heshy had only moved upstairs a few weeks before."

"Where had they been living?"

"In Rockland County."

"I've been told Miriam was . . . hospitalized?"

Aron nods. "Miriam is nearly twenty years younger than I. During much of her childhood and adolescence I was in Israel. I knew there had been difficulties. My father felt that the most important thing for the family was that she be safe. He felt safe meant away from other people. He found a place, upstate, for women. For years there were no problems. I returned from Israel while she was away. Rivka and I married. And then when Yakov was perhaps three years old, Heshy, whom I had known in Israel, arrived, looking for a *shidduch*. There was a dinner where they were introduced, and it was a match. They married and remained in Rockland County, where Miriam's home had been. We hoped they might have children. They did not.

"Rivka and Miriam were very close once. When my father passed away, she felt a responsibility to care for Miriam—just as my father had cared for Rivka in her childhood. After Shoshanna was born, we brought the baby upstate. Miriam looked well and Rivka asked if she and Heshy might come live at the house, in the suite upstairs. Heshy told me he did not think it was wise. He said Miriam wasn't ready to return to Borough Park. He was surprised when he learned Miriam had asked Rivka to make arrangements. I remember he told me, 'There are too many eyes in Brooklyn watching her. Too many hands to hold her down.' I thought it was strange, what he said. Later I realized he was using her words."

"She thought people were watching her?"

Aron sighs. "Of course people are always watching. At shul, at the market. You are Jewish?"

I nod.

"But you do not understand," he says. "In your article, your write that 'Shomrim' is Hebrew for 'guard.' This is not completely accurate. The more precise translation is 'watcher.' There are many in this world who hate the Jews. Who would see us gone from the earth. And so we must protect each other.

"Rivka felt we could protect Miriam. And I did not believe Miriam should be hidden away because of her illness. She told me that my father had been ashamed of Miriam's behavior, her outbursts. Rivka told me she had begun reading about mental illness and that she believed Miriam suffered from a condition that could be treated. She said that we should set an example to the community by welcoming her home. It never occurred to her, I don't think, that Miriam's illness—or what she had become in the years of isolation—should frighten her.

"And when she came home and found Shoshanna . . ." Aron's face is soft now, and he begins to weep. "We made a terrible mistake."

"Why did you let Miriam stay, after that?"

"We believed the baby's death had been an accident. We mourned together."

"What did Miriam say happened?"

"She said that Shoshanna had fallen out of her chair in the kitchen while Miriam was feeding the other children. But later she said Shoshanna took some food—a radish, I think she said—from the counter and choked on it. I should have known then. Rivka was hysterical. It was one thing or the other, she said. She fell or she choked. I felt perhaps Miriam was confused. That Shoshanna's death had been traumatizing and she was misremembering. I did not think she might be lying."

He pauses.

"Rivka asked me to ask Miriam and Heshy to leave."

"Did you?"

He shakes his head. "I did not believe that Miriam could have purposely harmed my child."

"And now?"

"And now I believe that she did. But it is much too late. I am so very, very sorry." His face, the one that had frightened me that night outside his office door, is slack with defeat. "I believed it was the right thing to do to keep our family together. I believed Miriam needed us. She had been sent away her whole life. I believed that she deserved our care."

He pauses. I wait. "Just before Rivka's death, Miriam became unmanageable. It began with Rivka." He purses his lips and looks at the table. "My wife was not in love with me. I believe she tried to love me, for some years. But after Shoshanna's death, she became restless." He pauses again. "We made a visit to a house in Coney Island. It was implied she may have become involved with a man outside our marriage. I also learned that Heshy had begun . . . following her to gatherings. Miriam learned this as well, and when Rivka came home the evening after we confronted her, Miriam became hysterical. She called Rivka names in front of the children. She screamed at me, demanding I divorce her instantly. She began throwing things. She smashed a heavy drinking glass on the edge of the countertop and sliced her arm. There was blood everywhere. But it was as if she did not see it. Something had changed behind her eyes. When she calmed down, she spoke in what almost seemed a different voice. She had become someone else, someone I did not recognize. Someone I know now I should have feared.

"Rivka told me that she was not going to spend another night in the house with Miriam. She said I could take care of her if I wanted, but that she was finished. My wife took the children and spent the last night of her life in a hotel."

"How did you find her?"

"She did not pick Yakov up at yeshiva. The rebbe called me more than two hours after she was due to be there. She had taken our minivan, and when I got home I saw that it was parked on the street. The house was very quiet. I walked through the hall and there was Miriam. She led me to the garage."

"I asked Miriam on Friday when she'd seen her last," I say. "She said Rivka had been gone several days."

Aron shakes his head. "She was confused. Rivka was still warm when I found her. Miriam had taken her clothes. She said she wanted to wash them. Heshy and I wrapped her in a blanket and carried her to the car. I could not leave Miriam alone. I instructed Heshy to . . . dispose of her."

"Why Heshy?"

"It was a terrible mistake. I was not thinking clearly. I thought of my son, and my daughters. I thought that if her body was gone, I could tell them—I could tell everyone—that she was just . . . gone."

SUNDAY

CHAPTER NINETEEN

Saul is already at the Starbucks when we arrive. He has a bouquet of mixed flowers wrapped in clear plastic on the table, and when he sees us he stands up and holds them out to me. It's an awkward gesture, and I appreciate it. He is not in the shapeless suit today. Instead he's wearing a sweater and dark-washed blue jeans. My father opens his arms to hug him, and Saul reaches out a hand; they collide, and laugh.

"Brian," says Saul. "You don't look a day older."

"I've been blessed," says my dad. I can tell he's not sure how to act. Neither of them are. Saul's feeling terrible because he almost got me killed, and Dad's feeling terrible because Saul almost got me killed. But they're looking at each other intently. It's almost touching. Each one seeing my mother in the other.

Maria sits down and my father starts asking Saul questions about people they knew in common from that summer he was in

New York—friends of my mother's, people from the Coney Island house. But neither ever says her name. I often wonder how Maria interacts with the ghost of Aviva Kagan.

"I feel as though I have explaining to do," says Saul, after the short list of names has been run through.

"You almost got me fired," I say. "I looked like a fool."

"I'm very sorry for that," he says. "Of course, I'm much more sorry for not seeing . . . For subjecting you to . . ."

I put my hand up to stop him. In the hospital, I spent time thinking about how I'd ended up in that garage. There were a lot of reasons. I'd been stupid, at turns, missing signals, mistaking my judgments for the truth about people and their motives. From the moment I encountered Rivka Mendelssohn's body and connected her to Aviva's Orthodox world, I was ready to pounce. It was easy. When I said I was a Jew, they spoke to me. But I misinterpreted what they were asking when they asked, over and over, You're Jewish? It wasn't, do you know this phrase in Hebrew or have you been bat mitzvahed. They were asking me: *Do you understand?* The fear of being a Jew. The baggage. The long legacy of hate and murder and discrimination. The rootlessness. The desperate need for self-preservation. And, of course, I don't really know. I only know the baggage of being me. But part of it, I think now, is being a Jew.

"You didn't think it was Miriam, did you?" I say.

Saul shakes his head.

"But you knew her history?"

"I knew she'd struggled. I knew she'd gone away. But your mother went away, yes? Many girls 'go away' for various reasons of . . . misconduct." He looks at my dad. "I'm sorry, not misconduct . . ."

My dad shakes his head ruefully and puts his hand on Maria's leg beneath the table. "Let's face it," he says, "it could have been considered misconduct."

Saul turns back to me. "But the police are only putting most of that together now," he says. "Miriam was taking very powerful medication. The autopsy showed all kinds of things. Antipsychotics, antidepressants, antianxiety. None of it should have been mixed. Who knows who was prescribing it to her."

I look at the table. It seems somehow inappropriate to say that I watched her take an almost lethal mouthful of lorazepam. She was just trying to feel better, she said. Less anxious.

"You spoke with Aron Mendelssohn, then?" he asks.

I nod. "Thank you."

"You know he's not talking to the police."

"I do."

There is a pause.

"What about Miriam's husband?" I ask. "What's he saying?"

"He's not saying anything, either," says Saul.

"Is he in custody?"

"No. He is in Israel. Aron Mendelssohn got him on a plane."

"Jesus."

"Rebekah," says my father. He hates it when I use Jesus as a swearword.

"Will they . . . extradite him?"

Saul raises his eyebrows. "I doubt it. They may try, but my sense is that they will not try very hard. And maybe it's enough already."

"Enough already?"

"The killer is . . . gone. The truth is out."

"Is it?"

Saul shrugs. "How much truth do you want?"

All of it, of course. But I don't say that.

We finish our coffee and Saul tells us he must leave for an interview.

"I have a lead on a job at the New York Aquarium in Coney Island," he says. "They need a security manager."

He and my father hug. My father promises to call when he comes back to visit me. We walk out together. Dad is making dinner for me and Iris, so he and Maria go off to do the shopping. Saul is going to drive me home to rest.

"He seems happy," says Saul, after my father walks away.

"I think he is," I say.

We're standing in the glass-enclosed vestibule between the Starbucks and the sidewalk. Saul hugs himself against the cold. He's shivering.

"What's wrong?" I ask.

"I didn't want to tell you with your father there," he says. "I had a call from your mother."

"Really?" The corners of my mouth rise involuntarily into a nervous smile.

Saul nods.

"She called you? Or you called her?" I'm almost giggling. Am I happy?

He looks at me. I've caught him in a lie.

"So you know where she is," I say. "You've known this whole time."

"She's upstate," he says, looking out across the street. "She read your articles. She wants to meet you."

And there it is. For twenty-two years I've been performing for her. Imagining she was watching, imagining her impressed when I showed moxie, repelled when I was weak. But it wasn't ever her watching. It was me, watching myself, wondering if I could ever win her love. She read what I wrote. She knew it was me.

"She wants to meet me?"

"Yes," says Saul. "She says she has a story for you."

ACKNOWLEDGMENTS

Thank you first and foremost to my husband, Joel, for pushing me to write, sacrificing holidays and vacations together so I could finish the first draft, and never wavering in your certainty that I could—and should—complete this book. Your ideas and imagination made *Invisible City* stronger, and your love has made my life a dream come true.

Thank you to my own personal literary dream-team: my cracker-jack agent, Stephanie Kip Rostan; and Minotaur's editor extraordinaire, Kelley Ragland. Your enthusiasm, intelligence, and support have made all this possible.

Thank you to Justen Ahren, Claudia Miller, and everyone at the Martha's Vineyard Writers Residency. You have created a truly magical place for writers. I would not have finished this book without you.

Thank you to Liora and Larry Fogelman, who invited me to

use their home as a writing retreat at a critical time in the life of the book.

Thank you to *48 Hours* executive producer Susan Zirinsky for supporting my work on this book. You have been my cheerleader, mentor, and friend.

Several people within the Orthodox and "off the derech" community in New York and New Jersey provided generous—and invaluable—service. Thank you to Ben Hirsch and Daniel Soskowitz for guidance early on and encouragement throughout. Thank you to Rebecca Schischa, Chana Schwartz, and Mimi Minsky for your close reads and honest notes. Thank you to Judy Braun, Pearl Reich, Shauli Gro's, and Chaim Levin for inviting me into your lives, trusting me with your stories, answering my dumb questions, and being such fun drinking partners. There are others I will not name, but you know who you are. Thank you.

Thank you to my incredible family: the "Chicago Dahls" and Nancy and Walter Urbach.

Thank you to my parents, Bill and Barbara Dahl, and my sister, Susan Sharer. Our two-religion household seemed odd to many, but we know it was exactly right.

This book is dedicated to my grandparents: Reba and Robert Blum, Jr., and Jeannette and Ernest Dahl. Your lives inspire me.